W

Contents

White Fire

Chapter 1 - Fall of the Casters

Our story begins, not in our world, nor our time, nor any place or age known in the world today.

This was a time where science and magic were one and the same; where the world was governed over by ordinary men with extraordinary abilities, who were commonly referred to as supernatural. They had an extraordinary affinity with the elements. They could control and create them using the powers of their minds, and used these tools to create and maintain peace. They became known as the Order of Casters.

However, there were some who craved power over others, and rose up against their equals in their lust for power. This became hatred, which in turn became something that they could use to defeat their equals, who had no anger, and they became twisted and proud in their power.

The first that the Casters knew of their friends' betrayal were the skies above the Torridon, their stronghold in the middle of the Three Realms, turning black with thick clouds, and blocking the sun.

The skies had never changed from a brilliant, sapphire blue before, and there was evil in the air. The Caster Elders sensed the true reason for the clouds, and sent out a warning for everyone to prepare for battle, so the Casters were not caught entirely unprepared.

The hastily erected defences were solid and

ready, and the protective spells were only just prepared, when the clouds broke and a sea of dark figures swarmed down.

The enemy was upon them.

From the heart of the multitudes came a great, terrible cry. The voices of the most powerful traitors were so strong; they shook the fortress right down to its deepest foundations.

From the hands of one of these traitors came blasts of white fire, then from another, and another, until a blinding volley of piercing white flame reached the supernatural barrier. But the defensive spells that the Casters had conjured were not able to defend against their own power, for the attacking forces were all once Casters and the white-hot blasts passed through them unhindered and plunged into the ranks awaiting them.

The Casters returned fire, and volley upon volley was fired from both sides, and Casters and traitors alike fell from their place in the sky.

And so the battle went on, with great losses on both sides for twelve days and twelve nights. However, the days were so dark and the air so full of ash and dust, and the night was so full of volleys of fire that the sun seemed deficient when dawn came.

And even on the morning of the thirteenth day, only five of the most powerful Casters were left, but still they were locked in combat.

The air around them seemed to shatter with each expulsion of immense power; each Caster matching one another's powers, water against flame, earth against wind, light against dark. The two Casters left were the leader of the Order, and his second in command. They fought with backs together, fending off even the most furious of attacks, but their retaliations were always to maim, not to kill their lethal opponents. Never was such grace shown in battle. These were true Casters; kind and forgiving.

This went on for seven more days, until finally, as one terrible action, the Traitors Three sent out a pulse of pure malevolence, and the remaining two Casters, being creatures of hope, and peace, had no barrier to match it. The pulse encircled them, and ripped through their very beings, and tore fibre from fibre, and when the smoke cleared, they were just clouds of dust, being carried by the prevailing wind towards the endless, deep, blue ocean.

But still there were the Three, and they revelled in their victory, for now there was no-one to contest their power. The Three towered above the battle field, soaring effortlessly, as if gravity had died with their combatants, and through their delusions of grandeur they did not see the Hell that lay beneath them, where the Torridon was no more or better than a pile of rubble, and Caster and traitor alike lay side by side, having died for a future that they never saw rise.

The Three became the ArchCasters, and because every other Caster was wiped out, they were the only conquering power left in the world, and swiftly took the Three Realms for their own. Kelthane took the dominion of the South, Solaxe took the dominion of the West, and Vanyol claimed the dominion of the

East. Together they ruled over the whole of Clas Muîr.

But still their lust for power continued to grow, and soon they began a bitter conflict between themselves, and across the borders of the Realms there was a great fortification, and in their paranoia of losing their land, the Three put up garrisons and watches, in an attempt to preserve what was never theirs to take.

As a result, an immense rivalry rose up between the Realms, and not just between soldiers, but citizens and peoples, and anyone who came from across-borders was met with the highest suspicion, and usually violence, until either they had been driven from that Realm, or, more often than not, killed.

But our story begins not with a great evil, nor a soldier, not even a hero. Our story begins with a boy called William.

Chapter 2 - Tursus

In the south of the East Realm, there was a small village called Tursus. Before the overthrowing of the Casters, it had been a merry place, with thriving markets and good food, and the people were happy, content in the knowledge that they were safe in the protection of powerful, but good, men.

Things were simple because the people had never known otherwise. There was never any trouble with bandits or wars; it was such a small part of the world that no-one ever really paid them any attention. If a family was struggling, every single person in that village pitched in to help them through. If there was a bad harvest, the able men would travel miles and miles to find food for their wives and children; to see them through until next harvest.

They also needed no authority figure. There was no mayor, no governor, and no king. If the village needed to sort out a problem, they would all meet in a committee and everyone, as a single unit, contrive a solution. Everyone's opinion was welcome; even the children, for they believed that if the world was simpler in the eyes of a child, maybe the solution was too.

But there was one child who seemed different to all the others. He was only very young when he was first recognised to be extra-ordinary.

When his parents were out, working in the fields on a day as ordinary and peaceful as any other, a panic-stricken woman came running out to them. It was a woman who knew the family well, but she was obviously in quite a flustered state, so they knew right away that this was an important situation. She was running at a considerable speed through the fields, cutting a swathe of broken stalks as she went. As she got closer, they could hear her shouting:

"Your boy! He is on the roof of your house! He will fall and die! Come quickly!"

The parents ran back to the house, now followed by a sizeable, and they saw that the boy had somehow managed to climb onto the very peak of the irregular-shaped house, and was slowly but surely crawling to the edge.

Despite the cries and screams of worried towns-people, he had reached the precipice, and he teetered on the edge for a second, and then fell, headfirst, towards the hard ground.

Before anyone had the chance to catch him however, the child seemed to glow white, like the faint luminescence of the moon through the mist, and just as quickly as he started falling, he stopped; toes in the air, head inches from the ground, looking at the crowd around him with wide, blue, bewildered eyes.

Nothing like this happened again, so, even though the whole village had witnessed this miraculous event, they soon forgot about it and moved on with their lives. Even the incredible was lost in the noise of the everyday.

Then came the fall of the Casters.

The whole world suffered beneath the rule of the Three. In the village, crops refused to grow and people started leaving to find work elsewhere, as food was becoming scarcer and more precious, and they wanted to find somewhere they could thrive.

Despite this, the boy had grown up into a good, kind, strong young man, and his name was William.

He was a dark-haired young man, tall and fair of face and with all the work he did in the village, he was strong and was growing into the body of a man. Despite this, he retained some of the lean body and energetic nature of a boy, and his deep, sky blue eyes were full of kindness.

He was so considerate and compassionate because all his life he had dealt with hardships, and had always had people to help him along, so his attitude was 'How can I do any different?' He helped out in the fields, farming what he could from the land and spreading it equally throughout the village, so everyone had enough to eat.

Then came the sudden arms-race between the Three, and all Three began to expand their armies; not only were many being lost in the battles along the borders, but the struggle to have a bigger and stronger army burned so bright in their hearts that they began to force any able men from villages in their Realm to join.

For the first few months Tursus was left alone, but one day, in the middle of summer, men in armour with long swords marched into the village square and started barking out orders. A very frail-looking old man walked into the captain, who threw him away as if he were a feather in the wind. The captain then demanded to see the highest authority in the village.

William's mother stepped forward and tried to explain that there wasn't anyone in charge, but before she could finish a single sentence, the captain drew his dagger and, without hesitation, drove it through her heart. Her face froze in surprise, and with her last ounce of strength she looked at William. There was only one message in that look.

I love you.

As her lifeless body fell to the ground with a dagger in her chest, her husband, with a strangled cry, leapt at the captain with unquenchable anger, but the soldier was faster. He stepped out of the way at the last second, grabbed the man's arm, bent it round behind his back, and despite a heart-breaking cry of defeat, pain and loss, forced him to the floor.

Another of the soldiers drew his sword, aimed it at the man's neck, and swung his sword down.

But the captain managed to grab his wrists with one hand, stopping the blade inches above the man's neck.

"We need the men. If you really want to hurt him, then we will put him on the front line of the West border. But he comes back to the camp alive. All of them do. Now, get in line!" This last was to the men of the village, who, seeing the brutal fate of William's mother, obediently formed into one long line, as the soldiers tied them together by their neck, with rope so rough it was as if it had been designed to grind off skin.

Once this was done, the captain turned round and saw a young man, on his knees, cradling the dead woman in her arms with tears in his eyes. "Leave the women and children, and anyone too weak to fight. It would be a waste to try and train them." He took one last look at the boy, and in his eyes were pure contempt; clearly love and attachment seemed like a weakness to the man, even enough so to warrant leaving a potential soldier behind. He spat, and then turned and walked away.

A fire burned up inside William that was fiercer than anything he had ever experienced. He could feel his body bristling with a new-kindled energy.

He lifted up the still bloody dagger from his mother's chest and prepared to leap at the captain with all his might and kill him, but as he looked at the deadly implement, he found that it was alight with a strange, white flame. The blade had been completely consumed by it, and there was no mark of blood on the white-hot metal. William's pure, unadulterated fury and pain seemed to have somehow manifested itself into this scorching flame, but it did not burn nor scald him.

It was hidden from most of the crowed who were transfixed on the soldiers marching their loved ones away, but upon seeing this, the elderly man leapt up from where he had landed to his feet with surprising speed. Just as William was about to make his rush at the captain, he grabbed him, bundled him to the floor, put his lips to William's ear and whispered *"Not yet, boy. You will get your chance. You have a power too special to waste. Meet me at the Eastern edge of the woods at midnight."*

And then the old man got up and walked calmly away through the crowd but they barely seemed to noticed through their tears and pained cries at the loss of their loved ones. William was left bewildered on the floor, looking in disbelief at the plain dagger he held in his hand. There were no gouts of blood left on the blade, but neither was there the curious white flame. Then he turned back, past the metal gates that had held together his life for so long.

As the soldiers lead the prisoners away from the village, William saw that the man at the front of the line of prisoners had his head hung down at the ground, as if his soul had left him, and only his body remained. He was sure that he would never see his father again.

Chapter 3 - Meeting at the Eastern Edge

By the time darkness fell, Tursus was in a bad way. Most of the women were cradling their children in their dark dwellings, weeping in vain for their lost husbands, brothers and sons.

There had been a ceremony for William's mother. She was not buried; there was a great pyre set up in the square, on the spot where she died, as a mark of respect.

Her body, wrapped in white cloth, was lowered elegantly into the flames with a cradle of ropes.

Much of the village came out for the sole purpose of saying goodbye to the person who was loved so much by so many. The woman, who many years ago had told her that her baby was on the roof, was standing in the midst of the throng; her eyes red and moist for the loss of a constant source of support and love.

William himself was standing at the front, staring at the intense fire with empty eyes. He barely felt the comforting hands on his shoulders. He barely heard the sorrowful words of the old priest, standing on a raised part of the concourse.

His voice was soft and melodious as he continued.

"She had a kind heart, and was loved by all that gather here. We pray that her soul will find its way to Heaven, and we pray for her son who is left behind on this earth..."

This last was too much for William, and he turned away from the flames with blurred vision and walked away, towards the house that he had fallen off what seemed lifetimes ago.

The service went on for another half an hour, and although William could hear it from his room in the eaves of the house, which had been left to him, the words seemed hollow and meaningless.

He lay on his bed, staring up at the crossbeams above his head, and thought of another time; a happier time.

So absent in his thoughts was he, that he had lost track of time. Then a sudden thought broke through these dreams and he leapt up, panicked. He stuck his head out of the barren window and squinted in the darkness to see the town's sundial. In his confused state however, he did not recall that the sundial did not work at night.

He pinched the bridge of his nose, sighed, and then tried to collect his thoughts. Only then was it that he remembered the words the mysterious old man had whispered in his ear; *"Meet me at the Eastern edge of the woods at midnight."*

He rushed from the window, and in his haste to put on his shirt, he hit his head on a crossbeam, lost his balance, and crashed onto the hard wood planks with a dull thud, in a muddle of limbs and fabric.

Five minutes later, he sped from his door, hair a mess, belt undone, shirt the wrong way round and one shoe held in his mouth as he hopped along, trying to put on the other one.

The side of his head was still throbbing as he successfully put on his second shoe and righted his clothes. But through this hectic confusion he had one thought; *"Am I too late?"*

He reached the edge of the Forest of Delsus properly dressed, but there was no sign of the old man.

William called out, but, not knowing the man's name, he was calling out rather improvised words.

He had been doing this for a few minutes and was very ready to go home. He must just have been a crazy old man after all.

Then a dark figure appeared in the corner of his eye, and William turned round to face him.

Yes, it was the old man, but he was no longer old. Gone were the grey, tattered rags and hood that previously bound him, gone was the long, spindly beard, and gone was the walking stick at his side. In their place was a man with black leather armour, trimmed, neat black hair and beard, and instead of a walking stick, a sword was strapped to his belt. He stood tall and proud, reminiscent of a bygone age of brave warriors and fierce battle.

Indeed, a memoir of these was in an obvious ridge that ran down the side of his otherwise solid face. The scar was straight; a direct, thin gash along the edge of his face, and stood there as evidence of the horrors those stern, kind eyes had seen.

William just stood there and stared, until a sturdy, powerful voice broke the silence.

"So boy, you decided to come after all. I must say I'm surprised. You're obviously very confused at the moment, especially after..." At this he looked through the trees to the orange, flickering light engulfing the houses around it. "...the events of today."

William did not need to follow his gaze to understand what he was looking at. He tried not to think about the flames, and how alone he felt inside.

"What's going on?" he said, hoping beyond hope that this man would have some answers. "What's happening to me?"

"I can't explain everything now. I have little time."

"Then why did you ask me to meet you, if it was only to offer empty responses."

"I can offer you something of far more value than that," he said, and William's eyes narrowed.

"What?"

"A chance, and only a chance, to be more than yourself. I am part of a rebellion against the Three."

William was taken aback.

"I take it that you have heard of the Casters."

"Of course," said William. His mother would tell him stories of the great and powerful sorcerers that kept the world peaceful for many hundreds of years.

"Well, the mark of a Caster's power is white. Any magic they cast has either a white sheen or aura around it, and that whiteness represents the purity of their heart."

The penny suddenly dropped with a clatter as William pieced it all together.

"But the dagger... The flame was white on the dagger," he said, barely able to string together the sentence.

"Yes, that's right," said the man. "It may be hard to believe, but you're a Caster; or at least you will be."

William just stared at him. His mouth was moving slightly, but no sound was coming out.

"You were born with incredible powers, but you have to train to be able to use them properly. That's what I'm offering. For you to join me on my journey and for me to teach you everything I know."

"What do you know about Casters?"

The man didn't as much try to avoid the question, as ignore it altogether.

"So what do you say?"

"It would mean leaving Tursus, leaving the house, leaving everything I've ever known... I really don't know..."

"You are almost eighteen."

"This time next week."

"So don't you think that it's time that you spread your wings, as it were?"

"Well, I don't have anything left here. My mother, my father, everything I've ever known has been taken from me..."

"And?" the man prompted encouragingly.

"And I intend to take it back," he said, with a fire in his eyes. "Yes. Yes, I will come with you. But on one condition. We have to find my father and save him."

"Agreed. But you have to train first. Otherwise we won't last a day."

"Well I'll need a few hours because I have nothing ready and my head is hurting terribly."

At this, the man put his hand up to the swollen, red lump on the side of William's head. He naturally flinched backwards, but soon moved back to his original position, as a white-hot light came from his palm onto the lump, and a searing pain shot through his body. But when the man lifted his hand away the lump had gone and the throbbing pain had completely disappeared.

"You're a Caster!" said William,

"I *was* a Caster; but not anymore." William noticed a flicker of shame in his eyes. "Meet me at the gates at first light with whatever you need. But don't bring too much. We have to travel light."

"Okay, I believe you. If you're sure that you can give me the means to track down my mother's killer, I'll gladly come with you. But before I do, what's your name?"

"My name's Ranson. And yours?"

"William."

As the men shook hands and went their separate ways, rising over the houses, the orange glow of the dying embers shone through the deep, dark night.

Light had just begun to creep into the sky when William met Ranson just outside the black, metal gates at the north-west of the village.

William had a pack tightly strapped to his back, which had in it a blanket, some food, and things he needed to start up fires; flints and tinder wood. He was leading his father's horse across the rough cobbles.

"Is that everything you need?" asked Ranson, holding his own horse by the reins, and it was grazing on a patch of grass that was sticking up at the side of the road, which was little more than dirt on the other side of the gates.

"I think so, but..." And with this, William looked back at the house he had lived in all his life. The house that his mother and father built and they has said that the whole of the village helped them too. He had left a note on the door that read:

I am going away and may never return, so I leave this house to anyone who needs it. The only condition is that whoever takes this house should be happy and live well. Goodbye Tursus, and thank you for everything.

William

"Is there anything wrong, William? Are you sure about this?"

He turned back to face Ranson, and said, "Yes, I am. I was just..." He took one last look at his house, through the dark metal of the gates, and said, "...thinking that I'm leaving behind everything I've ever known..."

"I know, but don't worry, I'll look after you."

And with this, the two men mounted their saddles and rode off down the track, their horses kicking up dust and dirt that flew up into the air behind them.

Chapter 4 - Camp Fire

It had been a hard day's riding, almost directly north, and the sun was just beginning to touch the horizon. The horses were tied up on an old, dead tree stump, and Ranson was standing with his legs and his arms crossed, leaning against a tree trunk at the edge of the clearing, looking out into the darkness of the thick forest surrounding them.

Meanwhile, William was crouching over the ordered pile of tinder, twigs and dried leaves in the middle of the clearing, striking the flints together, but only making as much progress as a couple of weak sparks.

Ranson looked over his shoulder, and sighed at the sight of William, trying to light the fire in vain. He turned and walked back over to him, crouching down beside him, and told him to put down the flints.

"I am going to give you your first lesson in magic. Now, the simplest spell in a Caster's arsenal is a blast of fire. By controlling the power and size of the blasts, they can be used for many things; from wounding enemies, to everyday practices, such as... Oh, I don't know... lighting fires."

With a subtle smile, he leant over the pile of kindling. He moved his hand into position over the mound, and shot a few blasts of bright flame from his palm into the base. The pyre immediately caught fire and bathed the entire clearing, from one line of trees to the other, in a flickering orange light.

He began to chuckle in his deep, strong voice, and soon William was laughing as well.

Once the laughing had died away, Ranson suddenly said, "Now you can have a go."

William looked at him doubtfully.

"But I can't control it."

"Well, I know this might be hard for you, but try and think about how you felt when... you ignited the dagger. Maybe that is the key to unlocking your abilities."

"I'll try"

"Aim for that tree. That one that's a little closer to the fire than the other ones. And remember; channel your feelings into that one spot."

So William stood with his feet slightly apart, arm raised, concentrating fully on the tree, about twenty yards away on the other side of the clearing.

His whole being was concentrated on one spot; the part of the trunk slightly below where it divided into two thick branches. He thought of his mother, of the years they spent living together in that village with friends all around; all the good times they had, and all the hardships too.

As his thoughts deepened, there was a static tingle in the air around him. He delved even deeper into his memories, and he seemed to glow slightly. Then the glow grew brighter, until the white-hot aura enclosed him, being brightest around his hand; at the very centre of his palm.

Then his thoughts turned to the terrible day when his mother died, to the exact moment when that cold dagger was driven through her warm heart. He could see his mother's last look, a look of love and compassion, in utter contrast to the twisted grin of contempt on the face of the captain. Tears fell from his eyes, and in this one moment of anger and pain, his feelings coalesced into a pulse of energy that rippled through his body. His eyes turned a pure, perfect white and the pulse, suddenly becoming palpable, travelled along his arm to his hand, and a piercing, white blast of flame shot from his palm and slammed into the tree, at the exact point his eyes were fixed on.

But the blast was so powerful that the wood simply could not withstand it. The resulting shockwave sent William and Ranson flying across the clearing, to land right at the perimeter of the ring of trees. The fire, despite being large and fierce, was instantly extinguished. Even the horses, being much sturdier and a good deal further away, were knocked from their feet by the blast.

After lying on the ground for a few moments, mostly as a result of pure shock, William groaned and pushed himself up from the ground. He looked around him with eyes that, despite being their normal colour again, were full of astonishment.

The smoke was still clearing, but he could still see most of what used to be the clearing. The major difference; it had got considerably bigger. The blast had uprooted trees for a good hundred yards from the epicentre. The fire was no longer any more than a small pile of sticks, and the horses were still lying on the ground. He looked a little closer, and with a sigh of relief, realised that they were both still breathing.

The space where the targeted tree had been was now a smoking crater, at least five feet deep, with no sign of the tree, except what might have been microscopic ash in amongst the dislodged soil.

He was broken from his awe by a familiar sound. He looked to his right and saw Ranson sitting up, supporting his weight with his arms, laughing long and hard. In the midst of this, he said;

"I think we need to find a new camp before nightfall!"

A new fire was burning bright in the new camp. They had set it up against a sheer rock face, with a fire a little way from the base, casting a ring of light around them. They were leaning up against the cliff, talking and laughing.

"I had no idea you had that kind of power in you!" exclaimed Ranson.

"It gave me quite a shock too!" William admitted. "So am I to become a weapon of the Resistance?"

"Not unless you want to be. And that reminds me. You'll need a weapon apart from your powers."

And with this, he sprang up and walked over to where the horses were tethered, just inside the band of light. He lifted one of the packs and retrieved a long bundle of fabric from underneath, and brought it over to William. He took a seat down beside him again, and removed the cloth.

It was a sword in a leather sheath. Ranson handed it over, and William drew it. It was not a long, thin blade with a heavy handle, but a short, wide-bladed broadsword with curious engravings down the length of it.

Ranson nodded towards the weapon. "That was my brother's. He died in battle, but I kept it to remember him by..." But then he shook his head. "It seems that you need it more than me."

"But it was your brother's. I can't..." said William, and tried to hand it back.

But Ranson pushed it back into his hands, and looked deeply into his eyes.

"It's yours now. And anyway, He'd be pleased that a powerful Caster like you was using it against the Three. Use it well."

They carried on talking for a little while longer, but soon they were both fast asleep, lying against the rock face, as the red sparks from the dying embers of the fire rose up, dancing into the black, night sky.

Chapter 5 - Swordcraft

William started as a cold bucket of water ripped him from his dreams.

He looked up, and the light of the bright afternoon sun devastated his vision. As his eyes adjusted to the light, he realised there was a figure standing over him.

As his vision returned completely, he recognised the man before him. He was staring straight into the sneering face of the captain; the soldier who murdered his mother, and took his father. He dropped the bucket and rested his hands on his belt.

"Well, well, well! Look what we've got here boys! Someone finally decided to stop crying over mummy. Maybe you're not too weak to train, but believe me," and here his sneer became a mad grin. "I am really going to enjoy breaking you."

His smile disappeared in a second, as he grabbed William by the hair and dragged him to his feet. He grabbed his hands and wrenched them behind his back, just as he had done with his father.

"Like father, like son. You are both as pathetic as each other." He used the same rasping rope to bind his hands behind his back. He also unstrapped his newly-acquired sword and belt from his waist. He handed it to the soldier beside him.

As William looked over to his side, he saw that Ranson was surrounded by three other soldiers. One was dragging him to his feet, while another took his sword from his side. The last had his sword drawn and readied it, just in case their 'prisoner' caused any trouble.

Then William realised that Ranson was looking straight at him. He never saw his lips move, but to his amazement he heard Ranson's deep, familiar voice in his head.

Use what I taught you. Concentrate.

As if to reinforce what he just told him, he nodded discreetly and William, now sure he hadn't imagined it, nodded back. He crafted together a message in his mind, being sure that Ranson could hear it. A simple message.

Be ready.

William closed his hand around his bonds and concentrated on them. He felt the coarseness of the fibres, the way that each one was wound tightly together, to form an unbreakable lattice. The rope began to glow, but the sun was so bright that if any of the soldiers had bothered to look, they would not have noticed the shine as it was lost in the sun's radiance, and his eyes were closed, so they couldn't see his eyes turn white.

As he concentrated more and more, the rope began to unwind. The fibres became looser and looser, until the only things keeping the rope up were his hands, tightly wrapped around it. He was free.

But then he had an idea. If he could use his mind to control the rope, then he had a weapon.

He used his mind to send a message to Ranson.

Now.

Then everything happened at once. William spun round with incredible speed, and on his second revolution he released the rope, at the same time as concentrating on its trajectory.

The rope, guided by unseen powers, flew at the captain, and caught him full in the face, knocking him momentarily off balance. As he stumbled, the rope coiled itself around his neck, and held there, fast.

As the soldiers surrounding him turned to see what had happened, Ranson used his mind to draw his sword from the scabbard held by the soldier that had taken it from him. It flew into his hand, and already he was in a battle stance; legs apart, his weight perfectly distributed on the balls of his feet.

All the men, including William, were looking at him in astonishment, apart from the captain, whose face was turning a rather vibrant shade of purple, as he tried to dislodge the rope from his neck.

William was the first to snap out of the awe, and took advantage of the soldiers' distraction. He managed to summon his sword in the same way Ranson did.

By the time the sword was in William's hand, Ranson had sprinted over to him.

Now the two Casters were back to back, swords in hand, ready and waiting.

The attacks came almost immediately; a flurry of blades from every angle. There was a total of four men, plus the captain, who was still writhing on the floor. That meant two men each.

William struggled to defend against all of the attacks at first, but then he heard Ranson's voice in his head.

Clear your mind. Think only about the fight.

William's ability became more confident, but was still quite wooden and stiff. Again, he heard the voice in his mind.

Your movements should be fluid. Parry an attack and launch one yourself in one smooth movement. And to finish of an enemy, append some fire onto the blade, like you did the first time.

Again, William's swordplay improved, but this time the difference was vast. He drove one combatant right back with a flurry of slices and thrusts, and as the second swung his sword down, William rolled beneath the blow and, burnishing his blade with a pale flame, drove it into his enemy under the arm, at the point where his armour gave way into simple leather padding. This was no match for the enhanced blade, and that soldier fell to the ground.

As the first soldier ran forward to re-engage William, he decided to end the fight there and then. He held up his arm in the soldier's direction and concentrated his thoughts into one spot.

The blast of fire shot from the very centre of his palm and slammed into the man's dark breastplate, propelling him backwards with inconceivable force.

The soldier slated onto the sheer rock face, and his back broke with a strident crack against the smooth surface. His body slid down onto the ground; limp and lifeless.

He turned around and saw that Ranson had already finished off his opponents. He was looking at William with a mixed look of wonder and disbelief as William's eyes turned back from a perfect, flawless white.

"You really do amaze me! Less than two days ago you were just a boy, and now you can take out three fully trained soldiers with ease!"

"I felt like my powers were guiding me. My mind told them what to do, and they controlled my actions; heightened my senses. It was like I was watching myself fight from inside my own head, like a dream."

Ranson smiled and was about to reply, when he realised something.

"There were five men that captured us. What happened to the one you... roped?"

William looked around. There was no sign of the captain, apart from the rope, cut in half, as if by a knife or a dagger,

"I don't know. He probably ran away when I was dealing with the other two. It's a shame I didn't get to deal with him, but it felt good to fight back."

Deep in his heart he felt a throbbing unease that he had just taken a life and that it had felt so good to do so, but he felt that this would appear as weakness to Ranson so he didn't let on.

"Well I'm sure you will get your chance eventually. Now, we must leave this place. Find our horses and we will go."

The horses were a little way up a ridge, grazing on the few clumps of yellowing grass that had managed to push its way up through the dust and rock. William caught them by their bridles and led them back down the slope.

Ranson met him on the path at the bottom and took his own horse by the reins. They both mounted and they were off, riding back up the sloping path to the top of the ridge, and from there they began to go north on a winding road over the mountains.

Their third camp was set up on the peak of a mountain; a round, wide, flat section with an area of settled dust, which was bordered by pilot fires that were lit in a circle, creating a safe haven against the dark night.

Ranson and William were sitting in the centre, leaning against their packs, talking.

"Now we've revealed ourselves to him, Vanyol will send armies to take us down. We have to reach the Resistance before sundown tomorrow, or we don't stand a chance."

"How far do we have to go?"

"These mountains are called the Beltzan Peaks. To the north of us is the highest crest; Mount Kanen. Our main headquarters are in a cavern behind the waterfall that flows down on the Western slope. It will be a hard ride, but there will be other difficulties. These lands may be ruled foremost by Vanyol, but they are watched over by terrible creatures called the Scarra."

"I have never heard of them before."

"Then you do not know how lucky you are. They were once mountain-dwelling men; joyous and plentiful, but the evil of Vanyol was too much for them. He tried to enrol them into his forces them but they refused, so, being disgusted by their disrepute, he cursed them to be creatures that walk like men, although they are anything but. They are cutthroats and cannibals; not much better than animals. They have inherited foot-long claws and fangs from the animals around them, but what makes them most dangerous is their minds."

"Their minds?"

"They are utterly without mercy, or compassion. You know from experience that Vanyol's men are not the nicest people in the world, but the Scarra are in a different league entirely. They do not only ignore their kinder thoughts; Vanyol's dark powers removed them completely, along with their spirit. When you fight them, and you will, do not hesitate. Kill them or be killed. It is that simple. They have no humanity left preserving."

"That sounds a bit harsh..."

"Trust me, it's what is necessary." And with this, he stood up and threw his pack to the edge of the ring of fires, and William did the same, still a little confused. But then Ranson drew his sword and swung it in a figure of eight around his body, and he understood.

The ring had become an arena.

"Now, to be a great Caster, you must also master sword-craft. Now, the sword that you have is called Melnhir."

William drew his sword and gazed at it. Almost as if he was naming the blade himself, he echoed, "Melnhir."

"Yes. It is a short, double-edged blade, with a heavy hilt that has enough room for two hands, but can be used with one. It is a very versatile blade."

"And what about yours?"

Ranson held up his own weapon.

"It is a two-handed, long, thin sword, with a balancing weight on the bottom of the hilt." He pointed to this. "This sword is called Triscant. It is only balanced in two hands, but can be swung in one with some difficulty."

"Ok, got it so far."

"Good. Now attack me."

William was taken aback for a moment, but then he raised his sword and ran at Ranson, who raised his own sword and parried the attack easily, knocking William to one side.

"Never run at an opponent. Keep your balance and let them come to you. The most likely thing is that he will be angry, and that anger with surely blind him. Keep calm, and focus on the fight."

So William readied himself and approached Ranson again, but more steadily this time; sword not wavering, but steady, and weight evenly distributed onto each foot.

He suddenly swung his sword and became locked in fierce combat. They were no longer friends, no longer allies. They were rivals; enemies; fighting for life and death.

Their boots kicked up dust, which skittered up into the air in clouds and burned with the light of the blazing fires surrounding them. Their swords rang with the almost hypnotic resonance of metal on metal.

Then Ranson drove William backwards with a flurry of blows.

"Don't let your guard down. Look for your enemy's weakness. Yours is your footwork. When you lunge, step forward with your strongest foot, while keeping most of your weight on the other one."

William smiled and retorted with surprising vigour, and knocked Ranson off balance by using all of the power in his body, and the weight of his blade.

Then with both hands he swung his sword in a curving motion from near to the ground to over his head, twisting Ranson's own sword from his hands, and it flew through the air and thudded into the ground; a good ten yards away.

He followed that up by taking advantage of his opponent's surprise. On the down-stroke of the same movement, using the flat and noticeably wide edge of his blade, he knocked his legs from under him.

Ranson smacked into the ground with a major jolt, and within a second, the tip of William's blade was pressed against his neck.

"Do you yield?"

"Not yet!" he cried, and discharged a blinding white flash of light, which caused William's arms to rise up and shield his eyes. Using his involuntary action to his advantage, Ranson swung his legs round and tripped him up.

Then, as William was lying on the floor, Ranson summoned white shackles around his wrists and ankles, pinning him to the dusty ground. He then used his powers to call his sword from where it was sticking out of the ground, and held it to William's neck.

"Now, do you yield?"

"Well, it doesn't look like I have a choice!"

Smiling, Ranson released William's bonds and reached out his hand to help him up. Smirking back, William took it, and once he was back on his feet he retrieved his own sword from where it had fallen.

"I can see that you will be able to look after yourself. Even against the Scarra! But now we must sleep. We meet the Resistance tomorrow, and you will need to be alert."

So Ranson collected his pack, unrolled his sheet and lay down in the centre of the ring of light.

But when William went over to the edge of the ring to collect his own pack, he was sure he could hear light feet falling all around just outside the reach of the light, and for a second he was sure he saw a dark figure with a vague outline facing him as he straightened up with his pack, but then it disappeared into the darkness.

He turned away and set up his bed close to Ranson's. Soon they were both asleep; blissfully unaware of the animalistic eyes watching them; waiting for the fires to die.

Chapter 6 - Tooth and Claw

William was woken by a hand clamping over his mouth, stopping from crying out. His heart skipped a beat, and he looked up in alarm.

He saw the familiar face of Ranson, vaguely silhouetted against the early morning sky.

But he was looking round frantically and a look of worry was etched across his face as evidently as the scar that was scoured down the length of his features.

He removed his hand from William's mouth, and the younger man sat up hurriedly.

"What's going on?"

"The Scarra. They've found us. They must have been watching the camp; waiting for the fires to go out."

"Can't we fight them?"

"There are too many and they have us surrounded. Our only chance is to break through the ring towards the horses, and make for the Resistance. They will have defences; the necessary defences to protect us."

"Let's do it then!"

And so William kept guard while Ranson collected his packs and strapped them to his back, and then Ranson did the same for him.

William had only just buckled his sword to his waist when the Scarra attacked.

The first assemblage exploded out of a line of bushes on their left flank, and they were running towards the pair. For the first time, William got a clear view of them.

They were the basic shape of a human, but they were covered all over in a dark brown, thick, fuzzy fur. They had no clothes, and William could see a musculature far tougher and tauter than any man's. Their arms were tipped by almost comically large claws, but William had no doubt that a slice from even one of those would have left him far worse for wear.

The Scarra had three on each hand; two fingers and one thumb, but the claws were not simply on the end of each, as nails would be if they were allowed to grow to such a length. They *were* the fingers; but it was hard to tell where flesh ended and claw began, as the entire hand was sheathed in the same long, thick fur.

The face was the most terrifying part of these monsters. The fur was absolute on the head; the hair and fur just seemed to merge until there could be no distinction between them.

The only parts with no hair were in smooth patches around the features, and even they were horrifying. The nose was upturned, shrivelled and horrible, and the eyes were dark. If the eyes really are the windows of the soul, then those led straight to Hell. There really was nothing left in them to hint that these were once proud, joyous men.

Below this was nothing to contradict. The face was forced into a crooked, insane grin by the twin, elongated canines that hung out of the corners of its mouth; almost as disproportionate to the rest of the face as the horrific claws were to the rest of the body.

And just to add to the animalistic nature, they were not in any particular order or precise arrangement.

They were a rabble. Some shambled along with their arms limply at their sides, some with arms horizontally raised and claws aimed straight to the pair, and some flailing their arms wildly, as if swatting away hundreds of flying insects, and nearly scalping the monsters around them as they ran.

But William and Ranson were ready for them. The older Caster stood with legs apart, in the battle stance that he had learned many years ago, and William was doing his best to copy him.

The younger man took the first blood of this fight, swinging his sword downwards, and took out the legs of the first Scarra. It flipped round and landed on its back on the ground, and before it could move, William had planted his sword into its chest, and it died with a final whimper of defeat.

Then Ranson took the next one, swinging his sword, high and fast, and beheaded it as it ran. It fell to the ground just next to him.

But now they were running in too fast to pick them off one by one, so both men were entirely focused on blocking those terrible claws and getting a kill in where they could. But more and more continued to join the fray.

Soon, there were so many in a ring of slashing claws and gnashing jaws around them, that they were forced back to back, matching each other's footwork, so that they were turning in a circle slowly, still fighting, until William was facing in the direction of the horses.

Now's our chance!

William heard Ranson's voice in his head once more.

They are scared of fire, like any other animal. I will create a ring of fire around us, and they should panic and run away. Then we make for the horses.

No sooner had his voice faded in William's head, when Ranson sent out a pulse of energy into the Scarra before him, knocking them back. He then had enough time and space to ignite the dusty ground before him with his mind.

The flames leapt higher and higher, and, just as Ranson had said, the majority and turned and fled, leaving only a few, and the dead behind.

A gap suddenly appeared in the wall of flame, and Ranson shouted to him.

"Go!"

So he jumped through the opening, swinging his sword and beheading a Scarra as he did so, and it closed straight after him.

He reached the horses and looked at the scene in dismay. There were two Scarra by them. One was crouched over the body of Ranson's horse, which it had obviously just slaughtered with its sabre-sharp fangs, feasting on its quivering innards; blood pooling around the Scarra's feet, and dripping of the tips of its twin canines. The other was coiled like a spring, ready to leap onto William's own horse.

But just as its feet left the ground a blast of fire hit it in the back of the neck. Its head snapped back, as if in surprise, and it fell to the ground just before the horse, and lay there; lifeless and still.

The other turned sharply round, and Melnhir buried itself into its chest, embellished with white flame.

William had begun running even as he threw the sword, and as the Scarra fell back onto the carcass of the horse, William retrieved the sword from its chest, made it burn briefly to cleanse it of blood, and sheathed it.

He then mounted his horse and rose back to Ranson.

Ranson had just seen William leap through the gap he had made in the wall of fire, so he closed it immediately.

Maintaining a spell this powerful was weakening him by the second, and he wouldn't be able to keep it up for long. So, once he was sure that William was out of range, he sent out a second, more powerful pulse of white energy, but through the fire.

The pulse carried the flame straight into the bodies of the few remaining Scarra, who not only got knocked back a few feet by the pulse but got burned heavily and, on some of them, their fur ignited, and spread from Scarra to Scarra like sallow wildfire.

But the pulse had extinguished the firewall protecting Ranson, and the Scarra that weren't burning to death attacked him once more.

Ranson did his best to defend against the attacks. Triscant was heavy, and swung quickly, so any flesh, bone or even claw that got in the way of it was lacerated.

But numbers were against him, and soon he did not have enough space to swing his sword well. He looked inside himself, but he was too weak for another blast.

Suddenly, a claw slashed down that he didn't see until it was too late, and it bit into his shoulder, and as he cried out, another sliced low into his leg.

Ranson was kneeling on the ground, defeated. A final claw arched downwards, this time aiming for his neck, and he knew that it was over.

Then, less than a foot away from his collar, the claw broke and snapped off as a blast of white fire hit it in a shower of white sparks. Another Scarra tried a swipe and another, and another; all with the same result. The fireballs seemed to be coming from where he had sent William, and the Scarra backed off; terrified by this new attack.

Then Ranson rose into the air; within a few seconds he was a good three meters above the ground. Various Scarra tried to take swings at him, but he was safely out of their reach.

Then he was propelled forwards at speed, until he landed rather inelegantly on the horse, just behind William, who seemed very drained from having to concentrate massively in order to pull off the incredible feat. Ranson clapped him on the shoulder with pride and he opened his eyes as they turned back to normal from a flawless white.

They were soon galloping at a speed that the Scarra simply couldn't match, heading north along mountain roads, towards Mount Kanen, and the Resistance.

They had little more trouble from the Scarra that day; just quick glimpses of dark figures dashing in-between the trees over to one side of the track. It still took them over two hours to navigate the winding, perilous paths over the mountains, but the sun had only just starting falling in the sky when they reached the Mount. The waterfall was obvious, but the way in wasn't to William, so Ranson explained.

"To enter the mountain there is only one way. A horse jump into the centre of the fall, which is only possible once the cave door is open, and for that you need to be a recognised member of the Resistance."

"So pretty well fortified then."

"Yes, but I'm here so everything should be fine."

"Should be?"

"Well, they don't really take very kindly to strangers, so don't expect the warmest of welcomes. They will treat you with the utmost suspicion until you prove yourself."

"And how do I do that?"

"That remains to be seen. But just be careful, and don't let your guard down. Keep your hand close to Melnhir; just in case."

They rode in almost solemn silence for a while longer, when a sudden, sharp voice cut through the air from somewhere amongst the rocks and made William almost fall off the horse.

"Who are you? What is your business here?"

William, rather startled, turned in the saddle and looked quizzically at Ranson.

Despite his injuries, he seemed completely unfazed by this. In fact, he almost seemed to expect it. He winked at William, smiled a subtle smile, and responded to the unexpected outburst.

"I am Ranson, and I have with me an addition to our cause. A boy with incredible abilities. He is a Caster."

For the second time, a loud, unexpected noise made William jump, almost out of his saddle.

It was a sharp, cracking sound, erupting from behind the waterfall. The gargantuan aperture was opening, an inch at a time.

As the maw continued to yawn open, they got glimpses of flickering torches; beautiful, dancing light through the shimmering water.

When the jaws had opened a little further, they saw the light of the falling sun glinting off metal.

Even further, and these glimmers were recognisable as the reflections of light off the unforgiving, fatal points of long spears, cold, callous plates of armour and smooth helmets. Even through the distortion of the waterfall, these did not look friendly at all.

William looked round, for the second time, at Ranson, and he realised how much he actually needed him. Ranson's head was held high. He was strangely regal and, despite his injuries, he seemed to be in control of everything around him, as if for that one moment the universe revolved around him, and the very earth was bent to his will, as the sun silhouetted his stately profile.

Suddenly, they met each other's gaze, and Ranson's monarchical composure faltered, and then disintegrated. As if this was a veil, it fell from his eyes, and William realised that he had seen those eyes before. Before the awful day when his parents were taken from him, even before he began working in the fields of Tursus. Ranson was someone from his old life, and had somehow commandeered this new one too.

Just before William made the connection, Ranson jammed his heels into the flank of the horse and it leapt forward, gathering speed, towards the dark, shimmering maw of the cave.

William righted himself in the saddle and saw the ground a way in front of the horse just end. It didn't slope downwards, or show any sign of a cliff beneath; it just stopped.

He heard Ranson mutter something as they galloped along, head close to the saddle, as if he was not talking to the horse, but to its legs.

Just as they were reaching the edge of the precipice, the horse's hooves seemed to glow a pale, deathly white. A little closer, and sparks flew from the edges.

Then, just as the front legs were about to leave the edge, it jumped. It coiled its legs together, and sprang seven feet upwards and many more across.

Everything seemed to happen in slow motion, as three worlds merged into one.

First was the pure ecstasy of motion as the bright, sun-filled world flew by. Then came the cold rip through the icy grip of the waterfall as it flowed over them, soaking everything on the horse. And finally they plunged into the ominous darkness of the cave, which was only punctuated by the shine of spears and armour, and the glare of torches.

Finally, the hooves struck the stone with a last discharge of sparks, and at once a dozen spears were thrust into unnerving proximity of their faces.

Ranson smiled and dismounted with a wince, painfully aware of the gash in his shin. William, feeling and looking far less confident, dismounted slowly, but landed more surely on the brownish rock.

The wall of leather and plate armour parted as Ranson approached, but the vicious points of the spears were still precisely trained on him. Through the gap strode an incredibly regal figure, dressed in similar armour as the guards, but decorated with gold around the edges, and precious stones. Similar gems also adorned a magnificent hilt, with a single, heavy, purple jewel in the pommel. This topped a golden scabbard, which hung at his side, and moved in time to the manly strides.

His face was similar to Ranson's own; his stern face was softened only by a short, dark beard. But not only in looks; in scars, some physical, some in eyes that screamed of battle.

He was obviously the leader of the Resistance. There was no doubt, because of the pure splendour of the way he walked, and even stood.

His face cracked into a smile as he saw Ranson, and they embraced each other. Then he looked over his shoulder, and noticed his counterpart.

William stood there, unsure of his whereabouts, but ready for anything; feet apart, weight even distributed on each, and hand on the hilt of Melnhir. He was still surrounded in a half-cirque of spears, but he looked surprisingly relaxed.

The decorated leader came towards him, and his voice echoed incessantly in the small space.

"So, young man. You wish to join us?"

This prompted a round of laughter from the soldiers around him.

"What do you have to add to the cause?"

William looked at Ranson, who smiled and nodded.

"This."

He flung his arms wide, and instantly ignited them with a flash of white fire. The resulting shockwave knocked soldiers off their feet for a good ten feet around him. The flames leapt high, and the heat was so intense that it caused all of the remaining soldiers to drop their spears and shield their faces. Even Ranson felt it gall at his skin from the other side of the cave.

All shadow was driven from that place by fierce light, and this was amplified by the wet walls of rock, so that the men were blinded from every angle.

Finally, once every soldier had dropped their weapons, the light began to fade, until only the flames could be seen in the cave; the torches had been extinguished by the blast.

Then, one by one, the flames began to shrink and perish on top of William's leather sleeves. Such was his power and control, he had managed to keep the fire a small distance from his clothes to prevent them from burning up.

The last flame faded from his arm, and he let them rest at his sides. Every man, including Ranson to a reasonable degree, was looking at him with a mixture of shock and awe, and he looked at the leader and uttered one strong, clear word.

"Interested?"

Chapter 7 - Secrets and Tales

William and Ranson were now sitting at an oval-shaped table, on which was spread out maps and charts of all three Realms, and marked by different symbols which William could only assume were different branches of the Resistance, or targets.

These were lit by a large candle, which exerted an almost pathetic flame in comparison; however this was somehow enough to bathe the entire table in a steady, orange glow, and the same circle of light was also imprinted on the low, flush ceiling.

Similar light, but stronger, was released from torches that hung in brackets on the walls of smooth, brownish rock, dyed a pale orange by the light. Because the room was an almost perfect circle, the torches were set at regular intervals so that the six beacons baptised the parts of the room that the candle could not reach very comfortably.

The table and the walls seemed at odds with each other, despite the men sat there. In some places, the table advanced until it was almost conquering the wall itself, whereas in others, it receded, leaving the wall greedy in its victory, and revelling in the great emptiness before it. The entire dance was bathed in seven surrogate suns, blazing in their watchfulness, fighting back the patient darkness.

This was the War Room.

The only escape was an arch in the brownish rock, lined with curious carvings and runes that William did not even attempt to understand.

49

This was guarded by two soldiers. In opposite hands they held a hexagonal shield, and a weapon that was somewhere between a halberd and a pike.

The men themselves wore armour which was a mix of leather padding and plate armour; the latter of which seemed to take precedence. Their helmets were smooth caps, but for five vertical lines where the metal bulged slightly, and an almost sheer drop that covered the backs of their heads and a small spur of metal in front of the ears.

But, unlike the other soldiers that William had seen, these had metal coverings over their faces, so that the only discernible features were their eyes.

These were entirely military; strong and obedient. This was identical to their body language as well. They were rigidly snapped to attention, but William had no doubt that they could disable anyone in the room in an instant.

William had seen the figure outside the arch on his way in, and, for all he knew, these could be the same pair. They were simply identical. These were called the Besiarites; the leader's elite guard and fighting force. They were hand-chosen from infancy and were trained to be compassionate but lethal; merciful but deadly. They were able to use any weapon with incredible efficiency.

Around the table were sat four men; two on each flatter side. On one side were William and Ranson, and on the other was the leader of the Resistance, who William now knew as Raimos, and his second in command; his trusted lieutenant, Garston.

He had learned their names during the journey into the bizarre room, but now he sat in silence while Ranson and the other two men talked.

"So how are things in the south?" asked Garston.

"Not good", replied Ranson. "Unfortunately the border conflict is still going fiercely, with many men falling every day." He glanced briefly at William. "That is why Vanyol's men have begun to abduct men from many villages, like Tursus and Macros."

William shifted uncomfortably in his seat at the mention of his old village, but his ears cocked interestedly and he sat up sharply as Ranson continued.

"The big problem is the Western Front."

William's mind flew back to what the captain had said as he took his father.

If you really want to hurt him, then we will put him on the front line of the West border.

"The stolen men are being forced into open battle, hemmed in by the labour camps on either side, where the men that aren't fighting or dying are being made to forge the weapons and armour used on the front lines."

But he comes back to the camp alive. All of them do.

"But what should we do about it?" posed Raimos.

"Either we do nothing, or we trek across many perilous miles to an almost impossible goal of releasing the prisoners, stop the fighting, and hopefully take down Vanyol." replied Ranson, barely able to keep the humour out of his voice.

"Let me rephrase that then, my friend. What are we going to do?"

"Well," answered Ranson, "we have the option between the right path, and the easy path."

"We cannot throw the lives of our men away for a fool's errand!" concluded Garston. "It would simply be folly. We cannot help."

"It would only be folly without method, conviction and a great deal of courage." retorted Raimos, with an air of imperiousness and superiority. "And you forget, we have a Caster on our side, and a powerful one at that."

William was taken aback for a moment.

"Just one?" he asked, half glancing at Ranson, who cleared his throat noisily, and shifted uncomfortably in his seat.

"Well, yes, unless you are expecting friends," joked Garston, but Raimos looked at him quizzically, as if guessing there was something more; something hidden.

William however, decided not to pursue the matter for now, and chose to concede a losing draw.

"No," he replied with feigned innocence. "I'm just quite new to your world. I don't really know how many of us are left."

He was lying; Ranson had told him that he was the only one he had been able to find in his years travelling the Three Realms, apart from the ArchCasters of course.

There was a moment of awkward silence that seemed to last an age, but then Garston continued talking. William was not listening to him, he heard Ranson exhale shakily, and felt him physically relax.

They looked each other in the eye and for the first time Ranson was looking at him with a look of pure gratitude. Again, William saw the story behind his eyes, as plans were made in the milieu.

William sat, with one leg resting on the edge of the precipice, and the other dangling down over the sheer drop, watching as the sun sank down over the golden edges of the Forest of Delsus.

The mists on the horizon would usually make the trees look blue and murky, but to the west, as the sun lowered in its course, the sunlight shone through it and made it burn a bright, tan flush.

He was sitting in silence, and neither the coldness of the dry rock, nor the slight chill of evening breezes could reach him through his thoughts.

Presently, Ranson walked up from the dark cavity that William had used, and sat next to him on the precipice in silence. His wounds had been tended to and bandaged, and they were healing fast.

After a short while, William broke the quiet stillness of the air.

"So why haven't you told them?"

"Well, I have no time for the fame, and the pressure on me would just be unbearable..." He glanced at William, cringed slightly, pulled a face, then said, "...Sorry..."

Silence overtook the crest again, and where not too long ago there would have been a man and a boy, two men now sat together as the sun continued its leisurely descent.

"So who are you?" The question had been burning in him all day.

"You know who I am." replied Ranson, with impressively believable sincerity.

"No, I mean who are you to me? I know that I've seen you before, back when I was little. I remember your eyes."

For a moment, Ranson tried to feign confusion and ignorance, but then the facade dropped, and Ranson sighed.

"Okay, fine. If you want the truth, and the whole truth, you should know that this won't be easy for either of us."

"Go on." William prompted.

"I have fought in many battles. You can probably tell by the little souvenir running down my face. And I have killed, many times." With this last, a haunted look glazed over his face, and still hung in his eyes. "But I never fought in *the* battle; the battle for the Torridon. I was a coward, and as it began, I ran. I ran so fast, and for so long; I thought I had died, and that it was merely my spirit fleeting across the ground. I headed east, where I hid in a hollow for many days without food or water, and I could hear the explosions and screams even from that desolate place."

William was looking at Ranson anew, but did not tell him to stop.

"By the time I got there, after realising my responsibility, the Torridon site was a wasteland. The fortress itself was in ruins, but the sheer quantity of the dead was inconceivable. Many black birds had flown down, and were feasting on the remains of my enemies and brothers alike. I searched through this Hell for many days more for any survivors, but not a single one did I find. After a while, I came across the body of my brother, and I wept; for my friends, for my kin. I wept for so long, until I thought that death would come to me through pure misery." Then his voice changed its note, back into the confident Ranson that William new. "But I took his sword. I took Melnhir, hoping that one day it could again do damage to the Three."

He laughed, but it was as empty as his eyes, and there was not even a hint of hysteria in it.

"In my grief, I wandered the wild. I went first to the north; to the beautiful, lush grasslands on the border, which is now little more than blood-filled mire. Then I journeyed through the forest, and camped in that very clearing that you destroyed."

And here, he really did give a genuine chuckle.

"I travelled on almost the exact reverse of our path from there, and came at last to a small village on the South border."

William finally understood, and nodded in comprehension.

"Tursus."

"Tursus." Ranson agreed. "But there I found not only shelter, but love. I met a young woman in the town square, collecting cloth, and fell utterly in love with her. I followed her home one day, and she kissed me. This was the first time I had even been touched by another human in over a year, and we spent one incredible night together. But in the morning she told me that she was engaged to be married, and she could not see me again. So I left. I wandered throughout the East Realm for at least six more months, making money the only way I knew how. By the sword. This went on for a while, until the newly-formed Resistance found me, and based on my reputation, asked me to join them. Of course, I took up the offer eagerly, and have been fighting for them ever since. It was in one such battle that one of Vanyol's men gave me this." And he pointed to his scar.

William was finally starting to piece it all together, and had come to understand, that he could have guessed what Ranson was going to say next.

"After a year and a half away from Tursus, I finally returned, only to find that the woman that I had loved was now married, and had a son. His name was William."

William nodded, but Ranson stopped him before he could say a word.

"But when I visited the house, your father was working in the fields, and you were being looked after by a friend of the family, so it was just me and her. And she told me that you were mine."

Ranson waited for this to sink in, but William just froze, and looked blankly at him, so he continued.

"I visited quite a few times as you were growing up, but you only saw me briefly, and it became increasingly hard to come back as I was needed elsewhere. But a while ago, I received a letter from your mother, saying that you were old enough to know the truth, and that I, she, and her husband would tell you together on your eighteenth birthday, and I was there, in disguise, ready to surprise you, but, well, things changed."

"Yeah, you could say that," replied William. This was the first time he had spoken since the beginning of Ranson's story.

"It was a great shock to me when your mother died, but when I saw that you had my abilities, I just had to intervene. And there is a reason that I said that we had to reach this mountain by today. Because this is your eighteenth birthday, I am telling you this now. It's what she would have wanted. So, here we are."

William did not know how to respond to the masses of life-changing information that had just been crammed into his head, and he just stared at Ranson with a mixture of perplexity and wonder of all that he had learned.

Finally, he spoke up.

"So... you're my... father?"

"Yes, I suppose I am. So, do you want to call me Father?"

"No, I think I'll stick with Ranson. It's just that my Father was my father. He raised me and turned me into a good person. Ranson, I think, suits you better."

"Fine, that sounds good to me!"

They embraced each other warmly, both being able to show their new-found love for each other for the first time. While in this tight hold, William talked up into Ranson's ear.

"But if you ever try to call me 'son', you will be forming a very close relationship with the sharp edge of a sword."

"Understood!" chuckled Ranson, although the reply was almost lost in the embrace.

Both men began laughing; still holding each other, and even when they released, the laughter had still not quite died away.

But then William noticed a large scurrying multitude; black under the trees, and he pointed to it.

"I don't like the look of them very much," he said, following the direction of William's arm.

The host was moving closer to the mountain with every passing second.

"Scarra. They must have followed the tracks. Or our scent. Either way, we have to warn the others."

William nodded in agreement, and both men leapt up, and sprinted towards the gaping mouth of the cave.

Chapter 8 - Ascent of Fire

The two men burst into the War Room, and immediately, a sharp point was pressed into each of their necks by the Besiarites. Raimos and Garston stopped talking instantly and looked up from their maps and charts. The torches flickered and roared at the interruption.

"What is it?" asked Raimos, after giving them a moment to catch their breath. They had obviously been running.

"Scarra..."

"...hundreds of them..."

"...must have followed us..." replied William and Ranson together, still gasping for air.

Raimos nodded, and said, "Stand down." This was to the guards, but even as he said it, they could see his mind working through and discarding different courses of action, until he called out.

"Garston!"

"Yes, sir?"

"Close all the crags and arm our army; wake them all and put a blade and a bow in the hands of each."

"Yes, sir"

"Ranson."

Ranson stepped forward.

"I'm putting you in charge of the battalion that will be our first defence; on the slopes of the mountain. The Besiarites will fortify the inside so that once you are outside there will be no way in. Not for those monsters anyway. Pick out our strongest men and get them into position now."

"Yes, sir."

And he ran out of the arch to go and do this. William was about to follow, when Raimos called his name.

"William."

"Yes?"

"Light the devils up!"

William beamed. "It would be my absolute pleasure, sir!"

And with that, he ran after Ranson, with Garston close behind.

In the space of about ten minutes, the mountain had been transformed. William and Ranson marched ahead of a contingent of strong, battle ready men, each holding a longbow and with an almost absurdly sized quiver strapped to his back, and a sword at his side; similar to William's, but with a thinner blade.

As they passed through the mountain in pairs, William noticed that the ground of any large, open space was now filled with smiths sharpening blades on whetstones, and even forging new blades, armour, and spear and arrow tips.

Then the outermost but largest chambers that were filled with lines of men in identical, gleaming armour, being given orders by Garston, and finally they passed Besiarites, with their long, curious weaponry, standing to attention without a sound, as their mission was booming out to them from Raimos.

He looked purely majestic in even more spectacular armour than before, and a helmet decorated with bright gold. William realised how glad he was to be on their side.

Ranson's leather armour had gone, and in its place was metal, shining plate armour, and a helmet with feathery wings engraved on either side. He held the hilt of Triscant out in front of him, so the scabbard pointed out almost horizontally behind him.

William realised how naturally Ranson fitted into this armour, and this life, as he must have spent most of his life in battle, whereas it was new to William, and he was not very confident about this fight. It was so much bigger than anything he had seen, never mind been in the middle of; although he felt some comfort in the fact he had more power than almost anyone in the entire mountain, and this thought made him chuckle quietly to himself.

William was dressed in a shirt of chainmail, covered with some kind of black, thick, polished leather, and shining metal guards over the joints. His feet were completely encased in metal, with padding on the inside, and the leather went a way up his neck, so the only flesh on show was his face, and his hands, so that he could perform magic.

He had been offered a full plate armour suit, but he wanted to have a decent amount of flexibility and movement as well as protection, so they had adapted this for him. Melnhir hung as his side, and he was determined to use it only as a last resort, and to rely on his abilities as his foremost weapon. He did not want to get too close to those awful creatures again.

Their journey had been going uphill for its entirety, with many twists and turns, and many men had gone down different paths as Ranson pointed to them and shouted orders to them, so when they finally reached fresh air and sunlight, William, Ranson and their men were high up on the mountain and significantly lessened.

They were on the west side, where there was much diversity on the gradient of slope; there were some sheer drops, like the one William and Ranson had sat at when the truth was revealed, and some almost flat areas.

These were defended by groups of Ranson's men all the way down to the road that led to the jump into the cave mouth, and around the north and south slopes too. The east side did not have much fortification, as it was an almost sheer drop down to the sea, but there were still strung some soldiers over it, on platforms at irregular intervals.

The sun was almost at the end of its daily path, so that part of it had already sunk beneath the clouds on the horizon, and the sky to the west was already growing dark and cold.

All around and up the mountain, torches were beginning to be lit; not only because of the ominously encroaching darkness, but the men were also taking advantage of the Scarras' fear of fire.

The dark shadow of hair and claws was shambling along at an almost unnatural pace, as if driven by some unknown force. They had been nowhere near this fast when they had attacked William and Ranson the first time, but they just assumed that it was their rekindled fury that drove them.

Then, all too soon, battle was joined.

The first line of defence was a line of brave men, blocking the way into the waterfall, but these were cut down without mercy by the monstrous hordes.

Then, some Scarra attempted to jump through the rushing water, but the cave door was shut and reinforced, so the Scarra that did not fall short crashed into hard rock, and were sent to join the others; plunging into the fatal abyss.

As was planned, the main horde was bunched onto the precipice, and despite a few that were pushed off the edge by the sheer number behind them, they stood there, trying to formulate their next move.

This was when William stood up from his hiding place in the rocks, and the Scarra looked up and abhorred him, as he stepped onto a plinth-like rock, and spread his arms wide. He was the absolute, undisputed centre of attention.

Then, he seemed to glow white, as if at any second he would be summoned up to the heavens, and his hands burned with a pure, unearthly fire. The Scarra saw a jerking movement, and the fire suddenly seemed to grow at an incredible rate, until an earth-shaking fireball smashed into the centre of the rabble, and some were incinerated on the spot, without realising what had happened.

The resulting shockwave threw bodies every way; forwards, backwards, sideways, and over the precipice.

Cheers and shouts of triumph were hurled from the mouths of men who, not too long ago, had jeered and laughed in William's face.

The blast had killed a great number of Scarra, and many more had been incapacitated. None of these would fight that day.

But from now on, it would not be so easy. They had lost the element of surprise, and despite their military advantage, the Scarra outnumbered them at least five to one.

The hideous beasts had finally found a way up the smooth cliff face.

One by one, they jumped at the wall and stabbed their horrific claws straight into it. From where the men were positioned, they could not see them making their way up, but they could imagine the monsters crawling up like Hell-born spiders.

Many Scarra misjudged their aim in the dark, and were beaten down by the tumbling water and thrown into the abyss.

Some Scarra had managed to claw their way over the precipice, and were now visible to the awaiting men; as fires were lit all around and up the mountain, lighting the slopes; almost as fully as sunlight.

Ranson was not going to let them get any closer, so he called out in his loud, clear voice.

"Archers!"

The men rose as William had, with bows already strung and arrows fitted, as William fired another blast. This knocked a great crater into the slowly levelling ground, and taking many more Scarra with it.

"Aim!"

Now it was the bows' turn.

"Fire!"

A volley of winged needles flew from their masters, in a cloud as thick as the hurrying darkness from the East, and practically shredded the first wave of monsters. Then, as the first group of bowman reloaded, a second cloud of arrows was loosed, accompanied by a third blast from William.

The long, slender arrows were enough to impale a man where he stood, but somehow, miraculously, the fire lit the metal tips of those deadly shafts while in flight, and the light cut back the darkness in a blinding cloud. Now, not only were their strikes piercing, but they ignited the Scarras' fur, causing new flame to burn on them, bright and terrible, in answer to the almost dead light of the sun.

As these Scarra fell, the ones behind had to clamber over not only the precipice, but over their fallen kin too. They themselves began to burn, and soon quite a number had perished to the flames. The bodies piled high, and the flames danced higher, until a wall of fire had arisen, close to the drop of the cliff.

William closed his eyes, slowed his breathing and concentrated, until the entire mountain appeared in his mind.

The dead Earth and sky looked as dark as they were when his eyes were open, but the surrounding plants glowed slightly green with eerie luminescence. The men around him glowed a pale grey, some brighter than others, but none as bright as Ranson. He was bright white, with a divine aura encircling him.

Down, on the feet of the mountain, behind the wall of glowing fire, there was an ugly, grimy brown aura. This was the Scarra.

William realised that, by reaching out with his powers, he was seeing the pure life-force of everything around him. But this only increased his loathing for the monsters.

He realised that how truly horrible they were, if their very life-force was corrupted and warped so far from human that they looked brown and dirty against the men's light grey sheen.

William had an idea.

He focused on the bright tongues of flame in front of the brownish smudge. Using his powers, he lifted the roots of the fires up, a couple of inches from the charred bodies, and it burned whiter and hotter than ever before. Using his mind, William pushed if forward.

Slowly, menacingly, the ever-hungry tongues crept towards the Scarra. Such was the fear in some, that they chose to retreat off the cliff and tumble into the abyss, rather than face the terrible incineration that inched ever closer. Those who stayed on the edge were consumed by the flames, and became piles of grey ash, with sparks rising from them, dancing into the dark night sky.

Finally, after its job was done, the wall of fire was extinguished, and William opened his eyes.

All around him were cheering soldiers, revelling in a victory that was not their own.

Suddenly, a cry rang out from the southern slopes. A host of Scarra were scaling the mountain from the south; from mountain paths over the lower peaks.

The men that were there fought incredibly well, and their kill count was awe-inspiring compared with their losses. But despite the fact that there were fewer Scarra on this slope, they were beginning to falter, as the sheer multitude of the monsters began to overwhelm them.

Ranson seemed divided, and for a moment he was frozen in indecision. William made the choice for him.

"Take your men and defend the southern edge. I will protect this one"

Then he smiled at Ranson.

"Less collateral damage if I blow up this side of the mountain!"

Ranson smiled back gratefully, and gave the orders to his men, who echoed them all the way down the mountain. Then, with one last nod to William, he ran to the other slope himself.

Meanwhile, William was planning his next move.

The Scarra were making their way up the mountain, but they were obviously warier. They were crouched, steadier and surer, with noses up in the air; testing it for even the faintest sign of what was awaiting them.

William saw this while crouched himself; behind a large rock, with sides almost polished smooth by the wind.

His right index finger traced the bottom of the rock, at the point where it met the brownish grass. The neck of the boulder was glowing with the same white-hot glare as the end of his finger.

With a sharp crack, the gargantuan boulder's foundation softened just enough to allow it to snap and roll down the slope. Its journey intersected with many of the Scarras', and it crushed the life out of more than half a dozen of them before flying off the precipice at the bottom.

However, such was its momentum, that it flew far enough to smash into and destroy the rock that jutted out and allowed Scarra to leap onto the wall, while crushing a few in the process. Now that this was gone, there seemed to be no way across, so the Scarra gave up, split, and shambled of in two separate factions; one to the North, and the other to the South. William wondered why they were so determined to take the mountain, if this was indeed a random attack by animalistic creatures.

He did not have much time to think on this however, as there were still a fair number of Scarra scaling the slope, so, once again, William closed his eyes and concentrated.

And then the waterfall moved.

It was only a little at first; wavering slightly from side to side while lit with a pale light that fought back the surrounding darkness.

But then, the origins of the waterfall changed, and the flow from the spring at the top of the mountain changed its course. Now it flowed down towards William, who sprung onto a neighbouring rock that lifted him from the path of the water.

As it reached the rock, it obediently parted and wound around the stone, until it re-joined itself on the other side.

As it flowed down however, it became stronger and faster, and as it rushed down the slope it put out many of the fires, and also took the legs out from underneath some of the Scarra, and cast them back over the precipice at the bottom.

But there were still some left in small clusters on the mountain.

Williams closed his eyes for a third time and summoned up globules of water from what was now no less than a river.

The first wave of blobs shaped themselves into mask-like bubbles that wrapped like steel bands around noses and mouths and squeezed; smothering and suffocating them until they lay motionless on the ground.

The next surge of water was atomised almost as soon as it was separated from the main flow, and when fired at the Scarra, the minuscule droplets practically ripped them apart.

Some particularly giant globules wrapped around the Scarra until they were entirely encased in the bubble, and were either left there to suffocate, or were hurled off the cliff at alarming speed.

Soon, there were no Scarra left on the mountain, and he righted the waterfall with mind, until it was flowing once more over the cave door. This in itself was so well camouflaged against the rock that it would be well enough hidden when closed that no-one would notice it unless they knew where it was; even without the waterfall in front. But as it was night, there was no worry of this.

But then William had a terrible thought. The Scarra that had gone to the southern slopes would be dealt with by Ranson and his men, but the group that went to the northern slope would find it far less defended and would overpower it in no time.

He ran north, but all the while, his vision was blocked by a ridge that ran round the mountain, but once it was cleared, he saw the northern slope.

What he saw made him wish he had come sooner.

The mountain was soaked with blood, and the bodies of man and monster alike were like chainmail on the slopes; numerous and uninterrupted, save for small patches of brown grass, now slathered with crimson. The men were fighting well, and were killing more than they lost. But there was something different about this fight.

It was more primal; more merciless. It was like two wild animals fighting over a scrap of meat. Whoever lost would lose far more than pride.

The men didn't even seem like men. They were just killing, as if they didn't care whether it was friend of foe that they cut down; as if they were as blind to the preciousness of life as the creatures that faced them.

William could not use his abilities on any grand scale here; the men and the Scarra were in such a tight fray that to kill one combatant would be to kill the other too.

So, reluctantly, he drew Melnhir and charged into the throng.

His first kill was a Scarra that was on all fours, with claws splayed out on the ground, and crouching over the partially devoured carcass of a man in armour, which might once have shone alongside its peers. William leapt over it and swung his sword downwards as he went.

His feet hit the ground at the at the same time as the hairy head after being sliced from its neck, but the stroke was so quick and precise, that by the time blood began to flow, William was in the midst of his next bout.

He fought his way through the scrabbling hordes until he came to the front lines. Here there was precious little space to move, never mind to swing a sword or claws, so the real battle was of strength; far more than skill.

The Scarra were just using brute force and bulk to push against the men, but their opponents were more ordered, forming something that resembled a phalanx, with their shields in front; the only thing separating them from savage monsters. They were also lit brightly by the light of the torches, whereas the monsters merely looked like a black cloud, and only the front ranks were illuminated; a line of horrific faces pressing in towards the men.

After a while of pushing and shoving, and not really getting anywhere, William knew he had to step in.

He told some men behind that still had their bows to ready them and find what arrows they could. He then told them to form up into ranks and aim over the heads of the Scarra.

As they shot, William closed his eyes and concentrated. Whilst in the air, the arrows glowed a sudden white, and turned, flying back, bright and low over the heads of the hairy hordes. They flew into the backs and neck of the monsters that were pushing against the hexagonal shields of the men, and they fell backwards onto their kin, knocking them over for many lines back.

Using this brief confusion and disorganisation, the men plunged forward and cut a great swathe in the ranks of the monsters.

Then, with a deep-throated roar, a multitude of men, lit by yet more torches, plunged into the other side of the hairy host and cut them down in a blizzard of blades and arrows.

William finished off a Scarra with a rapid slash to its stomach, and turned to see Ranson expertly cutting down three monsters in rapid succession.

He looked up and saw William, and the two men smiled at each other, just before a clawed slash almost took William's head off. He swung Melnhir round in his hand and plunged it into the stomach of the figure behind him.

Ranson nodded approvingly as the body fell to the floor, and they both turned and started battles of their own.

By the combined effort of Ranson and William's men, the Scarra horde was decimated, and the remainder was tiring and falling at double the rate.

To finish of the battle, William had an idea, but he needed Ranson's help, so he secretly transmitted a message in his mind.

Remember what you did against the Scarra the first time? Well I'm going to create a wall of fire, but I need your help to make it strong enough. Get ready.

Ranson and William stood apart, separated by man and monster, but in their minds they were one, with their eyes closed, concentrating on the task before them.

Now.

The ground ignited in front of the shields and the first line of Scarra exploded in an instant. The lines behind froze as the fire lit up their terrible, ugly faces, contorted further in pure dread.

The tongues of fire leapt higher than a man, higher than a horse, and then higher than any tree. The flames were opaque with bright, white light.

The Scarra could not cope with the blinding sight of the fire, never mind the searing heat, so they fled, running back down the mountain, some on all fours, and some even falling down the slope in their haste.

The men that they left behind them finished off the last of their kin; those who were blocked by the flames and could not get away.

William and Ranson extinguished the flames, and the men cheered with renewed vigour.

The sun was rising to the east over the sea, and the shadow of the mountain was stretching out like and arrow over the Forest of Delsus; pointing out the path of the Scarras' retreat.

But while the men were busy revelling in what was now a well-earned victory, William looked out over the forest, and saw that the dawn light and the long shadow of the mountain pointed to their doom.

Beneath the trees there was an almost rhythmic pounding. It was like the sound of a bass drum being beaten every second, crossed with sound of metal clanking together.

This was, of course, the unnatural, almost mechanical sound of a great mass marching with perfectly timed strides and precisely rehearsed clanging of weapons on shields.

The light betrayed them of their numbers, but even so, the glint of warm sunlight off cold metal chilled even the bravest heart held in its fleshy carapace on that mountain slope. Their lines were so numerous so that even though they were marching to the west slope, the lines were visible even to the men on the northern slope.

Ranson was called to the west, and as he reached the place where he stood before the battle begun, he saw the hopelessness of their plight.

A great, wide scar was being scythed in the once magnificent forest by a multitude that seemed to be emissaries of the sun, but came with hearts darker than the darkest cave on the blackest night.

Not only did they have numbers on their side, but they too dragged behind them machines of war. Foul, mechanic creations from a twisted, blood-thirsty mind. Vast, covered things they were; constructed of metal and darkened wood, but shrouded in some kind of leathery skin, unlike any animal skin Ranson had seen before, as if they had something to hide.

Some were shallow and wide, others tall and thin, but all possessed of a terrifying mystery somewhere under those unnatural coverings.

The men themselves were varied. Some had full plate armour, with long, two handed swords not unlike Triscant, strapped to their back. No flesh could be seen beneath that seemingly impenetrable armour.

Others were more terrifying for William, as they were battalions of men practically identical to the ones who killed his mother and taken his father. They were clad in leather armour with curious helmets, and long, slightly curved swords and oval-shaped shields.

They were in front and were considerably more numerous than the elite armoured behemoths, but were preceded by the terrible masked machines.

William was simply aghast. He had never seen anything like this vast army before. It almost tripled the Scarra host in numbers.

As for the rabble that escaped from the wall of fire, they were slain as soon as they came near the front lines of Vanyol's men; cut down like the beasts that they were, without mercy or compassion.

As the final animalistic screams died away, the men advanced again, and once more the curious drum-roll boomed and echoed under the trees.

William was simply terrified.

As he stood, Ranson rested a reassuring hand on his shoulder. They glanced at each other, but even William could see the lack of confidence in the other man's eyes.

A wordless chant became audible over the drum-roll of metal against earth, and it rose in volume and ferocity for each passing second.

Ranson snapped out of the terror that mesmerised him, and shouted to his men, also ripping them from their fear-induced trances.

He could have given an awe-inspiring speech, talking of victory and conquering all enemies, but each man there new that defeat was assured.

"Men! Today every man standing here had earned their place in the Resistance, but you know as well as I that we will not win this fight. Those who wish to may surrender, but I beg you, remember that the men that we face have less mercy than the monsters that we beat on this morn. Those who wish to flee may, but they will hunt you down like dogs! But those you who have it in their hearts to fight to the last man, fight now! With me! And die at my side for liberty and freedom in this world! We will not achieve it this day, but we will prove to the Three that the free arms which wield these blades and draw these bows are a force to be reckoned with all the same! Now what do you say? Do we fall with empty hearts, or do we fall with a cry on our lips and a fire in our hearts?! Do... we... fight?!"

Ranson's final words were met with a deep-throated roar from thousands of voices that carried up into the heavens and down into the earth and deep into the hearts of every man in the vast lines awaiting them.

Then, following their voices, the men ran down the mountain with their swords drawn and ready. About a third stayed, and readied their bows.

Then they shot, and a cloud of shafts, expansive and dense, flew from the mountain. These were then caught by the prevailing wind and carried over the machines, further on their path into the lines of the men that William scorned.

But they seemed to be expecting it, and raised their shields above them, and the arrows simply broke on the polished metal and fell, ruined, to the ground.

Some found their mark and plunged in between the scales of this massive animal, but far too few fell to hinder its advance.

The men pushing the machines at the head of the host stopped as they reached the gulley of emptiness that bordered the eastern slope of the mountain, and each one began to clink and clank out into various shapes and sizes.

The tall, thin tower-like structures all moved right up to the edge of the precipice, and the bases drilled into the ground with giant rotating tools, anchoring into the earth. The top section split and fell forward towards the wall of rock, as a felled tree does on its path towards the ground, and the top edge of the squared tower slammed into the top of the wall with metres to spare, so that the end just cleared the lip of the cliff.

Then the men above could see what these really were. They were tubes of metal, wood and skins with ladders all up the inside, so that men could climb up the sheer rock, ten at a time, and emerge without fear of being struck down by arrows. The skins protected them until they emerged in lines, with shields that would deflect arrows from then on.

This was happening all around the mountain, so the infantry was on the slopes without having to pay heed to cliff or arrows until they were in solid lines, ready to face anything.

Other, shallower shapes were uncovered. The sheets of skins were pulled off to reveal a line of large, metal crossbow-type machines that looked average enough, despite the fact that they were far taller than a horse, and double again the width.

Men loaded each one and directed others to aim it, and then two men each with levers wound them up. This all took around a minute, but as soon as it was done, the men pulled a lever and each giant machine fired.

At once, massive projectiles flew up and away from the lines of men at the feet of the mountain, and towards the hordes on the slopes, but as they reached the top of their arc, the large, thick missiles split into at least ten smaller ones, but each still had its own fletching and deadly tip, and each was still larger than any normal arrow.

On its own, one of these dividing projectiles would be devastating, but one was fired from each of twenty mechanisms, so the cloud of arrows, carried by the momentum of the larger projectiles, flew straight into the middle of the crowd rushing down the mountain. Not a single man survived within the perimeter of the deadly rainfall.

William and Ranson saw this devastation, and knew that they had to do something. The machines were almost ready to fire again, but the Casters had planned their next move.

They had moved to the giant ridge at the top of the mountain. From this vantage point they could see the whole of the mountain, which was already being taken up by bodies of men; and Scarra from the last battle.

Together, they began to send fireballs down the mountain, which had an utterly obliterating effect on the machines that they hit. Any wood on them was vaporised, and the metal either melted in a flash, or the joints were blown apart by the sheer force of the impact.

Almost half of the crossbows had been destroyed by the time the others fired again. At this point, the Casters ceased sending volleys of fire, and concentrated their powers onto the incoming bolts.

William managed to simply knock them off course, or straight downwards, but Ranson, being more skilled, stopped them in the air, flipped them round, and catapulted them backwards; at twice the speed and embellished with white flame towards the machines that fired them. The volleys practically shredded the men that operated them, and also set alight to many wooden components, crippling some machines beyond repair.

Only about a third of the machines were left, but by this time, many of the leather-clad soldiers had managed to clamber up the protected ladders and were now forming up on the slopes, despite the volleys of arrows from Ranson's men that killed some men and heavily disrupted the formations of the others.

The pair was determined that the machines would not get another torrent of bolts, and so they summoned up all of their power and formed fire from thin air. But such was their expulsion of power that they glowed a white as bright as the rising sun, and together they rose up into the air.

Men from both sides turned their eyes up to the sky to look, and saw a ball of light rise, shining, to the deep blue heavens. There could be no distinction between the two men, as the light was so bright that Ranson's men thought that it was just William, rising up in splendorous glory.

Suddenly, a noise like a thunderclap boomed out from the sphere, and giant balls of flame shot out, trailing smoke and steam behind them.

They slammed into the machines, but such was their power that they incinerated the machines in an instant, and send out a shockwave so powerful that soldiers for a hundred meters around them were instantly atomised. Once the light had died from each impact site, all that was left was a deep, smoking crater where each machine used to be.

Fireballs continued to fly out of the white ball of light, and tore whole battalions apart; and not only in the ranks of the leather-clad men, but amongst the metal colossuses too.

Then, suddenly, a deeper boom erupted from the West, and a visible shockwave tore through the air. It hit a fireball on its rapid journey, which dissipated without a trace, leaving its trail abruptly without a guide.

Then it hit the sphere of energy, which faded as quickly as it had appeared. The men who had seen it did not see two bodies fall from the sky, as their eyes had become used to the glaring brightness, and were unaccustomed to the sudden dimness.

William and Ranson fell back onto the ridge with a jolt, but despite a few bumps and bruises, they weren't too hurt. But William was looking in confusion at his father, who was obviously as ignorant as him.

"What happened?" demanded the younger man.

"I don't know. But I can't feel my powers."

Looking very worried, he lifted his hands to summon a fireball, but despite massive concentration and all of Ranson's effort, nothing happened.

William also tried, but his abilities were gone too.

"So what do we do now?" asked William, but Ranson was considerately more upset, and William realised that he had had his powers for the whole of his life, and now it had disappeared, he felt utterly helpless.

He put his arm around the older man, and spoke comfortingly to him, as a father talks to his son when he is scared of the dark.

"Look, I know that this is a bigger deal for you than it is for me, but maybe a while without powers will do us good. I mean, we can still fight, and it might give the other side a fairer chance!"

Ranson looked up and smiled at him, sadly.

"Maybe you're right. I'm glad I've got to know you now, but I never expected that you'd be the wiser of us both, especially in the middle of a battle!"

They both laughed, but behind both laughs there was an air of uncertainty felt by both, as they jumped down from the ridge and drew Melnhir and Triscant.

By the time they reached the men, the front ranks were already in combat, and the bowman, seeing that arrows would be little more use, dropped their bows, released the quivers from their backs, drew their swords, and plunged into the fray.

However they followed William and Ranson in, as the Casters had already thrown themselves into battle.

Chapter 9 - The Man and the Soldier

William swung Melnhir round and took out four enemies in rapid succession, while beside him Ranson did the same, slightly more expertly.

Suddenly, a sword was swung out of nowhere towards Ranson, and, having only just parried it, he broke off from his pairing with his son to finish off the battle.

William swung his sword round at a combatant that had just struck down a soldier of the Resistance, and they were suddenly engaged in combat. William could fight relatively well, but he was really missing having the advantage of his powers.

He blocked a downward blow by raising his sword horizontally above his head, but the force pushed him onto his knees, and the two men were locked in that position, as the bout became a battle of strength.

William shifted the strain entirely onto his right arm, and searched blindly on the ground around him with his other hand.

Then his hand came into contact with a hilt of some kind. Not caring what it was, William raised it and plunged it into the side of his opponent, where the armour joints were weakest.

It turned out that the weapon was a long-bladed dagger, and was perfect, as it was long enough to do serious damage, but was short and quick enough so that the soldier did not notice it before it was thrust into his flesh.

He dropped his sword, and fell to his knees with his face frozen in surprise, and a small stream of blood tricked out from the corner of his mouth.

William got up and stood over him, and was quite ready to finish him off. It would have been easy; one swing of Melnhir. But he did not have it in him, and so knocked the man out with the hilt, allowing him to die in peace.

He knelt down beside the man that the soldier had struck down earlier, and held his hand until he saw the light leave his eyes and his hand fall limply onto his chest.

Ranson was right. War was Hell.

He stood up from his kneeling position and raised his sword, ready to fight his next battle. He turned, and the whole battle, the whole world; everything around him, seemed to move in slow motion.

There, mercilessly skewering a young soldier, was the captain. The man that had killed his mother, and taken his father; the man that had shattered his life, was ten metres away from him on the battlefield. Ranson had said that he would get his chance, and here it was.

Their eyes locked, and as the young soldier fell to the ground, they strode meaningfully towards each other, with swords ready.

Another of Vanyol's men attempted to interrupt William's path by running at him; sword raised, but William just sidestepped, and, swinging his sword with all his might, he beheaded him as he ran. He fell next to William, and his head rolled off his shoulders as they hit the ground, but never did William's eyes leave the captain's as he walked forwards towards him.

They were separated by nothing now, but for five metres of empty ground, which despite the vivid stains of crimson, was brown and dry. Any grass that grew had been crushed beneath many feet, and was now plastered to the ground with dirt. It looked flat and smooth, but for the occasional body that lay there, covering it with blood and gore.

The men were bordered by fighting soldiers, but neither world seemed to acknowledge the other's existence.

The gap was closing fast, and soon they were only an arm's length away from each other.

At once, they were circling round each other; weighing up each other's weaknesses in this curious, hypnotic dance.

Finally, the loud silence was broken by the captain's harsh voice.

"Looks like I underestimated you, boy. You're even more stupid than I gave you credit for. Without your powers, you will die at the hand of a trained soldier."

He sneered, and William was taken aback. How did he know that he had lost his powers?

The captain saw the question forming in his mind, and before it could reach his lips, the soldier continued.

"It scares you, doesn't it; what I know about you."

They continued circling; in orbit of an invisible barrier, which kept them separated, but for a few feigned strikes that led the battle nowhere.

"But it burns you more to know that you had power; to feel special, to have the powers of the gods, only to have it taken from you, and to fall face down on the earth, with the rest of us mortals."

"Taken?"

William noticed something flicker in the other man's eyes at that one, simple word, and realised that through his arrogance he had revealed too much.

"It must kill you to know that you have failed your parents."

He saw by William's face that he had struck a deep blow.

"It must destroy you to know that you practically killed them yourself!"

At these words, William forgot his deductions about the captain's mistake. He forgot Ranson, and the damn, bloody war. He forgot the Scarra, and he even forgot his loss of powers.

All he could see was the captain, and the anger rose as he prepared to launch his blind attack.

But the soldier moved first, and lunged sharply towards him, and suddenly they were locked in combat.

Their swords rang and sung as they collided, but their sounds were lost in the fray around them.

Just two songs of metal in a million.

Morning was passing into noon, and still the clashes and ringing of swords rent the air above and around the mountain.

By now, many lives, on both sides, were lost.

The armoured behemoths had begun to climb the mountain, devastating anything in their paths, but the way was hard for them. Their armour was heavy and clumsy, and many were toppled over and rolled back down the slopes.

After this had gone on for a while, they were attacked from the rear.

By way of a miracle, and some secret passage, the Besiarites, led by Raimos and Garston, had appeared behind the ranks of the colossuses, and plunged head-long into them.

The two groups of soldiers were a good match; skill and speed against power and armour-plating.

Meanwhile, Ranson and his men were being driven back, albeit slowly, by Vanyol's men.

William was still locked in combat with the captain, and although the fight was draining them, neither let up in their ferocious strokes, and both tried hard not to show any outward sign of tiring.

But both men knew that, whatever the result, the battle would be over soon.

The sun was at its hottest through the clear blue sky, and the light and heat beat down on them more with every passing minute. Their feet kicked up dirt and dust, which choked them as they spun round in their lethal dance.

William's eyes began to glaze over. He wasn't just tired from the fight, although it was draining him fast. It was, he realised, that he had not had a full meal, or night's sleep, for a week.

The levels of energy in his body were so low, that he was running solely on adrenaline; and even this was running out rapidly.

His senses were dulling and his wits were fading slowly, and to his dismay, he saw that the captain was in far better shape than he was. After all, the other man was a skilled soldier; one who was trained to fight like this.

At one point, as they broke apart, he instinctively raised his hand as if to cast a fireball, but then he remembered what had happened, swore, and by the time the captain swung his sword, William was back in the combat stance and began fighting again.

The muscles in William's arms were screaming at him through the strain of swinging Melnhir and the jolts of each collision of the two blades.

Eventually they began to falter and weaken, and William was only just able to parry the captain's attacks.

Finally, his arms failed altogether. He swung his sword with difficulty into the path of the captain's, and the impact jolted through him, and it was too much for his wrists.

They twisted round and a splitting pain tore up his arms and Melnhir flew from his hands; landing a good few yards behind the captain.

William was woken from his tired trance by the realisation that he was dead.

He ducked and dodged the slashes from the captain's sword, but he could not keep this up for long. He was forced backwards, and tripped over the body of a soldier, and landed with a bump on the ground.

The captain walked slowly towards William, who was lying helplessly on the floor, with his feet raised on top of the dead soldier.

He was now towering over William, with his sword over his head, ready to slice down and slay his unmoving opponent.

Just before his arms began their journey downwards, two feet slammed into his ribs and winded him, knocking him back.

William had prepared himself as the captain walked towards him, and as he raised his sword, he coiled himself like a spring, and, using the already elevated position of his legs, planted his feet firmly in the middle of his chest.

As the captain stumbled back, William got up and desperately dived, past the staggering captain, and towards Melnhir. But the captain was not entirely without his wits, and as William flew past him the soldier swung his sword with one hand, and caught the young man a deep slice in his side.

The captain was still falling backwards, when William landed with his hand on the hilt of his fallen sword, rolled on his shoulder, and was up on his knees, facing the captain.

The man had just caught his balance back, and turned, still a little unsteady, towards William.

And just before he had turned enough to see him, Melnhir was plunged into his stomach, and went right through him, until the hilt was against his front, and the point was sticking out of his back.

His mouth was open in pure shock, and his sword finally dropped from his hand in defeat. A steady flow of blood trickled from the corner of his mouth, and mixed with the ample sweat on his face, until the horrible mixture dripped down from his chin onto the brown grass.

William was pressed against the man who had ruined his life; the man who had killed his mother in cold blood, and taken his father to suffer in some horrible camp, or die on the front line of a petty war.

But his thoughts were neither of them, nor anything else from his life until a few hours ago.

The captain sank to his knees, and now William stood above him; triumphant.

He knelt himself, and as their faces were together William almost spat as he hissed at him.

"How did you know?"

No reaction.

"How did you know about my powers?!"

Still nothing, and William began to twist the blade inside the captain, causing him pain beyond belief, but the only reaction he got was an insane grin through the agony.

Infuriated, William wrenched his sword violently out of the captain, and blood gushed out of the wound like a mountain spring.

He collapsed onto the dry ground, which was rapidly being conquered by the circular stain of crimson beneath him. He began to convulse on the ground, and through the obvious pain and the stream of blood that he was choking back, he spoke.

"You don't understand yet, do you?"

William stood up, but was listening intently.

"You are all dead. Every single traitor will die."

He coughed, and blood speckled his lips.

"Because he is coming, and he will kill you all. He took your powers, and now there is nothing you can do to stop him."

He closed his eyes, and was fading fast, when William knelt down beside him, not caring that his knees were thrust into the dying man's warm life-blood, and shouted at him.

"Who?! Who is he?!"

For a second, the captain opened his eyes, and through a shaking breath, and another convulsion, he spoke his last two words. Simple and devastating.

"Your doom."

Then, with a final breath, his head fell back, his body went limp, and the man died.

As the stains continued on their journey, they did not see the scene they left behind them.

The body of a dead soldier lay, with a red break in his armour over his stomach, and a young man standing above it, with his head hung down, his sword coated with blood, and some of his own running from a wound in his side.

Triumph in a hollow victory.

Chapter 10 - The Lightning Fall

William looked down on the man that had ripped his life apart. The captain was still, lifeless, and lying in a rapidly cooling pool of his own blood.

But as he stared down entranced at the bloody site, he realised something.

He had begun his journey and his training as a Caster for the sole purpose of revenge, but now the deed was done, he felt no overwhelming peace; no feeling of pride or achievement in what he had done.

He felt empty; cold and tired, and he realised just how short the time had been since he had started.

Two weeks ago he had been farming and working with his father in the fields of Tursus, but now he was a killer; a warrior for a cause whose aim is to overthrow the leaders of the world.

How short a time for a boy to become a man.

Through his dense thoughts, William caught a flash of light in the corner of his eye.

Suddenly, William was thrown off his feet by an immensely powerful blast that carried him metres away from where he was standing.

He slammed into the ground with great clods of earth and pieces of metal cascading down around him. He tried as best he could to shield his head from the falling debris, but he felt the showers bounce off his body.

After a few seconds, the dust settled and William got up onto his hands and knees. His ears were ringing and his hearing was muffled beyond comprehension. He put a hand to one ear, and when he looked at it, it was stained with blood.

He got to his feet, but he was so dazed that he lost his balance, and fell over almost immediately.

Another flash appeared in his vision, but this time he was looking in its direction, so he saw what it was clearly.

It was a gargantuan fireball, bigger by far than any that he or Ranson had produced. It flew through the air trailing thick smoke, and as William got to his feet once more, everything happened in slow motion.

The fireball smashed into the mountain at a point, which from where he was standing, William could not quite see the point of impact, but he saw rocks, earth and dust fly out diagonally from the slope, creating a great plume of ash and dust that billowed out into the sky.

William saw bodies fly up behind the cloud, and fall far lower down the slope. The number of men thrown up like ragdolls was so massive that they formed their own swarm under the dust cloud.

A split second later, the shockwave blasted out, and William was thrown from his feet once again, but this discharge was so much more powerful that it threw him twenty metres backwards and into a big boulder. His back connected with the rock with an agonising thud, and he fell to the ground with a shuddering pain searing through his body.

He looked up, and raining all around him were bodies and pieces of armour. His eyes scanned across the departed, but the corpse of the captain was nowhere to be seen.

Once again he tried to get up, and once more he overbalanced and fell down against the rock. After a few tries, he managed to clamber to his feet and remain there, but his armour was rent and broken from the blasts and the impact with the rock, so he released the straps and let it fall to the ground. He was now dressed in leather padding and his old clothes underneath. Finally, with a hurting back and blood running from his ears, he walked towards the epicentre of the blast.

Soon, after walking through a dense field of bodies; some of which were piled higher than his head, William reached the edge of the precipice.

He was standing on the edge of what was now a sheer drop at the edge of a simply vast crater. The fireball had penetrated through thick rock until it had blasted through into the hollow halls beneath. He could see a little way inside, but there was merely ash and fragments of metal where once there had been forges and furnaces. The crater was smoking and steaming, with bodies of friends and foes alike lining the smooth inside edge. William gazed on so much death and destruction that silent tears ran their course down his bloodied face.

The ground shook him out of his mourning, and he almost toppled off the edge of the precipice.

Another fireball had hit the mountain further from him, but he barely had to imagine the horror and destruction that it caused.

He tore his eyes away from the depressing sight, and as he turned his aching body away, his mind was spinning with thought.

What was happening?

He is coming, and he will kill you all. Your doom.

The words echoed round his head, as the shroud of mystery parted in his mind, all his thoughts coalesced into an evil that was not nameless. It had a name that William had heard many times, but he had detached himself from iniquity so readily that he had not even considered the possibility of that name becoming palpable.

But now it had.

Vanyol had come.

Suddenly, an ear-splitting thunderclap ripped like a knife through his thoughts and juddered his heart. The sky suddenly darkened as thick, black clouds rolled out over the mountain, strangling the light and blanketing the peak and the lands around it in shadow. The world turned grey and dreary, as if the colours of the world had carried any hope of happiness away with them.

Under the clouds came the only discernible colours in the drained world.

Great flashes of light blazed out from the cloud cover, but as if to counteract the yellow flares, a steady, red luminescence glowed out from an epicentre directly west of the mountain. The nucleus of the glow was just far enough out of William's vision so that he could not see it clearly, but he no doubt as to what, or who, it was.

Bright bolts fell downwards from the cloud cover in such numbers and ferocity that for a fraction of a second, nothing could be seen between the blinding glare of the searing deluge.

What no-one saw until afterwards was that in the small crater that each bolt had left behind were men, wielding spears with vicious-looking tips and fully plated body armour. Even their faces were covered completely by metal. There were no breaks in the smooth surface to see or even breathe through; they were guided solely by Vanyol, so that their own senses would not betray them.

As the smoke and blindness cleared, the men left on the mountain saw that hopelessness of their plight, and surrendered immediately. All of the stirring fire from Ranson's earlier speech was gone, and fear overtook them. Even William, without his powers and weakened and bleeding, felt like giving up.

But the decision was made for him, as two sharp points were jabbed roughly into his back, forcing him forward.

Together, the three men walked quite a way before anything around them changed. For ages it was just bodies and gore spread out across the ground, until at last, Vanyol arrived at the mountain.

He positioned himself above the western slope, and in an incredible red aura, floated downwards. He hovered over the Besiarites, who had just won over the metal-covered behemoths, and sent down blankets of crimson flames over them.

William watched as men trained from infancy; the toughest men in the world; the ultimate, elite fighting force screamed in implausible, unbearable pain as the hungry flames burned the life out of them. But amidst the high mantle of flames, two areas were not burning; one around Raimos, and one around Garston. They were obviously perplexed at being the only ones to survive. Surely they would be the most dangerous to the Three, but nevertheless, the flames refused to envelop them.

One Besiarite flung himself, screaming, at Raimos; his head bald, and his skin charred and flaking, and despite the attempts of his leader, the man was pulled back by the flames, and consumed in screams of agony.

The two men that lived both walked towards the edge of the flames, where the rest of the surviving men, including William, were now assembled, surrounded on all sides by faceless figures.

The circle of guards broke to allow the two through, but only Raimos was grabbed and thrown down with his men. Garston stood above him and looked down on him with a face that could barely contain his insane glee.

"Finally!" He almost screamed the words out. "Finally you know how it feels! To be at the feet of a man who makes your life miserable! Twenty years I have been by your side, but ever since I got there you have paid heed to none of my counsel, and disregarded me and degraded me at every turn! Well now you will die with the other traitors, and the Three will rise!"

But what Garston had not realised was that in the time that he was crazily screaming at Raimos, Vanyol had landed at the foot of the western slope, and was now directly behind him.

The most striking thing about him was his cloak. It flowed out behind him like water, but not into the ground; into the air. Dozens of tattered arms swum around in the air about him, making an ominous silhouette against the flickering fire that had become a mass-grave.

His skin was pale, ghostly white, but around his eyes were dark patches, which only further emphasised his blood-red pupils.

But as the dark figure spoke, his voice was a hoarse whisper, but that only added to the terror for William.

"We had risen long before you came. You told us where to find you, but now your usefulness has run its course."

Garston turned around in surprise at the voice, but his expression changed first to confusion, and then to dread, and he stuttered as he tried to appeal to the dark figure before him.

"B-but sir. I betrayed my comrades to serve you..."But Vanyol cut off his bumbling with a voice that was quiet, but commanded power and authority.

"And you could betray me in the same way. Traitors are like spears. Use them to pierce enemy armour, but once they are broken and blunt, cast them away so they will not strain your arm any further. And you have become blunt and useless. You must be taken care of."

Any further bumbling was ended immediately. Quite calmly, Vanyol touched an index finger on Garston's forehead, and it suddenly glowed red with anger. The light seemed to ripple down inside his body; from his head to his toes, and he convulsed slightly as the energy ate him from the inside out.

Then the inward light faded as quickly as it appeared, but Garston froze, and his skin began to peel where Vanyol's finger had touched him, and then like a wave from there, his body seemed to fall apart.

Skin flaked away, and bone showed for a moment, until it crumbled in its turn. Nothing further could be seen inside, as the crimson energy had atomised his insides. Finally, the structure of his body collapsed, and the remaining ashes and dust fell into a pile on the dirty ground.

And Vanyol simply walked past.

He looked as if he couldn't care less about what had just happened; as if the dead man was merely dirt beneath his feet. In a way he was now.

And William abhorred him; he loathed him. The way he just disregarded the preciousness of life made his blood boil and his skin crawl.

But now the horrific sight had passed away on the wind, and Vanyol stood over the group of kneeling soldiers, who were surrounded by a horse-shoe of spearmen, and addressed them in his ghoulish whisper.

"Your Resistance is crushed. Your army is decimated, and your spirits are broken. Your heroes are drained of their powers. But who is this sorcerer? Who is this magician? Who is this...Caster?"

This last word almost made him laugh with derision, but the crowd before him stayed deathly silent.

"Why do you defend him? He has not helped you. You are on your knees, and what does this unsung hero do to save you? Nothing!"

Still no reaction, and Vanyol became frustrated. He sent fireballs into the crowd and obliterated some soldiers, but still nothing, and he was just about ready to kill them all, just to be sure, when he saw a face he recognised that stared straight at him out of the sea of bowed heads.

"You!" Vanyol's voice rose in sudden intensity, and he pointed madly towards the crowd.

Towards William.

Men rushed to him from the horse-shoe, and William prepared for the inevitable.

One soldier pushed through the crowd from Vanyol's direction, and reached out his arms towards him.

But then he pushed him aside and grabbed the man behind him, as other soldiers grabbed the figure from the sides and behind.

William watched, helpless, as Ranson was dragged through the kneeling men with blood running down his face from a dull wound on his forehead. As he passed William, they locked eyes, and the look that Ranson gave him was as heart-breaking as a lamb taken to slaughter. But there was only one message in that look.

I love you.

Tears fell from the younger man's eyes, as they both knew what was an inevitable future.

Finally, the look was broken as Ranson was half-carried, half-dragged towards Vanyol.

As the group of men eventually broke out of the crowd of kneeling figures, Ranson was pushed forward, and he overbalanced, falling onto his hands and knees in front of Vanyol.

"I know you. I remember your face from years ago, from the Order." he hissed. "Your name is Ranson." No reaction. "Why were you not slain in the Battle?"

William knew what his father was about to say, and he also realised that by saying it, he was admitting that he was a Caster, and had lied to all of his men.

Ranson's head was hung down in shame at Vanyol's feet, and his willpower and nobility was completely gone as he monotonically verbalised his confession.

"I fled." His voice sounded so empty; so sad. "I ran away before the real battle started."

These words were met by murmurs from the crowd, but Raimos was looking at Ranson with a complex expression on his face; something between understanding, disappointment and awe.

"So this is your hero?" Vanyol addressed the crowd, but spoke almost directly to Raimos. He was almost laughing as the words left his poisonous mouth. "A coward who runs away instead of fighting his own battles!"

He used his mind to flip Ranson over onto his back, and as he lay there groaning, Vanyol looked him over. Then he knelt down beside him, and almost hissed in his ear.

"You have power, but you are foolish to contest us. We cannot be beaten. Your leaders were slain by our hands, so what did you hope to achieve by revealing yourself against us?"

With his eyes still closed in pain, the floored man replied.

"I cannot expect you to understand nobility or honour. And without them you will lose."

"There is no one to contest me now. You are as good as dead, and even if you still had your power you would still be nothing but an insect on the bottom of my foot."

Then he stood up, and addressed his men, but William guessed that he did not even need to speak to them; that they obeyed his very thoughts.

"Form around each man in groups of three, and keep them still. You will be sent to the palace."

No sooner had he finished speaking, when the faceless figures grabbed the men from the crowd and each stood in identical formation. Each rebel soldier was flanked from either side and behind by men, with spear tips pressed against their backs and necks.

Crimson bonds suddenly appeared from the air and wrapped around Ranson's wrists, ankles and neck, lifting him clean off the ground, and held him there tightly, ceasing any struggle or squirm. He was held with his back to the ground and his front to the sky, until he was jerkily turned to face Vanyol.

Then, as William watched, lightning bolts tumbled down around him, and each one hitting a four-strong group of men. One by one, the groups of men vanished instantly, leaving only clouds of smoke behind them.

He stared with a look of alarm as the men around him were vaporised in an instant.

After most of the men had gone, he looked up at the black clouds above him. They were fizzling with a pallid energy, and William knew that it was his turn to die.

He closed his eyes, and a second later he felt the shocking, violent energy all around him. The smell of burning filled his nostrils, and he could almost taste the static tang of energy at the back of his throat. Glaring yellow light flared and flickered beyond his eyelids.

And then all was dark and silent.

Until he opened his eyes.

And within a second of seeing his surroundings, he knew that he didn't want to be there.

William was standing in a shadowy room. The bricks were so dark that they were almost black, and behind the high windows was pure pitch, and only a hint of starlight could be seen through the criss-cross of ugly, metal bars.

The room was lit with torches and a table with dice on it was lit by candles, with two chairs either side of it. This was in the corner of the room, which was long, narrow and straight; ten metres wide, but over one hundred metres long. In the opposite corner to the table was a door that was heavily set, and bolted, and locked from the outside.

Half of the room was taken up by cells. Most were full, and some were eerily empty.

It was towards one of these that William was pushed at spear-point, and as a wall of bars clanged loudly shut behind him, the wistful truth sunk in.

He was trapped; he was alone.

Chapter 11 - A Light in the Darkness

Days passed.

The cell was dark and cold, and William was already nostalgic at the mere sight of the dark bars.

The only solace he could find was at the back of the cell, where the only solid wall to flank the cell cast enough shadow for William to wrap himself in, hide from himself and dream of happier times.

The cell was an almost perfect square. The stone wall that provided William's solitary escape stood at the back of the cell, and was the only solid construction to border the chamber; but for the cold stone-flagged floor and the rough ceiling of rock.

The other walls were just a criss-cross of dark, metal bars; similar to the windows, but on far grander scale. Of course, this meant that he could see down the entire length of the row of cells. Either way he looked, he saw misery and squalor.

The cell directly on one side was empty, but there were few beyond it that were desolate.

However, on the other side, the cavern was inhabited by a dark man with dark skin, crouched over something with his back stuck out in William's direction.

The guards that paced the length of the cell wore the same armour that the faceless spearmen did. The only way that William could tell that they weren't the same men was that he had seen the original three leave and another triad had taken their place, just

107

before he had woven himself in shadows and drifted away into unconsciousness.

The table with the dice on was almost certainly for the men to relax on, but for as long as William had watched them the faceless figures had not stopped patrolling up and down, forwards and backwards, with a scarily equal distance and speed between each man. They were in perfect, mechanical synchronisation, and seemed to have no need to communicate, and not even to rest. For hours they marched, checking and guarding each cell, but not even breaking their step as their heads whipped sharply round at each cell and back as they turned away.

So the table was for someone else. It couldn't have been for a prisoner or an interrogation table, as there were dice laying on it. No guard would let their inferiors play games. But there were two chairs; one either side, which suggested that the people sitting they had an equal power balance. However, given the fact that they were facing each other and engaged regularly in a competitive game, they were in contest about something other than dice.

William had stored this information in his head, in case it could prove useful. Despite his defeat, he still clung onto what wits he had left.

But for now he was wrapped and clothed in dreams of Tursus; of his mother and father, of the happy times in his life. Back when he was a boy.

A dark shroud descended over his thoughts, and they morphed into nightmares. Dark visions of the

Scarra formed in his head, then of the war, then of the Besiarites screaming as they were burned alive.

His breathing rate increased rapidly, his heart almost jumped out of his chest. Sweat formed all over his face; foremost on his brow, and ran off onto the stone floor like a stream. He kicked out and convulsed in response to the images behind his eyelids.

Finally his thoughts settled on the captain and the look on his face as he died, and he jolted awake.

For a split-second he was blind, as the pale light consumed his vision. William sat up and rubbed his eyes with his index finger and thumb.

Even though he was gone, the captain haunted him still.

The light was streaming in through the barred window, and cast an intricate shadow over William's stooped body. But even the light had a darkness to it; it was somehow grey and cold, and offered no warmth or comfort to him.

Slowly, as his strength and sight returned to him, he got to his feet. But he winced as the half-healed wound in his side tore at him, and the parts of it that had begun to heal tugged and ripped at each other. But the fibres of his flesh stayed intact, and the pain was lessened by a slight application of pressure onto the wound from his hand.

Finally, he looked at his surroundings, and he sighed. The cell was small, but because of the light effect and his fading dreams, the cell looked impossibly big and empty.

So solitary; so alone.

"Who did you lose?"

The voice cut through the silence like a knife, and William turned towards the source.

The man with dark skin was looking at him through the pattern of dark bars, and his eyes were kind. William knew that he had a good heart.

He looked at him and sighed.

"How did you know?"

"I have lost many of both friends and family. I know the look of a man who has lost everything."

William nodded, but he was looking at the floor.

"If you want, I can tell you my story..."

Here he looked up and through the window into the greyish light.

"But it may take a while."

The sun had reached its full height in the sky, and from its steep angle, its light no longer streamed into the cells.

The dark man exhaled noisily through his lips. "That's quite a tale. I can see why you feel so empty."

William nodded, once more looking downwards. He had left out the part about him being a Caster.

They were now sitting directly opposite each other through the bars, cross-legged, with their knees almost touching the bars. The faceless men continued to march, but although they were checking each cell, they seemed not to have heard what the two men had been talking about.

Both men started as a loud clunk echoed through the cells. In each door, a tiny hatch was opened in the bottom, and loaf of bread and a metal plate were pushed through. The food on it, if food was the right word, was grey and slimy, and the bread was stale and rock-hard. It did not look at all appetising to William.

"Is this what we have to eat?"

"Yes." answered the man, who used the provided spoon to greedily scoop the lumpy mixture into his mouth.

"You'll get used to the texture."

William tried a small spoon of the gruel, but spat it out almost immediately. He grimaced, and his face contorted in a dramatic way.

"The taste on the other hand..."

The dark man began laughing at William's expense, but not cruelly, so soon the younger man was chuckling as well.

"I think I'll skip dinner."

"It might taste like the back end of a horse, but it's all you're likely to get for a long time. If I were you, I'd keep my strength up."

William looked at the older man doubtfully for a moment, but in the end he knew that he was right. So, preparing himself for the coming onslaught of his taste-buds, he took another spoonful.

But once again, he spat it out. The taste was just too overwhelming.

"Don't let it stay in your mouth for too long; try and swallow it quickly and all in one go."

So for the third attempt, William followed his advice, and in a few minutes, both men had set down their empty bowls.

They began talking once more, and soon tales were drifting back and forth between the bars. It was from these tales that William got some information.

He was in Vanyol's palace on the north edge of the East Realm, with its back to the sea and surrounded by desolate, deserted plains, where the only things that managed to grow were brown and thorny, and looked already dead as they poked through the dusty ground.

But something still vexed William.

"Why am I here? Why am I still alive? I'm only an average soldier."

At this, William's conscience stabbed at him. Of course, it was true that he was, at present, merely a normal man, however he truly wanted to tell this man everything. But he just couldn't. He knew that he must guard his secret with his life and be extremely careful who he told. He was finally beginning to understand how hard it must have been for Ranson; not telling anyone the truth for all those years.

The man did not answer for a second, as if he was preparing himself for what he was about to say.

"When I first came here, the men that occupied these cells talked about the experiments that Vanyol was performing with dark spells. One of his first was transforming the men of the Beltzan Peaks. When they would not obey him, he turned them into horrible, animalistic creatures called the Scarra."

"I have seen and killed enough of them for a lifetime."

The man nodded, remembering William's story.

"But then the Scarra became too volatile to control, so Vanyol abandoned them into the mountains and set his eyes on the human heart. He has always considered love and compassion to be a weakness, so his next experiments were on how to control it. He removed love and kindness from many men, and therefore breaking their will, making them opinion-less slaves. Some were set to work forging weapons and armour, but some were made into Vanyol's personal guard."

He gestured towards the men patrolling outside their cells.

"They are elegant, cold-blooded killers. Nothing can stop them, save maybe the Besiarite warriors of the Resistance, and from what you have told me, I don't think they are on hand to help."

Everything that the dark man was saying was making William more and more afraid. Could this really be his fate; to become a faceless, heartless warrior for his enemy? He could barely even stand the thought of it.

"Look, is there any way out of..."

William was interrupted by the thick door slamming open with a loud toll. Through it scrabbled four figures; three masked men were attempting to manhandle a fourth person down the length of the cells. The figure in the centre of the precession was writhing and struggling with all his might, but it was no match for the trained hands of three utterly focused men. Suddenly, a foot flew out from the struggling mass and kicked the only lit torch off the wall. It snuffed out as it hit the floor, head down. The rebel's feet were dragging across the stone-flagging, attempting to find a foothold, or a means to anchor against their captors, but this was in vain, and the soldiers finally forced him to the front of the empty cell next to William's. Another masked individual held open the door, and the figure was bundled into the prison.

Through the darkness, which was only broken by the small candle on the table and the slight grey light through the barred window, William saw the figure in the cell charge back at the men before the door was closed, but once again they caught him by the arms. They dragged the squirming figure to the back of the cell, where they fastened irons around their wrists. These were connected to the back of the cells by strong metal fastenings, so when the figure once again tried to charge out of the cell, the chains held him fast.

The faceless soldiers picked the torch up and relit it using the candle on the table. The room was suddenly lit up again, and William's eyes took a second to adjust to the light.

Once his sight had returned, he looked at what had previously been an empty cell, and he was taken aback.

Chained against the wall was no great man; no muscled figure or scarred, battle-worn face.

It was a girl.

She looked about the same age as William, and in her, brown eyes burned the same fire of rebellion that he himself had experienced. Her face was shockingly beautiful, and her hair was a woody brown colour, but was smooth and reflected the light, and tumbled down over her padded shoulders. She was dressed in leather armour, and William could see the scrapes along the left side of her waist from where a scabbard had hung, so he knew she had fought with a sword in some kind of battle.

She finally gave up struggling, and sat down on the cold, hard floor, slumped and breathing heavily.

William moved over to the other side of the cell, close to the girl, and tried to talk to her.

"Are you okay? Are you hurt?"

The girl offered no response.

"My name's William. What's yours?"

She looked up at him, and through her expression, she conveyed a louder translation of 'stop talking' than words ever could.

Clearly understanding the message, William turned away and began talking once more to the man with dark skin.

The girl looked up once more, and examined the boy. He was slightly younger than her, but looked very tall for his age. He seemed quite good looking, and his tangle of brown hair seemed to almost match hers for colour. And for that second that their gazes had locked, his deep blue eyes seemed to contain genuine concern. She pondered this, as she saw an intriguing contradiction. He was obviously a soldier, from the wound in his side and the haunted look buried deep in his eyes, but he seemed genuinely kind and caring. There was clearly something special about the boy. William, wasn't it? She would have to keep a close eye on him.

But she had had a devastating and shattering day, so she let her thoughts float away, and knowing there was no escape from her bonds, she sat with her head between her knees and her arms resting limply upon them. Slowly the mist of unconsciousness descended upon her, and she drifted off into a surprisingly easy sleep.

William, however, continued talking to the man. In the midst of conversation he suddenly realised that he had no idea of his name. To mask his unintentional rudeness, he wrapped up and disguised his question in others.

"So who are you? Where did you come from, and how did you come to be in such a place as this?"

"I am a member of the An'tiamo tribe. We dwelled on the river Tiamo, or Delsus to you. It runs from within the Southern Realm, and it joins with the ocean on the north border of this Realm. We lived there quite happily, until Vanyol seized control of these lands. We were forced out of our home; some were taken prisoner like me, but most were not so lucky. They were most likely killed."

"I am familiar with having to leave your home due to events you can't control." replied William, sympathetically. "But who do you mean by we? Your people?"

"In a way, but more than that. I lived with my wife; my great love. She was taken from me while I was held at sword-point; whether she was taken prisoner or killed, I still do not know. But the soldiers were merciless. They needed the land to build this palace, and they slaughtered men, women and children of a peaceful people to get it. The ground this fortress is built on is stained with much blood. Its foundations are hundreds of my people's wasted lives. If I had the chance, I would tear this place down piece by piece."

William nodded. A while ago, he may have been the man to give him that chance, but now he felt almost shameful that he couldn't help.

"My name is Aniik'arim An'tiamo, and my wife's name is...was... Kei'arim An'tiamo." He sighed, and William saw the pain in his eyes.

"I have been in this pit for so long that I must remind myself of her name every day, lest I should forget it. I can barely remember her face. By now we should have grown-up children, and they would soon have children of their own."

He sighed once more, and gestured to his face.

"But now my heart is broken, my body is weakening, and my skin begins to wrinkle. I know in my heart that she is gone, and that I will never see her again."

The man's voice was so dull and flat that it brought tears to William's eyes, but he blinked them back and choked back the lump in his throat. He felt so sorry for the man, and it broke his heart that he could do nothing to help.

A solemn silence overtook the cells, and as the older man had his head bowed towards the ground, William could think of nothing to say. So his mind wandered, and his eyes idly roamed across his surroundings, until his gaze settled on the black bars over the small window. Some diminutive part of his old being wondered silently, and the tiniest spark of hope of escape echoed, becoming brighter as he delved deeper into what he once would have thought, what seemed a lifetime ago.

"There is no escape that way."

The voice cut through the air and his thoughts with equal vigour, and very slightly startled him.

"Believe me. I spent the first years of my imprisonment trying to escape from this awful place. Of all the information I gathered, none proved useful to me. I accepted it years ago."

"Accepted what?"

"That there is no way out of here. I would have liked to have died by a warm fire with my beloved family by my side, but instead I will slowly die in this cold, God-forsaken cell, watching through the bars as the world I love tears itself apart and all comes to ruin."

William watched as the man's sadness glazed over his eyes once more, but this time he could not take it.

"You will not die in here! I will do everything in my power to let you breathe free air once more."

"What can any of us do against such powerful evil?!"

William hesitated. He knew he shouldn't divulge his secret, but he also knew that it would give the man hope; false or not, it would stay with him through the dark times. So he made up his mind, but played his hand carefully.

He leaned in closer to the man, and whispered.

"What if the Casters still existed?"

The older man looked up in disgust at William for making such horrible humour, but when he saw the seriousness in the younger man's eyes, he knew that this was no joke.

"And what if..." William continued, more hesitant with every passing word. "What if one of them was in these cells?"

Aniik'arim just stared at him with utter disbelief. Not only was William looking at him with such sincerity, but also by the intensity of the hurt deep in his eyes, the older man had no doubt of whom this remnant of a bygone age was.

The blank expression on the older man's face lasted for a good few minutes, and William wished he would say something, even if it was to report him to the guards; the long silence was killing him. Had he cemented his one and only friendship, or had he destroyed it forever?

For seconds that felt like years, William scanned the older man's face for any sign of reaction, and finally he saw his face twitch into a quizzical expression as a question formed in his mind.

"But if you're so powerful, why are you stuck in this place?"

"It's complicated..."

"I think you better retell your story, don't you?"

William nodded in silence.

"But this time, truthfully."

Chapter 12 - Path to Freedom

Dawn was just creeping into the sky when William's true story was finished; he had been talking all night.

It had taken so long for a couple of reasons.

Firstly, because he had to talk at a ridiculously low volume, and regularly checking that the guards had not heard, but also because so much more was included in the story.

William felt an overbearing sense of relief telling Aniik the truth, but he also heard a tiny voice in the back of his mind saying that he just made a huge mistake. After all, the older man could easily be an enemy spy, or he could think that the story he was hearing was enough to sell to Vanyol for his freedom.

No, he decided. He trusted this man. And in prison, all you have is your word.

The older man was just looking at him in awe once more, but in his eyes was a new found respect for the boy.

After a while he spoke.

"So Vanyol has no idea you're a Caster."

"He thought my father was the source of the magic on the mountain. Once my armour was gone, I looked just like a normal soldier. I suppose I actually am now. But it's a scary thought that his ignorance is the only reason I'm alive."

"And your powers are utterly gone?"

"Completely." William agreed. He raised his arm towards the wall, and tried to summon fireball, but with as much result as he expected.

The familiar clang from the cell door slightly startled the two men, but this time, finally, William turned to look at the source of the noise; and what he saw seemed simply alien in this world of harshness and severity. Two men were walking down the length of the cells; one carrying a pile of bowls and bread on a rusty tray, and the other sliding open the hatches in the cell doors and pushing the food, if food is the right word, into the cells.

They were wearing almost vivid, brown fur clothing which only just fastened over their over-ample guts, and their matching hats only just covered their bulbous, flabby heads; which were decorated by matching facial hair. They both had dark moustaches and beards that lazily merged into one another in the folds of fat that made up their faces.

After a few minutes, they had got to the end of the row of cells and the tray was empty, when a voice made their heads turn back the way they had come.

"So do I not get anything to eat?"

William turned, and saw that the strong, defiant voice came from the girl, who was still chained to the back wall; even in bondage her body language and attitude shouted out that she had the upper hand.

The men sauntered up to the bars of her cell, the tray having been put down onto the table, and, sensing that she was no threat, unlocked and opened the door. The girl's composure faltered slightly as the two large men approached, but she was determined not to lose face.

"Well?" She kept eye contact with the closest man. "I'm hungry. What do I get to eat?"

The man laughed unpleasantly. Then he suddenly leaned forward and kissed her roughly. Her eyes opened wide in surprise and disgust, and making use of her free limbs, she thrust her knee up between the man's legs as hard as she could. He backed away, the colour suddenly drained from his flabby face, and he collapsed; much to the enjoyment of his counterpart, who burst out in roars of laughter and almost collapsed himself.

The first man recovered from the initial pain, and got up, quite unsteadily. As soon as he was on his feet, he slapped the girl, hard, across the face, and her head snapped sideways against the wall.

The two men turned to walk away, but just before he did, the injured man looked once more at the girl, and spat unceremoniously at her feet.

Once the door was locked and bolted, the men sat down at the table, and began to roll the dice while talking quietly to each other.

William was staring daggers at them, but neither seemed to notice. How could they treat a prisoner like this? They may not be controlled by Vanyol, but they were just as bad.

He heard a muffled sobbing, and he looked over at the girl. She was slumped against the wall, and her hair had fallen down over her face, but he could see her shoulders quivering as she softly cried.

William looked down at the floor, but then glanced at the food that had been pushed through the hatch. And then he looked once more at the girl.

In silence, he stood up, walked over to the door and picked up the bread. Then he went back over to the girl, getting as close as the bars would let him, and slowly threaded his arm through, presenting the bread to her.

"Here," he said simply.

The girl looked up, and William saw the glowing red mark across the right side of her face. He saw that the only clean parts of her face were the tear-stained streaks where the evidence of her misery had coursed down to the floor.

She looked at the bread, then into his eyes. Then her head turned once more towards the floor, and once more her hair fell back over her face like a veil.

"Come on," William insisted. "You have to eat."

The girl looked at him once more, and this time, she timidly reached out her hand, and took the bread before William retracted his own arm.

"Thanks," she said softly, and began to nibble on her breakfast.

William turned back to his own breakfast, and, slightly less gratefully, began to lap up the gruel, as Aniik was doing the same in the next cell.

"I heard you talking," stated the girl, in a quiet, soft voice. William put down the bowl, but did not turn towards her.

"Is it true?"

William had no need to clarify the question, and nodded silently.

"You're our only hope."

In those four words, he felt the weight of his responsibility fall on him like a ton of bricks, but the fact that this hope now had no basis completely crushed him.

"Not anymore."

"What happened?"

William sighed. He probably shouldn't tell her, but she did know his secret anyway, and over his time in this place, his willpower was at an all-time low, so said this.

"If you are willing to listen, I am willing to tell you."

"Well there doesn't seem to be anything else to do here," she replied, and William was glad to see some of her attitude coming back; at least she wasn't as upset now.

"Okay, but it may take a while." William was so used to similar words that it was bordering on cliché, but he did actually like telling his story, apart for the sad parts. It was almost like every time he shared it, the listener was with him and supporting him through the trials and tribulations.

So he began.

"I come from a village called Tursus, on the south border of the East Realm. My parents and I lived there quite happily, until one day Vanyol's men came…"

William finished his tale, and the two young people sat in silence.

He could see from the look on her face that she had truly lost all faith in him. Her eyes seemed empty; gone was the fire of rebellion that he had seen before. But in the end, after an excruciatingly long silence, she spoke.

"We heard that there was a Caster in this Realm, and we rejoiced. We waited for so long, but you never came. We fought and we died, because you never came."

She looked at him, but there was no gratitude in her eyes now.

"And now you're stuck in here, like the rest of us. You're useless to anyone. I hope Vanyol finds out, and kills you in the slowest way possible."

There was an edge to her voice that he could only compare to Garston's, as he finally rose above Raimos in the illusion of victory. But William knew what it meant.

Hatred and contempt.

She was blaming him for what happened to her. It was safe to assume that it had hurt her deeply, and whether she meant what she had said or not, William had enough wits left to know not to press the matter.

He watched as the faceless men marched out of the room; they changed every morning.

As the door closed behind them, a laugh caught his attention, and he looked over at the men at the table. It was obvious that one of them had just won whatever game they were playing. Then, as he watched, a small, half-eaten loaf of bread hit the closest man on the back of his flabby head.

He turned round instantly. William could see that he was the loser in the last game, and he had been further aggravated by this blatant insult.

The two men instantly saw that it was the girl who had thrown the stale missile, due the look of surprise in William's eyes, and the look of pride and derision in the girl's.

"Who gave this harlot that bread?!"

"It was him!" shouted the girl, pointing at William.

The boy's eyes widened even further at this. Aniik had suddenly woken up from his usual morning daze, and was still confused at what was happening.

"What's going on?" he hissed at William, but the boy had no time to answer, as the two men had opened the door and barged into the cell, one behind the other. William could not be sure, but he thought that the closest was the un-injured man.

"How dare you give food to her when we deliberately did not!" the first man said.

William tried to form a sentence, but his babblings were cut off when the man grabbed him and dragged against the wall. He was completely pinned.

And then the man drew a knife and held it to William's neck.

"I would not have a problem in cutting your throat right now," he said, surprisingly calmly. "If you ever help another prisoner that I have not, then I promise I will kill you on the spot."

William struggled but it was no good. He could not escape from the man's clamp-like grip.

"If I see another person in trouble, I will always help." William looked into his eyes as he said this. His voice seemed calm as well, but in his eyes was a hint of rebellious danger. "That is my promise to you. So kill me if you want; I don't care. You can't stop me from doing what is right."

The man sneered.

"You do not fear death, so there would be no point killing you. But what about your little girlfriend?"

He nodded to his associate, and the other man walked over to the next cell. He unlocked the door, and drew his dagger. The girl struggled as much as she could, but with no luck. The chains held her fast against the wall. Aniik was shouting something, but William could not hear. The words seemed to be muffled, and he heard the blood pumping in his ears.

He felt an anger rise up in him, such as he had never felt before. He began to shake with pure fury as the man advanced on the girl.

Suddenly a white spark flashed in the corner of his eye, and just as this happened the man in the girl's cell tripped dramatically, and everyone involved in this affair turned towards him; waiting for him to get up. But he did not get up, and too late did the group see the crimson puddle spilling out from under him.

He had landed on his own dagger, and he was quite dead.

The other man backed away from William in disgust, and ran over to his colleague. He turned him over, but he could see the dagger hilt sticking out of his chest, and he watched the steady flow of blood.

His grieving turned to anger. He let go of his friend and shouted at the girl.

"What did you do?"

"Nothing!" she replied, suddenly very scared.

He raised his dagger once more, so the tip was pointing right at her face.

"What did you do?!" he shouted far louder; so much that he almost screamed the words.

"Nothing, I swear! I could not have touched him. Look." She stretched as far as the chains would let her. "These chains are too short!"

The reply was not good enough for him, and he raised the dagger above his head with both hands. From this distance his could not miss his helpless target.

As he brought the blade down on its lethal journey, he suddenly burst into bright flame. He did not even have a chance to cry out before he exploded into bright sparks, which faded as quickly as they had appeared, leaving nothing left of him, or of the other man.

The girl's mouth was open in shock, but through the rapid events, she had not had a chance to scream.

She looked over at William.

And as he opened his eyes, just for a second, a white light made them seem brighter than the searing light of the sun.

As the light in his eyes faded, he looked at the girl. She just stared at him, with unbelieving eyes.

He was standing up, almost regally, above the many captives. All of them had seen what had happened. The first death had looked like a lucky accident, but with the fiery demise of both bodies there was no doubt whatsoever.

It was magic.

He was a Caster.

Vanyol fired another crimson blast at the wall. His anger was violently evident.

He was sitting tensely on a high dark seat in the throne room of the palace, which was a vast, circular and poorly lit room; but for the torches lit around the room at regular intervals.

Even though there were many torches, the light was lost in the vast space flanked by black stone.

The roof was incredibly high and was made of glass, but the clouds were so thick above it that not even a trickle of light leaked through. The height and span of the room created a vast, empty void, and any sound in that place was amplified to deafening proportions.

The throne itself was raised up on a squat tower of slabs that formed wide, shallow stairs.

A lone man was kneeling half way up the steps; his face was towards the ground, and he was sweating profusely. He flinched at every room-shaking explosion, but he was far more terrified when Vanyol spoke; not for the fear of the words that would be spoken, but for fear of the man who would speak them.

"It was magic! Here in the palace! I felt it!"

"Yes master..." The man replied hesitantly.

"How could this happen?! I took his powers!"

"I know master. I had already stationed many guards to secure him, even the ones guarding the cells. Nothing seems to have changed, but just in case..."

"Ranson is not stronger than me!"

Another fireball hit the wall, and the unfortunate man practically jumped out of his skin. His breaths were becoming shallower and more rapid, and waterfalls of sweat coursed down onto the black stone slabs.

The fireball had left a smoking crater in the high wall; it must have been thick indeed to stop the scarlet missile dead.

Vanyol was sitting with one hand stroking his chin, thinking.

"What would you have me do?"

The ArchCaster smiled unpleasantly.

For a while, William just stood there and the prisoners stared up at him.

He was just about to sit back down, when a voice from one of the cells shouted.

"Our saviour has come! We are free!"

This was met with other calls and cheers from around the long room.

"Sorry, but I did not come here to save you," he admitted.

The cheers suddenly died away and were replaced with ominous murmurs. William's face fell, and he turned round to look for support from Aniik, and the older man gestured from him to continue.

"I came as one of you; a prisoner, a normal man, but now I have power, and now we have a chance. A chance for freedom."

He looked down both sides of the lines of cells, and he saw the smiling, nodding faces of the many captives.

"Those who can fight must fight. Those who cannot must be aided. So are you with me?"

William was not prepared for the mind-blowing roar of approval from hundreds of souls crying out as one. The sound was so amplified by the black stone walls that the cell doors shook, and every heart in that place was stirred.

Even before the call had ceased, William closed his eyes and concentrated. He focused on each cell door and saw in his mind what he wanted to do.

A few seconds later, each cell door exploded outwards off its hinges, and when the smoke cleared the people were cheering and walking out of their cells.

William fired a fireball at the thick wooden door, and it disintegrated in an instant. Just as the mass of once imprisoned peoples was about to pour out of the door, a voice called out over the continuous cheering. Many hands were clapped on William's shoulders, but he did recognise one of the figures in particular. Raimos came out of one of the cells, and looked him in the eye.

"You truly are your father's son," he said, clearly not having missed a trick.

William smiled, and pointed to the rabble running out of the door.

"Help them," he said, and Raimos smiled and went through the door himself.

"What about me?!"

The girl was still chained to the wall, and although the door of the cell was no longer intact, she could not escape.

"What about you?" William said, knowing he now not only held all of the cards, but was in control of the deck itself.

He looked at her with obviously feigned puzzlement, and the girl looked at him with almost enough contempt to melt the chains themselves.

"I would quite like to escape too!"

William raised his eyebrows, and she sighed exasperatedly.

"I need your help..."

"Oh, really?" William replied with mock realisation, but he didn't move.

"Yes! Hurry up and save me before the guards come back!"

William finally moved to help her, but still obviously taking his time.

He raised his arm, and just as he was about to summon another fire-bolt, Aniik grabbed his arm.

"No, you cannot use any power against the wall. It would bring the roof down on top of us, or at the very least injure her."

William brought his arm down again.

"Shame."

He smiled, and walked over to her. Then he wrapped one of the chains around his arm, and summoned fire around his hand. It burned so bright that the man and the girl had to look away, but William looked unfazed.

Soon, the chain turned white-hot, and then snapped. Then William moved to her other side, and did the same to the other chain.

Once the girl was free, she couldn't help but smile at William, who beamed back.

She blushed and broke the gaze, and pushed past him to get to the table. It had been knocked over by a cell door, so she picked up the keys that had fallen off it and undid the shackles that were still clamped around her wrists.

Then the party off three joined the main group, who were waiting just outside the door. They were hiding just before a right-angle in the corridor, and as William peered tentatively round the corner, he saw why.

Two faceless figures were standing, blocking the corridor. William turned back to the party and put his finger to his lips. Then he signalled for them to stay where they were.

The Caster stepped out, now full of confidence, and the two men realised his presence. Their hands moved for their swords, but one man was incinerated on the spot before his fingers touched the hilt.

The second man seemed unfazed by this, and ran at William with his blade drawn, but William concentrated and held out his hand. A second later, the man's sword was in the Caster's grip, and if he could see the man's face behind the mask, he was sure it would look very surprised.

William concentrated once more, and summoned the man towards him as he had done with the sword. The man flew towards him, and was skewered by the outstretched sword.

Once the man's unmoving body fell off the blade, William realised he would have no need for it. Then he remembered the scrapes on the waist of the girl's leather armour, and he knew that she could use it more than him, so he handed it to her. Then he instructed his followers into formation; anyone who could fight on the outside, and anyone who couldn't on the inside. There were one or two who couldn't walk at all, so they were carried on in the middle by any men that could be spared. He also told the men at the front to pick up the spears that the guards had dropped, and pass them to the men at the back.

So, as they walked down the dark halls of the palace, they were quite a procession. William and the girl led from the front, and dispatched any person in front of them with ease. He was impressed by how incredibly she moved, and how blade and body

135

worked so perfectly together, so that they may as well have been one unit.

They were followed closely by Aniik, and then behind them were the weak and the old, flanked by the strong, who took out anyone who appeared from doors or side passages.

Finally, at the back were more of the strongest men; defending the rear of the party with spear, strength and just plain rage.

As they ventured through the palace, led by William, who was led himself by his powers, some were cut down on the flanks or the rear. But because of their sacrifice most of the men were now armed with swords and spears, and for every guard that they encountered, some might be lost, but far more was gained, and soon practically no-one was falling. Even the men being carried were armed, and were helping wherever they could with the defence.

The palace itself seemed to be an incredibly expansive maze, but William could see the right path like a map in his head.

After a good half hour of this, William suddenly raised one of his hands, and the party stopped.

"We are about to enter the main courtyard. This will be our hardest challenge yet. Vanyol's guards are everywhere. There are many of them, and we will be open to attack from all sides. I will do what I can, but there is a good chance that many of you will die."

The faces around him looked doubtful.

William looked at Aniik.

"You know this place. Is there any other way out?"

The older man shook his head, and the Caster was suddenly very concerned.

A voice called out from behind the party.

A young man was limping slightly as he ran to them, and another from the back line called out to him.

"Cedric! I thought we had lost you some time ago, my friend."

"I was cornered, but they found out that there is life in me yet!" he called back, smiling slightly. Then he addressed William.

"There is a company of guards on our tail. They easily outnumber us, and I only just escaped. They will be here soon."

There was murmuring from the crowd, and they turned to their leader to see how he would react to this ill news.

"We have no choice. We must fight for our freedom, if not our lives."

The company nodded approvingly, but still not confidently. But then an old withered man, who was being carried by two other men, spoke up.

"Come on! I've lived too damned long to be scared of death! Just let me at them!" he cried, swinging his sword above his head.

This lightened the mood of the crowd, and they cried out as one.

William took this as the signal to attack.

The doors that stood before them were easily thirty feet high, and encased in metal, but William summoned all of his strength and blasted them outwards into the courtyard, crushing a few guards before they knew what was happening.

At the others looked up and drew their swords, they saw an immense and furious horde charge down the steps towards them. They saw the faces of men ready to fight for the right to be free, and they saw one figure rise in splendour over the others, with white light steaming from his face, and from the searing white bolts that flew from his hands.

The horde's wrath was like nothing William had ever seen. They cut down many of the guards without even slightly slowing down, but eventually they were slowed down to a snail's pace. Not many were falling, but they were struggling to find space to fight.

To his delight, he saw the old man cutting down guard after guard, and laughing gleefully as he did it. Then he noticed the girl. She had separated from the main group, but was having no problem in holding her ground. William was suddenly very glad to have her on his side, if only for the moment.

Movement caught his eye, and for a moment he stopped sending down his fiery deluge. Along the high walls that encased the battle were scurrying many faceless figures carrying vicious-looking crossbows. Before William could react, the first sharpshooter took aim and fired, and William almost cried out as it hit the old man in the chest, and he fell into the fray.

Implausible anger overtook William, and his bright, white aura suddenly became blinding. He rose until he was perfectly level with the crossbowmen, and sent out a horizontal pulse of power. It disintegrated anything it touched, and every single archer was wiped out.

William's outline became visible in the sky once more as the light faded once more.

But suddenly William realised his mistake, as he saw that the blast had freed many stone slabs, and he watched in horror as they fell into the courtyard. He swooped down at incredible speed and, using his mind, caught them. He grunted under the unendurable weight of the stone, and knew he could not hold them for long. He manoeuvred them in the air until they were in a circle over the front lines of the guards, who had now surrounded the rebels.

"*My* men! Get out of the way!"

As soon as the rebels on the front line had broken combat and taken a few steps back, the incredible crushing weight of the irregular boulders fell on the front line of the guards. The boulders had formed a wall around the group, and they were safe for a moment.

William descended into the centre of the party, but then had a terrible thought. The girl had been fighting outside the main circle, but to his great relief he saw her face next to Aniik's on the furthest side of the circle.

"Now is our chance. Once I clear the stones you must run for the gates. I will open them, and then any who can escape must do so."

The men around him nodded, and at that exact same moment William saw the masked heads of guards as they tried to scale the impromptu dam.

The Caster closed his eyes, and concentrated once again. The stones shot outwards like the points of a star, and devastated the guards. So many were crushed that only about a fraction remained. The men that had been scaling the wall had landed hard on the ground, and as the horde of men coursed out towards the gate they were either trampled or had a fatal experience with the end of a blade.

William was at the back of the throng, covering their escape with various powerful expulsions, but he suddenly turned, shouted 'Get down!' and sent a mammoth fireball towards the main gates. To everyone's surprise, they were not destroyed. They must have been very strong to withstand the uncompromising power of William's fireball. The only thing that broke were the thick wooden beams that fastened across the gates, so that they swung open, and the mass charged through the breach.

William alone stayed behind, preventing any guards from hindering their escape. He faced the palace, and sent volley after volley of scorching missiles into the guards. Soon there was nothing left but bodies on the stone-flagged courtyard.

He nearly wept to see the corpse of the old man, and lying next to him was the former leader of the Resistance; Raimos had died during the battle.

One man who had somehow climbed up onto the high wall over the gate drew his long, two-handed sword and jumped down, with the blade pointing straight down at William.

The Caster looked up just in time to see an arrow imbed itself firmly into the man's chest, knocking him clear of William and onto the ground a few yards in front of him. He looked behind him, and saw the girl lowering a bow that she must have acquired at some point during the battle. She looked around for any remaining guards, and then walked towards him.

"Thank you," she said, and William was taken aback. He could see the sincere gratefulness in her eyes, and there was no aggressive edge to her voice.

"You too. I suppose that it's thanks to you that I got my powers back."

She nodded.

"And my goodness you can handle a sword!"

She grinned, but then as his face became serious she realised what he was going to do.

"You can't go back in on your own."

"I have to. My father's in there. He needs me."

"Then I'm coming with you."

"You can't," William insisted.

"You are going to need help. You don't have the time to argue with me. I'm coming in with you whether you like it or not!"

141

She pushed past him, but froze as she saw what was before her. William turned too, but even he looked noticeably anxious.

The company that was following them earlier had reached the courtyard, and was forming on the steps.

William looked at the girl. They were now standing side by side.

"Can you handle yourself down here?"

She smiled at him.

"Let's have some fun."

He was pretty sure that this meant yes, so as she drew her sword, he rose up a little way into the air, so he was over the very centre of the courtyard.

He summoned as much of his power as he could, and, using his mind, he lifted the heavy doors that he had blown off its hinges earlier, until they were level to him. It took all his mental strength to hold them in position, but then he began to spin slowly around, and the doors spun with him, gathering tremendous speed with each rotation.

Soon, body and bulk blurred into one, but suddenly the gates flew out of their orbit, one after the other; towards the waiting guards.

The first sliced horizontally through the first few lines and then thudded into the stone, holding fast. The second slammed into the guards face first, and crushed them against the steps.

Thanks to William's door projectiles, the number of guards had been halved, and once the makeshift missiles had stilled, the guards charged forward as one.

The girl prepared herself, and cut down many of them easily, with accurate, perfectly timed strokes. But the guards vastly outnumbered her, and William realised that they would soon surround her and cut her down.

He descended quickly, and landed next to the girl. As she looked at him, he nodded and they stood back to back. William used his mind to summon a sword from the hand of one of the guards, and just as he had done with Ranson what seemed like a lifetime ago, they fought back to back, matching each other's footwork immaculately, so that they slowly turned as they fought.

William embellished his blade with fire, and he cut down man after man. The fire on his blade was so intense that he actually began to cut through the guards' blades and armour as if they weren't there at all.

The girl noticed this, and shouted to William while still fighting two guards at one.

"That fire, light me up; quick!"

William concentrated for a second and did what the girl said. Her blade burst into flame, and she cut down the two guards that she was fighting, and shouted once more.

"Duck!"

William skewered a guard, and then ducked.

The girl jumped up and over him, swung her sword wide in one hand, and felled two of the guards with one stroke. William then brought down some stones from the wall that towered above them and each man was struck out cold. As she landed, all of the bodies fell to the ground.

The flame faded on the blade, and William looked at her in shocked awe.

"Well come on then!" she said, as they reached down, unclipped the belts of different deceased guards and clipped them onto their own waists. The belts held scabbards, so both young warriors sheathed their swords and walked towards the entrance of the palace.

As they crossed the threshold, William closed his eyes, and concentrated. The palace appeared in his mind, and the walls seemed transparent, so he could see every person. He saw a bright white aura surrounded by many shadows that had none. The white one was obviously Ranson, but he had not realised that the faceless figures had not only lost their identity, but their souls were gone too. That was why they had no aura.

Then he saw an even bigger crimson aura near the centre of the palace, and realised that Vanyol was more powerful than Ranson. He also realised that the ArchCaster was on the move, and was about to leave the massive void that William saw in his mind, and he was heading in Ranson's direction.

William panicked, and there was only one thing he could think of doing. He focused on the black walls of the great cavern, and in his mind he pulled with all his strength.

Vanyol felt a twinge in the back of his mind, and knew that more magic was being cast somewhere within the palace, but he did not understand how this was possible.

So caught up in his thoughts was he, that he did not notice the movement of the stone above him until it crashed down on top of him, and as one particularly heavy rock hit him a glancing blow on the side of his head, everything went black.

William opened his eyes, and the light faded. He was panting loudly, and he looked noticeably out of breath. Whatever magic he had performed had obviously taken something out of him, however it was not particularly hard to guess what it was, as one of the towers of the palace had just fallen in on itself.

"I've stopped Vanyol for a while, but he will soon be fighting back with a vengeance. We must get my father quickly, but there are many guards watching him."

He looked around the courtyard, and chuckled.

"Although I don't think that should be a problem."

She smiled back, so they stepped into the palace, and drew their swords.

The door was ripped off its hinges, and William and the girl walked through the smoky haze. As the dust settled, the two young people saw what they were about to face.

Ranson was strung up by his wrists to the low ceiling, so that his feet only just touched the floor. His arms were spread wide, and his head hung down. He didn't even seem to react when the door was so violently dislodged.

However, the soldiers around him definitely reacted. They had been stood in a circle around Ranson, with their spears pointing inward towards him, but when William and the girl made their explosive entrance, they immediately turned round and brandished their weapons.

Suddenly, to the girl's horror, William doubled up and fell to one knee, but as he stood slowly up she realised that he wasn't hurt. He was building up power, as she could see from the dazzling aura that surrounded him. His eyes were closed, and his arms were tensed over his chest. The light became more and more intense, and just as William disappeared into the light, he threw his arms wide, and a pulse of pure energy boomed out from him. All of the guards were thrown backwards and were still, but curiously, Ranson barely moved.

The girl's eyes were wide in shock.

"What did you do?!"

William walked into the room, crouched down over the body of a guard, and waved a hand in front of his face.

No response.

"I created a powerful blast of power, which, if I'm right, severed the hold that Vanyol had over them."

William tried clicking; still nothing. Then William poked him in the stomach.

"Okay, okay, he's dead. I think you've checked enough. Stop messing around."

"They're not dead; they should just be unconscious. But I have to check that they're not…"

As he looked up, he saw a masked figure standing just behind Ranson, holding his hair with one hand, and pressing a knife to his exposed neck with the other. Only, he wasn't a masked man anymore. He had removed his mask, revealing a psychotic, erratic face with constantly darting eyes. He was clearly unstable, and neither William nor the girl wanted to do anything to provoke him.

"…awake," finished William hesitantly, and he stood up slowly with his arms held out in surrender.

The man had positioned himself perfectly. William knew that he could not use any of his power without either hurting Ranson or giving the man a chance to cut his throat. Even if the girl still had the bow from earlier, she wouldn't have a chance to fire it.

No-one moved for what seemed like years, but William sent Ranson a message.

Don't worry. We'll think of something. Just stay calm.

Ranson just stared at him. Of course, William realised that his father hadn't seen him since his powers had returned.

Meanwhile, the previously masked man's face got more and more erratic, and the group could see that he was seconds away from killing the imprisoned man.

But then the girl perked up some courage, and tried to talk to him.

"What's your name?"

"No... no, no..."

"It's okay. We're not here to hurt you."

"No... no, no, no..."

The girl repeated herself calmly, and crept slowly towards him with hands uplifted, like William's.

"No... no, no..."

A little closer.

"No, no, stay back!"

The girl backed off again.

Beads of sweat fell down his face, and his eyes were darting from boy to girl and back again, waiting for someone to make a move. The knife shook in his hand, and it inched further into Ranson's neck, pressing hard enough to draw a little blood.

The man was once more seconds away from slitting Ranson's throat, but no-one said anything, as they knew that this would mean certain death for the older man.

Suddenly the man froze, and he dropped the knife. His mouth was open in shock, and he fell aside.

Behind him was a masked figure, holding the knife that had just been thrust between the man's shoulder-blades. He pulled off his mask, and William froze just like the man that was now lying dead on the floor.

It was his father, or his step-father as William now knew he was.

It was the man who brought him up, the man who had been with him for his whole life; the man who was so cruelly and suddenly taken from him.

William looked him up and down, wondering if this was some kind of trick, but his step-father must have realised what he was thinking.

"I'm real, William. As real as you are."

William nodded, but was silent.

Ranson was looking down at the body.

"He must he been under Vanyol's control for a long time. His mind was completely broken. The rest are most likely the same." William was surprised by how much genuine pity there was in his voice.

A couple of seconds later, the young Caster snapped out of his trance of confusion.

"We need to go," he said, walking over to Ranson. "Vanyol will recover soon, and this lot could wake up just as unhappy."

William tried to melt the chains, but there was some kind of crimson barrier around it; obviously an extra defence put there by Vanyol. The joints between the chains and the walls were also protected, but the irons round his wrists weren't. He put his hand onto the shackles, and looked directly at the older man.

"This is going to hurt a lot, but there's no other way. Are you ready?"

Ranson nodded.

William closed his eyes, and the shackles lit up; red hot. Ranson winced and gritted his teeth. Then white hot, and smoke began to rise up from underneath. Tears formed in the corners of the older man's eyes, and his mouth opened and closed in pure agony.

Then, finally, when the strength of the metal gave way, William wrapped his fingers round each one and ripped them off his wrists.

Ranson fell into William's arms, and his step-father nodded to the girl. They threaded their arms under the older Caster, and helped him walk to the archway where the door used to be. William took one last look at all the men on the floor. He was sorry that he couldn't help them too, but there was nothing he could do. He turned followed the party of three.

As they worked their way back through the corridors of the palace, William had swapped with the girl, so William and his step-father were supporting Ranson; he was incredibly weak, and unable to walk at any kind of pace. The journey was painfully slow, and the girl walked in front with her sword drawn; ready for anything.

However, about five minutes into their journey, William felt a stab in the back of his mind, and it told him the news he didn't want to hear. They stopped, and everyone turned towards him.

"Vanyol's awake."

A second later, he had to drop Ranson, as the man on the other side of him collapsed in agony, holding his head. William caught Ranson just in time, and helped him sit up against the wall. Then he rushed over to his step-father, and held him in his arms, resting his head on his knee.

The man's face was completely red, and he was almost writhing with pain.

"What's happening?" William asked frantically. For all his power, he had no idea what he could do.

"I know Vanyol's mind. He has a backup plan in case any of his slaves disobeyed him. Although the link is broken, he can still communicate with us because we used to be in tune with him. But that also means he can do this."

He cried out, as the pain increased dramatically, but then he raised his head and looked past William; towards the other man.

"Ranson, you look after him. You're his real father. If you don't keep him safe, you'll have me to answer to."

Ranson nodded with moist eyes.

"And you," said the dying man, looking deep into William's eyes. "I am so proud of you. I'll give your love to your mother, shall I?"

William nodded as tears streamed down his face. He tried to speak, but the words caught in his throat.

The man tensed, and struggled to breath, but the light in his eyes slowly faded, and his head sunk backwards. The man slowly slipped away, and his body went completely limp.

William couldn't hold it back any longer, and he completely broke down holding his deceased step-father. He planted his face into the man's chest, and sobbed, rocking backwards and forwards.

The girl walked slowly towards him, and put her arms around his shoulders.

He straightened up on his knees, and looked at the man that spent years bringing him up. His eyes were still open, and William reached out his shaking hand. He slowly brought the man's eyelids down, and he suddenly looked so peaceful, as if he was sleeping.

William's grieving turned to anger, and his hand was no longer shaking but steady.

"I'm going to kill that bastard." His voice was low and quiet, but had an incredibly angry and dangerous edge to it. "This ends here."

He looked at Ranson, and then at the girl, who had stepped away from him.

"Get him out of here," he said to her.

She nodded.

"And quickly. You don't want to be here when it starts."

She nodded again, but then stepped towards him and kissed him on the cheek.

"Good luck," she said simply, meeting his gaze.

Then he broke the look and went to help Ranson up. As William and his father embraced, he whispered to his son.

"Don't do anything that you'll regret."

But the look in William's eyes told him that this advice was pointless.

Then he limped over to the girl, and she helped him as quickly as possible to walk down the hall.

All she had to do to find her way out was to follow the path of dead guards that they had left on their way in to rescue Ranson.

William, however, was rooted to the spot. He closed his eyes and concentrated on the massive scarlet aura that he knew was Vanyol.

He sent a message that even Vanyol would understand.

You made a mistake killing my father. You made this personal, and now I'm going to kill you for it. I'll face you above the palace, where you can't be cowardly and summon slaves to fight your battles for you.

William got a message back almost immediately.

You have not chosen the place of your victory, boy; you have chosen the place for your death. I do not need slaves. You will get your battle, and you will die.

The Caster shot a fireball directly upwards, and as his eyes lit up and the white aura surrounded him, he shot up through the impromptu channel and out into the open air, which was choked by the thick clouds that oozed out from a massive tower; that itself rose up from the centre of the levelled palace.

However, through the gloom, William noticed a piercing red light. He summoned a fireball in each of his hands, and prepared himself as he flew carefully towards his opponent.

And then the battle started.

Chapter 13 - Momentum

As soon as William was sure where Vanyol was, he suddenly lit up with a piercing white light, so that his outline could barely be seen, and as charged through the air at Vanyol, he all but screamed out his pain, but this only sped him up.

He covered the distance between them within seconds, and Vanyol did not have time to react.

The Caster slammed into the ArchCaster with enough force to knock him back dramatically. As the men flew backwards, their auras mixed and writhed together as if they were fighting a battle of their own; red against white.

William had planted himself into Vanyol's midsection and, try as he might, the ArchCaster could not stop himself or his opponent on their swift journey.

Suddenly, a tower appeared in their path. It was the main tower; the one that the black clouds were coming from, and it was approaching too quickly to avoid, so it hit Vanyol full in the back. But such was the force of William's charge that the two actually went through one wall, then the other, then out into the air again.

Only Vanyol could see it, but the tower began to topple and fall, smashing through the roof of the part of the palace that William had come from.

They had now cleared the high walls of the palace, and were flying over the bare, dry, rocky plains that encircled it.

But they had reached the top of their arc, and began to fall faster and faster.

As the ground rushed up, William spun himself around, planted his feet into Vanyol's chest, and kicked downwards with all his might.

A second later, William landed on one knee on the dry ground, causing is to fragment in a circular pattern, with him as the epicentre. Behind him, closer to the palace, Vanyol smashed into the earth, and the impact was so tremendous that it sent a vast cloud of dust and dirt far into the air. As is began to clear, William saw that Vanyol was lying in a deep crater, but he soon got to his feet, still a bit unsteadily.

"So it was you." He seemed genuinely surprised. "You were the one who cast the magic. You're Ranson's son."

William did not say a word. He had a million ways to kill Vanyol, and only a few of them would work, but he no longer cared about being careful.

"Do you speak, or are you dumb as well as stupid?"

William's eyes lit up, and he shouted.

"I am here to kill you!"

He charged through the air once again at Vanyol, but he was expecting it, and dodged the attack easily. As William passed him however, he fired a blast of crimson right into his side.

The Caster was thrown away from him with incredible force; the blast had not been big but it was extremely powerful. He hit the ground, but was still travelling, and used his own momentum to roll onto his feet.

Vanyol had his hands raised to the sky, like he was having one last prayer to the heavens, but William realised only too late what he was doing.

Lighting began to crash across the sky, and William prepared himself for the imminent attack. But, to his surprise, the bright bolt of lightning came down and hit Vanyol. As soon as he had built up enough power, he threw his arms forward, and scarlet lightning sliced through the air towards William.

The Caster raised his arms by instinct, and the lighting split into hundreds of tiny forks about a metre in front of him. But the lightning was constant; like a river, and even though William was stopping it from hitting him, the force began to push him backwards. The faintly glowing barrier that was shielding him from the deadly forks was being pushed back, and, acting like a solid wall, it was pushing William back too. His feet were sliding slowly over the dirty ground, but his power remained strong enough to counter Vanyol's vicious attack.

As soon as the searing barrage has ceased, William rose into the air, and began to spin rapidly around. The dust below him began to spin too, and it slowly joined the aerial vortex that was now surrounding him, until before the stunned Vanyol was a giant tornado. But it was doubly dangerous; the sand was moving so fast on the wind, that it would rip flesh to shreds in seconds.

William however had left the cyclone almost as soon as it had started, and he was now hovering behind it. He raised his hands, and using his mind he pushed it forwards, towards his enemy.

Vanyol shot fireball after fireball at the twister, but every single one got blown off course by the winds. Soon they got so strong that the ArchCaster was having a hard time staying upright. He raised his arms, but this was mostly to protect his face from the cold bite of the sand. Soon this became far too much for him, and sent out a blast that fragmented the cyclone, and the sand and dust fell into a large pile around him. William was knocked off his feet too, and landed on his back a few metres away.

Vanyol then summoned up the sand, and launched all of it towards William as a cloud, embellished with crimson magic.

The young Caster covered his fist with magic to give it extra power, and slammed it into the ground. Dirt, sand and even the rock around him jumped into the air, completely surrounding him, and he shot blazing hot fire out of his hands, baptising the entire covering in implausible heat. What remained was a completely smooth glass casing, which the sand, even magically enhanced sand, barely even scratched. It just slid over the sleek surface, and that was the end of it.

Vanyol walked over to this translucent casket, and looked at the severely obscured outline of his enemy. He sneered unpleasantly, and then blanketed the glass with constant flame, as the contents heated slowly up.

Inside the glass dome, the heat was becoming very uncomfortable. William was sweating, and he has to slow down his breathing to conserve what air he had in that small void.

He knew that now Vanyol was this close to him, he could not get out of his self-made trap without being burned alive in a second.

Through the glass, the fire, already mesmerising, was warped and strangely moving. It cast intricate shadows across his face, and it was incredibly distracting. The heat was also beginning to get to him; his wits were dulling fast and it was getting hard to breath. Every second he spent in that prison was another nail in his coffin.

Then, he heard an almighty crack, and he looked straight up. A rather unnerving fracture had appeared in the glass, and tiny wisps of flame seeped through.

The casing was melting and would not last much longer.

He had to get out.

Vanyol heard the glass crack, and he knew that William could not survive for much longer. But maintaining this spell for so long was incredibly draining. He was not only manipulating the fire; he had to create it, and that took a lot of effort. Sure enough, the stream of fire that was flowing from his hand was beginning to wane, and soon failed altogether.

The ArchCaster studied the glass dome. The air around it seemed to warp and bend out of shape, and the surface was glowing faintly red. More cracks had appeared, and it was a wonder how the structure was still in one piece.

He looked closer, and thought he could see the outline of his enemy, but there was no movement from within.

Vanyol raised his hand, and the dome glowed red for a second, before blowing outwards, revealing its contents. William was lying completely still on the dusty ground, and did not react as some pieces of glass reigned down onto him. The ArchCaster walked over to the body, very slowly. He couldn't feel any power coming from the corpse, and there was no sign of life.

But he was taking no chances. Vanyol reached under his dark cloak and drew out a sword. It was a relatively squat sword with a short handle and a wide blade.

It was Melnhir.

Not caring whether or not the boy could hear, Vanyol spoke.

"This sword was owned by one I slew in the great battle. He was brave, but weak. I killed him with his own blade. And now I realise that he was your uncle."

Vanyol looked down at his unmoving enemy.

"How convenient."

He stood over William and raised the sword.

Suddenly he doubled up, as Triscant was plunged swiftly in and out of his side. Vanyol looked behind him from his stooped position, and saw a girl holding the sword, with his own blood amply covering the tip.

He threw her back with a powerful pulse that knocked her unconscious before she even hit the ground. He removed the hand that had been covering his bloody wound, and pointed it at her.

"The price for treachery is a heavy one."

As he spoke his hand glowed with a crimson aura. But a voice made him turn sharply.

"Get... away from her."

He turned to see William pull himself to his feet, and he laughed loudly.

"What will you do to stop me? You may have some power, but you're just a boy!"

William's voice was calm and quiet, but was full of strength.

"I'm a Caster."

And with this, his eyes blazed with white light; as did the aura that lifted him off his feet and into the air.

Vanyol fired a blast of pure energy at him, but it didn't hinder him in the slightest. If anything, it made the glow brighter. Vanyol tried a fireball, then a lightning bolt, but the glow grew brighter still.

Then the glass around his feet suddenly glowed with a bright white aura, and rose towards William.

The fragments began to orbit him in ever accelerating circles, whizzing clockwise and counter-clockwise.

Vanyol began to shout at him in pure desperation.

"No, you can't do this! I won!"

If William's eyes had been visible, Vanyol would have seen a slight edge of pity.

"You lost. You will always lose. Because I have something that will always overcome."

William floated towards him.

"Something that you never understood."

Vanyol dropped Melnhir and backed away, but could not retreat fast enough.

"Something you lost the right to have many years ago."

There was nothing the ArchCaster could do. His eyes did not leave the rapid orbit of shards.

"Love."

The shards shot out from the Caster, and stabbed into Vanyol's clothes, pinning him to the ground.

William looked down at the man, who suddenly looked simply pathetic.

"If you have love, then let me live!"

"I would," said William, his soft voice somehow amplified by his powers. "But you killed my parents."

He raised his hand, and the dull clouds gathered and merged into one purely black entity over the place where Vanyol lay.

Then, before the ArchCaster even had a chance to cry out, an immense lightning bolt sliced down, past William, and immersed him in crackling, powerful light. He was instantly vaporised, and the lightning bolt disappeared just as quickly, as the clouds thinned and began to move away.

William descended, landing next to the girl. He put his hand on her forehead, and she felt cold. So he clasped one of her hands in his, and the gaps between their fingers were filled with white light. Her whole body tingled with a pale aura, and her eyelids began to flutter.

After a few seconds, she was fully awake, and as soon as the image of William focused in front of her, she pulled him down by his collar and kissed him tenderly. He was taken by surprise, but did not object. As their lips separated, she looked at him and blushed.

"Thank you for saving me," she said quietly.

"I was only returning the favour," William replied, smiling as he gazed into her deep brown eyes.

Ranson was waiting with the other freed men and women. As he and the girl had walked through the palace, he had noticed a familiar sword in the hand of one of the dead guards, and had picked it up. He had carried Triscant all the way through the halls of that awful place, and as soon as the girl had brought him to the rest of the escapees, she said she was going back to help William. He had given her Triscant to use, as she had given up her sword and scabbard in order to carry him.

But she had been gone a while, and although the entire party had been audience to William's charge and the tower falling, after that the two combatants had disappeared behind the expansive palace. They had noticed some strange cloud activity and heard odd blasts of noise, but that was it.

Ranson hoped his son was okay, but he had a horrible feeling in his gut telling him that he was dead and the world's last hope for freedom had died with him. It also infuriated him that, since he had lost his powers, he could not detect other power, meaning he did not know which great Caster was left.

He looked longingly at the horizon, beyond the furthest corner of the palace, but he thought he saw movement.

Yes, he was sure of it; a figure, no, two figures.

Suddenly, sunlight struck him on the side of his face, and its alien warmth was comforting in the extreme. The gloomy clouds that had covered the fortress for so long had begun to move away and disperse. Then he looked back at the figures. As they walked, one of them seemed to jerk their arm, and white blast flew up into the sky, exploding into bright, brilliant spark above the palace; sparks so dazzling that they could be seen clearly even in the bright sunlight.

As the people around him cheered at the celebratory explosion, Ranson looked at the approaching figures, and smiled.

As William and the girl approached the crowd, they were met with rolling cheers and a hearty dose of back-slapping.

As the girl embraced Ranson, William saw a familiar face in the throng and ran over to him.

Aniik'arim An'tiamo was beaming at the Caster, and they embraced warmly.

"You did it," the older man said. "You found your power. You saved us."

William nodded.

"But there is a promise I have to keep to a good friend." He grinned and led the older man to the front of the mass, close to the palace.

William closed his eyes, and concentrated with arms uplifted.

The stones of the palace began to move, and then separated from each other entirely. First one, then another, then another flew up into the air and began to spin around each other. Once every stone was in the air and the palace was no more, the stones began to fall. But not randomly; each stone landed on the one that fell before it, creating walls, then rooms, then houses, and soon where once there had been an ugly, unaccommodating palace, there was a nicely ordered city, enough to house every person there with ease.

"And I believe a city needs water."

His eyes were still closed, and far away, at a little blocked spring in the Beltzan Peaks, a dam exploded into nothingness, and the water coursed forth. Not too long after, a fully-fledged river flowed through the centre of the city.

William opened his eyes, and looked at Aniik.

"This was what you wanted, wasn't it? A place where people could be happy, on the banks of the river Tiamo. I wish you the happiest life that anyone could have."

"Thank you," the older man said simply, but his moist eyes and warm smile said more.

William turned to the crowd before him.

"There is enough here for everyone; enough space, enough water, and there will soon be more than enough food. You may have this city on one condition; that you treat each other with kindness and love, and thrive in that love until the stones themselves fall."

The crowd roared their agreement, and rushed forward to find their new homes.

Only a couple of people remained.

One was a man, and one was a girl, and they both held a special place in his heart.

He walked over to Ranson, and the older man spoke first.

"You did well. I knew you had it in you."

"Thank you."

The girl coughed quite deliberately, and William realised he was being rude.

"Oh yes, father, this is..."

His voice trailed off, and it struck him that he had never found out the girl's name.

But she saved him the embarrassment and introduced herself.

"My name is Alayna. I am a member of the Resistance."

William remembered the War Room charts in the mountain, and remembered that he had seen symbols that he thought were other branches of the Resistance.

"So are we," said William, gesturing to himself and Ranson.

"I think I am the only one left of the men who fought with me. We were overrun by Scarra and most of us died. The rest were killed in spontaneous fires in our camp. I understand now that it was Vanyol."

William nodded and then turned to Ranson.

"How many branches of the Resistance are there?"

"Quite a few, but we have to assume the worst. If Vanyol attacked two camps, there is no reason to believe that anyone else is alive. As of now, we are the Resistance."

They all nodded to each other.

But then William had a thought. An incredible thought. An incredible, game-changing thought.

"We could rebuild the Resistance."

The two others just looked at him like he had two heads.

"We could. There must be others like me; children of Casters. If we could find them, we could fight back. I only just managed to kill Vanyol, and that was mostly on the element of surprise. We need more power to win."

Ranson nodded.

"You're right. But how do we find them? You're the only one with any power."

William smiled.

"That's not entirely true. As Vanyol died, I felt power go into me. Not his, but the power he took from you."

William reached out his hand, and Ranson took it. White light suddenly shot from the gaps between their flesh, and Ranson's eyes lit up with pale light. He was surrounded by a pale aura, and the burns on his wrists faded to perfectly healthy skin. The older man was full of energy once again, and he shot a fireball into the air in joy at the return of his powers.

The girl brought him back to the problem at hand.

"But how will we find them?"

"Ranson and I have an ability to see life energy in our minds."

Ranson took over.

"Each Caster has a bright white light, far brighter than any normal person."

At this, the girl looked at him with sharpness in her eyes.

"Sorry," the older man said. "You know what I mean."

William continued.

"If we can find a way of surveying each of the three Realms, we can find each potential ally and then go into battle with the ArchCasters."

"There is one thing that I can think of," interjected Ranson. "The Torridon was the centre of the Casters, and therefore the centre of their works. The founding place of magic had long since been lost, but a stone was recovered from that hallowed place. The Caster Elders used it to amplify their power of foresight, allowing them to see into the future. We could use it to magnify our power so that we could find each Caster. But there is one problem. The stone was sealed in the vault underneath the citadel, and even the Three, with all their power, could not open it."

"Maybe they were not meant to," replied William. "If this stone is as powerful as you say, maybe it stopped anyone from using it that had evil in their heart. Maybe, if we are truly doing what is right, it will let us use it."

"It's not much to go on," said Alayna.

"It's all we have. But we must do this as soon as possible. News will quickly spread of our actions here, and Kelthane and Solaxe will rain down their vengeance callously on the entire Realm."

William and Alayna nodded at Ranson's words.

"But we have no horses," said the girl. "It would take far too long on foot."

William smiled and whistled a long, sharp note, clearly amplified by his powers.

"I sent my father's horse away before the battle on the mountain for fear of what would happen to it. After all, it is the only thing I have left of my father. It knows the way to me, and will be here by dawn tomorrow. But for now, we must plan our way to the Torridon. Our path will be treacherous."

Aniik appeared behind the group.

"Do you have anywhere to stay tonight?"

The group shook their heads.

"Then please, stay with me. I know that there are many empty houses, but I would like to get to know you as much as I can before you go. After all, I have heard so much about your father. It would be a shame to miss this opportunity to meet him."

Alayna replied for the group.

"We would love to stay with you, thank you."

As they followed Aniik to his new home, Ranson walked with Aniik, and Alayna moved beside William. She took his hand in hers, and they smiled at each other as they followed the two men towards the hundreds of new homes.

William was lying awake on the floor of Aniik's new home. He could not sleep; every time he closed his eyes he saw once more the horrors he had witnessed. So he let his mind wander and his thoughts played out in the air around him.

Ranson and Alayna were asleep beside him on the stone floor. Aniik was in the bed next door, which was a flat stone that stuck out of the wall. William had created each house like this.

He heard a quiet voice, and turned his head to find Alayna lying on her side, looking at him.

"What are you thinking about?" she asked, quiet enough to not wake Ranson.

"The war," he replied. "Every man I've killed, every man who has died because of me, still remains in my mind. They haunt me every time I close my eyes. I hear the sounds of the battle and of many dying cries. I smell the blood and sweat in the heat of battle, and feel the bitter chill of warfare crawling on my skin. I had once thought that war was glorious, but now I understand that it is beyond Hell itself."

William turned towards her.

"And it has to continue. I have to kill more to end it all. Sometimes I wonder if I am good, when I have killed so many."

"You have only ever taken the lives of those who would otherwise have killed you."

"But does that make me any better than them?" Alayna saw the raw pain in his eyes. "Every soldier has a cause that he thinks is right. Maybe I am the true enemy, taking lives, kingdoms, none of which are mine to take."

"Do you believe that you are doing the right thing?"

The boy nodded.

"Then you must fight for it."

William turned once more onto his back, and studied the stone ceiling.

"I believe in you," she whispered, and then turned away from him. William opened his mouth to respond, but seeing that she had her back to him he realised that the conversation was over.

Once more he stared sightlessly upwards, but then noticed a spider in the corner of the ceiling opposite him. It was trying to string a web together, but the surface was too smooth for the web to cling onto, and it kept falling apart. He watched as the tiny creature ventured further and further towards the centre of the ceiling to try and find a decent lodging for its silk, with no luck. Suddenly it completely lost its grip and fell, and William caught it using his mind, much to the spider's surprise. He lifted the creature up the original position of its web, and using his mind broke tiny flakes of stone away from the wall and ceiling, creating a rough surface that the web could stick to.

Once the spider was securely grasping the wall, William got up and crept out, past Aniik's bed, and out into the night. The house had a flat roof, and William lifted himself up onto it. He lay there looking up at the dark canvas above him, punctuated by tiny, brilliant points of light, and became lost in its massive splendour.

He used to lie under the night sky and watch the stars back in Tursus. How long ago that seemed.

He was always encouraged by how small his problems looked when faced with the magnitude of creation. Even now, when his troubles were so much bigger and more hideous, this simple thought gave him an overwhelming feeling of release. His mind became peaceful, and all troubling thoughts were lost to the magnificent night sky.

Slowly, tenderly, the cloud of unconsciousness began to lull him, and as his eyes closed it embraced him. His thoughts swam out into the inky blackness and dreams began to weave a haven for his mind; a sweet escape from the tiring tribulations of the day.

Far above him, the last stars blinked into existence, standing as sentinel, unfaltering against the surrounding darkness. They looked down on the earth from their high seat in the heavens, and saw a white ray of hope shining back at them.

Chapter 14 - Love in the Time of Magic

William was woken by a loud whinnying, and sat up on the roof to see his father's horse stomping its feet on the dry, dusty ground, kicking up small clouds of dirt.

The Caster smiled and jumped down onto the ground in front of Aniik's house. There was ample room, as the house was on the edge of the empty desert and faced outwards into it.

William took hold of the horse's bridle and patted it lovingly. He was genuinely thrilled that the animal had survived.

He summoned up a length of rock from the ground, and tied the horse off. Then he went inside to wake the others.

First, he woke Alayna gently, then Ranson a little less ceremoniously.

"The horse is here. We can go as soon as we are ready."

Ranson nodded, and sprang up immediately. Alayna took more convincing, but eventually rose too. All three grabbed their belts and packs, and began to move towards the door.

William glanced upwards, saw a complete, elegant web in the corner of the ceiling, and smiled to himself.

But then he noticed Aniik standing in the doorway, arms folded and expression serious.

"Did you think you were going without saying goodbye?" he said, and his face cracked into a smile.

The group each embrace the man, and William was last. As the two friends were in each other's arms, the older man spoke.

"Thank you, my friend. For everything. I cannot ever repay the kindness that you have shown me."

"You don't have to," replied William.

But Aniik reached into a pouch on his belt and brought out a necklace.

"This was my wife's. I would like you to take it. It would bring her joy to know that my saviour has it." He pressed the necklace into William's hand.

"Thank you, I will treasure it."

Aniik smiled warmly, and Ranson patted William on the back.

"Time to go," he said.

William nodded one last time at Aniik, and then left his new home, closing the door behind him.

Outside, Alayna was busy strapping their packs to the horse, when she stumbled across something. Underneath one of the packs that the horse had on already was a long, slender bow. The girl unclipped it and drew it out.

"That was my hunting bow. I had completely forgotten about it."

Alayna also pulled out a wrapped quiver that contained about a dozen arrows.

"Well, you seemed handy with a bow in the last battle. I would be happy for you to have it, if you want."

"Thank you," replied the girl, still looking the bow up and down. Then she looked at William and grinned. "And it's not like a powerful Caster has any need of it."

"True," he admitted, smiling back. As she strapped the quiver to her back and strung the bow, he walked over to the horse.

"All of the things I packed from Tursus are here," he informed the pair, while carefully studying the contents of the packs. "We have water skins, blankets, a little food, flints and kindling. I think we have everything we need."

Ranson looked at him suspiciously.

"You planned this didn't you?"

"Maybe," William replied with a grin.

Alayna was less optimistic.

"If there's only one horse, which of us will be riding it?" she asked.

"Well, how many of us here can't fly?"

Alayna gave William a look, and Ranson smirked at their exchange. He saw a lot of himself in William, and he saw a lot of his mother's spirited spark in Alayna. They were certainly quite the pair.

The girl turned to him.

"So, we have established that I am taking the horse. What about you two?"

Ranson answered for them.

"One of us will stay by the horse and one of us will scout ahead in the air. We will take in turns so neither of us gets too tired. We should get to the Torridon by the end of tomorrow if we start now and ride fast. I'll take the air first. Alayna, get going and go as fast you can. William, stay with her."

The trio nodded to each other, and Ranson took off into the air. William got onto the horse, and Alayna got on behind, putting her arms round him.

Suddenly William heard Ranson's voice in his head.

Get going now!

William agreed, and jabbed his heels into the sides of the horse. Suddenly, the animal charged forwards. It was so sudden that Alayna almost fell backwards off the horse, but she tightened her hold around his abdomen and clung on as they charged across the dusty ground.

Soon, they came to the edge of the desert and a line of trees defined the perimeter of the Forest of Delsus. As the horse and its riders reached the border, Ranson descended and landed next to them.

"I scouted ahead but I couldn't see anything through the trees. We could go round the forest but it would take far too long and far too close to the border. We have to go straight through, which means we have to make our own path."

William nodded, and Ranson looked at Alayna.

"You will have to ride as fast as you can through the path we will create for you. If you see or hear anything unusual, tell us straight away. We don't want to be ambushed by Scarra."

"Okay," Alayna replied. "Let's go."

Ranson and William lit up with a white aura, and rose up into the air. They held their arms out in front of them, and the first few line of trees in one area burst rapidly into white flame and then evaporated in an instant. The Casters began to fly into the forest, and every tree within a few metres of them instantly atomised into nothing.

Alayna began to follow, and soon they were picking up speed. The horse soon realised that it had to follow the big white light in front of it, so Alayna no longer had to steer. So she drew an arrow from the quiver on her back and fitted to her new bow, just in case.

And her carefulness was proved useful, as to either side of them she saw fleeting shadows through the trees, only for a second, and then they disappeared, and then appeared again. Alayna was incredibly surprised that they could keep up with a horse going at full speed.

"I hate these things," she shouted.

William looked back to see what she was talking about. "Scarra," he muttered. Then he continued louder, "They must have been attracted by the light."

Alayna's complaints were short lived however, as one of the monsters launched itself out of the tree line towards her. She lifted her bow, drew and fired it purely by instinct. The arrow hit the Scarra between the eyes, and it was knocked back. But they were travelling so fast that the body was soon out of sight behind them.

She turned in the saddle one way, then the other, shooting down monsters with each arrow. Soon the Scarra were leaping at her with such numbers and vigour that she was simply beating them away with the bow itself. She drew her sword, and with the bow in one hand and her sword in the other, she was defending the horse well, but soon she would be overrun.

At the front of the party, William and Ranson were incinerating any Scarra in front of them as well as any trees. But, seeing that Alayna might need some help, Ranson sent William a message.

I'm fine here. Go and help her.

William nodded and decreased his speed.

He matched the horse's velocity and held up his arms. A slightly luminescent barrier appeared around the horse and its rider. Monster after monster jumped at them, but each one was repelled. A few were propelled back into trees, and their backs broke with loud cracking noises.

Alayna was looking at William with awe, but he had his eyes shut in concentration.

Ranson noticed that the light was increasing between the trees. They were getting closer and closer to the other edge of the forest.

All we have to do is hold out a little bit longer and we will be out of the trees. The Scarra will not follow us beyond the forest.

Ranson sent this message to William, who relayed it to Alayna.

The brightness grew stronger and stronger, until with a final burst of light they were out of the forest. Ranson and William both stopped, and landed in front of the horse and its rider, who had come to a halt a second after the Casters. Dozens of Scarra appeared on the edge of the forest, and roared at the escapees.

The two men lit up with incredibly bright white auras as a reply to the snarls, and the Scarra, knowing that they had been beaten, slunk back into the forest.

Alayna sheathed her sword and strung her bow across her chest. She was the first to turn around in her saddle, and she was practically speechless at what she saw. But she had enough energy to release some sound, which caused the two men to turn too.

Towering over them stood part of the outermost wall of the Torridon. It had been blown away from its place by powerful magic, and had landed here in the ground. Even though it was merely a tiny fraction of the original palace, it left the party awestruck.

"It's a good sign that we're heading the right way," commented Ranson, who was the first to snap out of the trance, as he had seen things like this before.

"Now we have left the forest, the Scarra will leave us alone. They have lost their advantage, and even at night they know we are more powerful. They have neither the numbers nor the conviction to win. And by the time they do, we will be long gone. But we should go a bit further just in case there is one who fancies its luck. We don't have to ride hard. We should just walk until dusk and then set up camp."

Alayna nodded and clicked her tongue at the horse. It seemed to understand and began to walk, seeming very happy to put its tail to the trees. The two men walked either side of it, and while they were walking William reached into one of the packs and pulled out a water skin. He took a swig and then passed it up to Alayna, who took it gratefully.

"That was some fancy shooting back there," commented William, once he had swallowed the water.

"Thanks," she replied. "Not all good warriors need powers. I've gotten by well enough without."

She passed the skin down to Ranson, who finished off the water that was inside.

"So how did you come to be in prison?"

"Our camp was attacked by Scarra. We were completely unprepared, but we rallied our forces and drove them back. But then Vanyol's men attacked us and we realised that it was not a random attack; that the monsters were merely pawns, driven forward to weaken us by the more powerful pieces. We did not have the strength to hold them. Within a few hours we had lost almost everyone. The brave souls fought to the last man instead of allowing themselves to be captured. I tried to do the same, but still managed to end up in that horrible place. Someone must have told Vanyol where we were."

"The traitor was in our camp. He paid with his life, but with all the blood that was on his hands, it was far too low a price," replied Ranson. He seemed incredibly angry, and William realised that he had worked and fought beside Garston for so many years that the pain of betrayal ran deep indeed.

"Anyway," William began; eager to change the subject. "Tell us about this stone at the Torridon."

Ranson calmed himself down and replied.

"It is called the Stone of Draoidh. It is believed to have come from the cradle of life itself; which is also the birthplace of magic. The cradle itself has long since been lost, but this one stone was recovered many years ago; no-one knows how or by whom, but it fell into the hands of the Casters. It was noticed straight away that it amplified a Caster's powers, and after many, many years studying it the Caster Elders were able to harness its power to see a little way into the future. That is how they predicted the betrayal of the Casters a few hours before they attacked. But it also showed then great truth and knowledge, and gave them the assets necessary to perform incredible magic. They built the Torridon from mere dust."

"And to dust it has returned," interjected William, poetically. Ranson nodded.

"The ArchCasters wanted the power of the Stone for themselves, and that is why they fought for it. But unbeknownst to them, before the great battle began, the Stone was sealed in the vault below the fortress, protected by worldly strength and powerful spells. Their corrupted magic could not open it, so they laid waste to what was left of the palace, making sure no-one else could ever lay their hands on the Stone."

"And you want me to open the vault?"

William looked doubtfully at Ranson, who nodded.

"If I am right, opening the vault is the easy bit. The Torridon is huge and I have no idea where the vault is, apart from the fact that it will be under tons of broken stone and rubble."

"Is there any way we can detect it using our powers?"

"Almost certainly not. The spells that guard the vault would block its emanations."

Alayna was feeling slightly left out of the conversation being the only one not to have powers, so she allowed her eyes to take in the striking scenery. But it was not impressive; it was striking because it looked so normal. After being in that horrible palace for days, she loved the looked of natural, normal scenes. But her eyes settled on a thicket surrounding pile of rubble. It was still quite far away, but it was undoubtedly remnants of the Torridon. It was a good place to camp, but when she suggested the idea to Ranson he said they should keep going for a bit longer. After all, the sun was still quite high in the sky, and they wanted to get as far as they could in one day.

So, on they went, seeing reminders of their quarry on a regular basis. The sun had just begun to dip down beneath the horizon, but there was still light in the sky, when they came across something that they really did not expect.

A small village had set themselves up on the banks of a river, no doubt a branch of the Delsus. But the entire township was towered over by a gigantic piece of wall, which half encircled the buildings. The rest of the houses were surrounded by a far less impressive wall, made of something similar to wicker.

Alayna and William sighed in unison, incredibly relieved see civilisation.

"Rest," William muttered.

"Hot food," sighed Alayna.

Ranson smiled.

"Aren't you glad that we kept going now?"

The trio laughed, and Alayna dismounted and led the horse on foot.   As they passed through the gate of the village, they looked at their surroundings.

The houses were quite simple, and they each surrounded by fenced off green patches, some containing crops, some housing animals, some holding wood and metal used and forged by smiths.

The people smiled at them as they moved through the rows of houses, and responded helpfully to Ranson's inquiries to certain places. Although it was not much, this place was home to them, and they were glad in it. A longing for Tursus suddenly loomed on William, and despite the cheery faces he saw around him, he felt a deep emptiness.

The party seemed to be making good progress to wherever it was they were going; they were simply following Ranson, who apparently knew where he was headed.

Eventually they arrived at the tavern, and tied up the horse. As soon as they opened the door, they were glad to be there. There was merry music being played by the band in the corner, and people were laughing heartily, clanging their tankards together and swigging hearty glugs of mead.

Ranson walked through the throng and up to the counter. The barman recognised him instantly and they exchanged pleasantries with smiles on their faces. William and Alayna followed more slowly, and reached the bar slightly later. The boy coughed deliberately and Ranson introduced them to the man. Then he did the opposite.

"This is Arthur," he informed them. "After the great battle, this was the first place I came to. Back then it was just a village, and the giant wall outside had landed in the middle of it. They all moved to this side for better protection. Back then, Arthur was only a worker at this tavern, but he was the first person I talked to on arrival. I told him where I came from and he let me stay in one of these rooms until I was strong again. He hid me from his master and brought me food and water."

"And now I'm running the place," chortled the man. He was generously proportioned, but jolly all the same.

"You can all stay here tonight, free of charge. Your old room is empty at the moment. Have it. I'm sure you remember the way."

"Yes, thank you," said Ranson. He led the two others past the bar, up two flights of stairs, and into a room built into the rafters of the building. It wasn't all that big, but it would be warm once they got a fire going. There was also one big double bed and plenty of furry skins on hooks on the walls for anyone wishing to sleep on the floor.

While Ranson and Alayna were sorting out the packs, William collected some pieces of wood from the pile in the corner, built them up in the fireplace, and with a small blast of fire the pyre lit up and bathed the room in orange light.

He stood up.

"We need to get an early night," he said.

Ranson nodded.

"Tomorrow will be a difficult day for all of us."

"So what are we going about sleeping arrangements?" the girl asked.

"You have the bed, we'll sleep on the floor," Ranson answered, glancing at William. The younger man nodded, and walked over to the skins on the wall. He took two down, and then threw them to Ranson. Then he took two down for himself.

Within half an hour everyone was in bed. William had his eyes open, and with a flick of his wrist all the candles in the room went out.

He glanced up at Alayna, and she seemed to be fast asleep. Then he looked round at Ranson, who was lying face up, staring at the thatched ceiling.

"You're stronger than me, you know," he said quietly.

"Of course I'm not," replied William.

"Of course you are," insisted Ranson. "Vanyol took my powers, but he could not take yours. He only suppressed them, but you were stronger than him. That's why you never lost your fighting ability. It stems directly from you powers, and you did not lose them. I only had my experience to see me through. What makes you a great Caster is your heart; your soul. Promise me you will never lose who you are. I have no doubt that you can win against the ArchCasters if you stay true to yourself."

"I will," William replied.

"I can see how you feel about her," he said, nodding towards the bed. "But never let that cloud your judgement. Your heart is strong but it can betray you, and sometimes weaken you. Do not get too attached to her."

William nodded, but did not say anything.

"When we get to the Torridon tomorrow, I will not be able to help you. I am not strong enough to wield the Stone. You will be on your own."

The young Caster looked at him doubtfully. Nonetheless he said:

"I will try and make you proud."

"You already have, son. You are already a better Caster than I am, and I am sure that you will be a better man. Whatever you face tomorrow I am sure that you will do what is right."

William looked at Ranson for a while longer, even after he had stopped talking and began to drift away into sleep.

William's eyelids also became heavy, so he too nestled down into the warm, soft skins, and fell sound asleep.

William was woken up by a small click, and, after a second of being dazzled by the morning sun, looked towards the source of the sound.

Someone had unlocked the door to their room, which was the cause of the click, and had just walked out of the door. In his drowsy state, he could not tell who it was.

He looked at Ranson, and he was still asleep, face up, just as he had been the night before. He then glanced at the bed, and the familiar outline was still visible under the sheets.

William began to panic slightly, and woke up Ranson with a couple of nudges.

"I just saw someone leave the room, but we're all still here."

Ranson looked around dopily.

"It was probably just Arthur. Go back to sleep."

William could tell by his barely open eyes and slurred voice that he was too tired to be of any help. So William stood up, drew Melnhir, and rapidly studied the room for any sign of an intruder. Everything that should have been there was there, apart from the pack and bow that William had given Alayna.

He realised immediately that something was wrong. William rushed over to her bedside, and whipped the sheets off. Underneath was a bundle of skins rolled up and positioned into the shape of a person.

William sheathed his sword, quickly put on his shirt and shoes, and ran out of the door.

He caught up with Alayna just inside the village gates. She had her pack on her shoulder, and she was walking very fast.

He finally drew level with her and as he grabbed her shoulder she stopped. Once she was still, William was able to get his breath back; he had run as fast as he could through the entire village trying to find her, and he was panting heavily.

"Why... why are you leaving?"

"I heard you two talking last night! Your father was right. I can't stay with you. I don't fit in anyway."

William shook his head.

"I want you to stay. I don't care if you don't have powers. You've managed to save my life without them."

The girl smiled, and looked at the floor to hide it. William smiled too and stepped towards her.

"So please stay with us, because that's not the only thing my father was right about."

"Do you really care that much about me?"

William said nothing, but nodded.

Alayna smiled, and pulled him towards her. Then she planted a kiss on his lips which lasted for what seemed ages on end. When it finally broke, William was a bit flustered.

"Right... so, okay..." he said, stuttering a bit.

"That means yes, genius," she said softly through a thick smile caused by William's blatant discomfort.

Alayna pushed past him, brushing against him deliberately, and then began to walk back towards the tavern, leaving William just standing there in stunned silence.

"Well come on then!" she shouted back.

William snapped out of his trance, and turned round just in time to catch the pack that Alayna had thrown at him.

"And you can carry this too," she said, then grinned and walked away.

William chuckled, and then followed her.

Within a few minutes they had returned to the tavern. They walked through the door, navigated their way through the almost empty bar, nearly walked into a barmaid carrying a tray of empty tankards, and up the stairs.

Just as William was about to reach for the handle, he heard the creaking of floorboards from inside and, after putting his finger to his lips as a silent instruction to Alayna, knelt down carefully.

He heard more creaks, and he aligned his eye with the keyhole.

Suddenly and without warning, the door opened sharply and struck William hard across the face. He was sent reeling into the opposite wall.

Ranson was hurrying out of the doorway, but he stopped in his tracks at the sight of Alayna. He looked down and noticed William propped up against the wall, holding his face, with a pack lying next to him.

Ranson sighed audibly with relief.

"I thought that you had left."

"Well..." began Alayna, ready to admit the shameful truth.

"We just went for a walk to get some air and look around for supplies," William said, interrupting her.

Ranson smiled.

"Next time, leave a note or something."

He walked back inside to put his pack down, and Alayna glanced at William gratefully.

He picked himself and Alayna's pack up, the side of his head still throbbing with pain. Together the two young people walked into the room to make preparations to leave for the Torridon.

Chapter 15 - In Ruin

William, Alayna and Ranson walked out of the village gates as the sun had reached its peak in the sky.

In the last few hours, they had procured everything they would need for the journey ahead from the village; some were acquired through Ranson's relationships with the townsfolk, and some using the money that William's horse had brought all the way from Tursus. It was actually his parents' inheritance.

They now had plenty of food and water each, and new clothes and armour, plus skins and sheets. All of these packs were strapped to their horses. William still had his father's horse, but Alayna and Ranson had new ones.

William was now clad in leather padding, covered by chainmail, which itself was covered by plates of armour, which were not thick but layered over each other to form an impenetrable barrier that was easy to move in. There was also a red mark on his cheek from where the door had hit him, but the pain had mostly gone, as had the swelling; only a tiny patch of broken skin remained.

Ranson and Alayna also had new clothes, but were so similar to their old clothes that they could just have been the same ones. The major difference was that this leather armour was not covered in stains, scuffs and cuts from the many battles they had seen.

So now the three were not merely wanderers of the wild blessed with nothing; they were now prepared for anything they would meet on their journey to the Torridon.

So, as soon as they left the gates, they mounted their horses and began to ride; William and Alayna following in Ranson's wake.

They had been riding for only a few hours when they noticed an irregularly-shaped rise on the horizon. They were getting close to the remains of the Torridon, and the results of the catastrophic destruction were already becoming apparent.

The outline of the wrecked palace was far closer and clearer now, and rubble and broken stone was blocking their path more and more frequently. Soon they either had to navigate them carefully, or the Casters had to move them with their minds.

Before long, the fortress was so close that they were able to pick out the tiny slit windows in the part of the ruin that was still standing.

But by then, the broken stone blocking the way was now too treacherous for horses, so they tied them off and continued on foot.

The gargantuan pile of stone before them was steep, and it took all of them a long while to scale it. Alayna was more nimble than the other two, and the two men were a few metres behind her for the most of the way, however when the slope became steeper, about half way up, the gap increased a lot.

William was considering using his powers to catch up to her, when he heard the skittering of rocks, and a pained cry.

He looked behind him, and he saw that a few yards behind him Ranson had fallen. Maybe it was a loose stone that came away under his feet, or maybe he had tripped. Whatever the cause, he was now laying on his side amongst the rubble. William stifled a snigger and went back to help his father.

He put a hand under each of his arms, and went to lift him up, but Ranson swatted his arms away.

"I'm not that old yet," he chuckled, but then he spoke more seriously. "I just needed to talk to you."

He got up on his own in a second, and dusted himself off.

"I'm sorry about what I said last night. I know that she meant to leave. I saw the skins on her bed, and I realised it was my fault that she was leaving. You two belong together; I see that now. I had no right to get involved."

"No, it's fine," William reassured him. "I understand; you were just trying to protect me. But you were right. When I face the ArchCasters, I cannot be distracted at all." He looked up at Alayna, who was far ahead of them, springing nimbly from one stone to the next. "I really do care about her, but I know that, before the end, I have to let her go; for both our sakes."

Ranson nodded.

"It was the same when I had to leave and your mother. But let me tell you something. Don't make the same mistake I did. Don't choose any course if it means that you have to forsake love. Life is too damn long to live it on your own. Don't push her away unless you have to."

William looked at Ranson anew, and realised that it was hard for him to tell him to choose someone else, when he was all the older man had. He knew he was right, but didn't want to hurt his father any more.

Alayna called down to them form the summit of stone, and they looked back up at her.

"Come and look at this!" she hollered.

William and Ranson began to scale the slope as fast as their legs would carry them. But the older Caster knew what was beyond the ridge, and he was dreading having to see it again.

Even so, they reached the top in a very short time, and even Ranson looked at the scene before them with sombre awe.

The pile of rubble was completely encircling a massive area of land, in the centre of which lay what was left of the fortress Torridon.

But around it, inside the valley, was IIcll.

The dust and fog covering the scene never seemed to settle, but it was thin enough for the trio to see what lay beneath.

The floor was carpeted with bodies; decayed skeletons littered every inch of the ground. The flesh had been eaten away by carrion, insects and time itself. But some jet black birds remained; either circling overhead or picking at the already bare bones to try and find any morsel of meat they could.

Some bodies were covered by armour, some still had swords in their hands, but most jaws were open, as if their final, dying cries were still on their lips.

William suddenly understood why Ranson had run.

He looked at the older man, and saw that a tear was edging its way down his face, parallel to his scar. He muttered some words over the horrific scene; words that may once have been a poem or a song, but were now merely a whisper on the lips of a man who was looking on the bodies of his friends, and the words a final prayer spoken over memories by a man who should have stood and died with them.

For peace and for love, from dust we once came
We stand far above, until us it claims

No evil will rise, no pain and no shame
Until from our hearts, fades every flame

We stand together, brothers through strife
We never shall fail, while in us is life

By the strength of our backs
And the strength in our hearts
We will all stay strong, we brothers in arms

As Ranson finished, his voice cracked slightly, and William laid his hand on the man's shoulder.

"Come on," he said quietly. "We've got a job to do."

Ranson nodded in silence, and after a second more of staring at the macabre sight, they began to make their way down the slope.

The going was easier, as not only was the slope steeper so they had a smaller distance to go, but they now had gravity on their side instead of against them.

In sombre silence, they began to walk through the silent ranks of the dead; towards the ruined palace. Every now and then, William had to freeze mid-step to avoid putting his foot through a ribcage or a skull.

Most of the skeletons were complete, but some had been literally blown apart, and scattered around the battlefield. William grimaced when he saw a skull with an irregularly-shaped hole in the forehead, and instinctively knew that it was where a fireball had smashed into the man's brain. He put the horrific image out of his mind and moved on.

Most of the rubble had been blown outwards into the gigantic piles that acted as a barrier to the outside world, so the ruin of the palace, for the most part, was clear.

The main archway, which clearly used to hold gigantic gates, was no longer whole. As they walked through it, they saw the bottom of the structures poking a few metres out of the ground, but the rest had simply mixed with the rest of the broken stone.

Some parts of walls had stayed standing, and offered the only evidence that this had ever been a building. There was no ceiling, but the pure magnitude of the rooms was impressive enough to force silence upon the group.

They followed Ranson through the amply spacious hallways of the palace, and as they walked behind, they passed corridors to the left and to the right, and saw cave-ins of rubble and many blocked doors. The way they were going seemed clear enough, until they got to a tall metal gate. It had a lot of rubble around and in front of it, but it looked especially strong and immovable.

Ranson and William looked at each other, and they both closed their eyes. Then they both brought back their arms and then swung them forward, perfectly in sync with each other. As their hands sped forwards, they became ablaze with pale fire, and by the time they left the men's hands they were large, fully formed fireballs.

At exactly the same time, they slammed into the base of the pile of rubble and all of the broken stone flew outwards and peppered the group; or at least it would have if William had not summoned an invisible force-field to protect them.

Once the stone had stilled, William let the barrier fade, and the group looked at the gigantic door.

Amazingly, it was still on its hinges, and it had barely been scratched by the fireballs or the flying stone.

The girl sighed and spoke curtly.

"Well, what are we going to do now?"

William really had no idea. This was the problem with having little experience. He turned round slowly, pinching the bridge of his nose; hoping for some kind of miraculous epiphany.

However Ranson, having been blessed with the advantage of experience, knew what do. He instructed William, "Do as I do," and laid his hands a good deal apart onto the metal door. A moment later William did the same, and noticed the air bending around Ranson's hands. Then he saw a faint glow emanating from under the older man's palms, and he understood.

They were going to melt their way through.

The metal under their hands was now red hot, but their power and control was so incredible that they did not let the heat touch their skin; it was completely under their power.

But the door was extremely thick, and it was not melting quickly enough, so both men suddenly increased the intensity of the heat, and the metal suddenly sprung into blazing, white life. The ripples around their hands became more and more accentuated, and the metal began to peel off in bright white flakes. The red glow spread a good meter each way from the heat in the centre.

Then, without warning, the metal became soft. William had his weight pushing against it, and his hands suddenly sunk into the door. He felt the ends of his fingers push through into the open air, and he knew that the void he felt was the room on the other side of the door.

William turned his hands round in the molten metal so that his dorsa were together, and his palms were pointing away from each other.

Once he was happy with the position of his hands, he pulled then apart, and the effect on the door was almost absurd. Although some metal was molten, the rest was merely weakened, so his hands went through a few inches of the metal, but the rest obediently parted into a concertina fold on either side, leaving a large, diamond-shaped hole in the door.

He looked over at Ranson, who did the same thing a few seconds later. Then he looked back at Alayna, who was smiling in awe at the two men, and walked forwards to climb through the holes. William rested his hands on the edge of one hole, and then the other. As he did so, the red glows disappeared; he absorbed all of the heat in a matter of seconds. The holes, now cool, were just about wide enough for the trio to clamber through, feet first, and land inside whatever room Ranson had led them to.

The first thing that hit them was the dust.

The air was chokingly thick with tiny particles that made it hard to breathe. The walls and ceilings were an unbroken cocoon, which offered no breeze or escape to disturb the dust.

After the trio had regained what little breath they had, they looked at their surroundings. They were inside a vast, empty hall. Windows flanked the high walls along one side, and the sunlight that streamed through was strikingly visible. The angle was very slanted, and Ranson realised that it was getting late.

But the room wasn't entirely empty. In the centre of the floor was a single stone pedestal. It was about a meter high and had curious markings and engraving all the way up it. The wooden flooring around it seemed broken at regular intervals, but William could not work out what shape the breaks were in.

"This is the hall of the Elders of the Casters. They would come in here to get answers from the Stone. It is probably only due to its own magic that this hall managed to stay in one piece during the battle, so we must be in the right place."

"So that is the Stone," William said doubtfully, pointing at the pedestal in the middle of the room.

"No, I don't think so," replied Ranson. "But I've never been here before. I don't know what to do next."

Alayna sighed exasperatedly, and then laughed somewhat hysterically.

"We may as well search. It must be here somewhere."

"And if it isn't?" asked Alayna.

"Then we have to find everyone the old way; by looking."

"Through the whole of the Three Realms?"

Ranson nodded, and the other two understood the hopelessness of their plight without this key advantage.

"Fine," William said, slightly down-hearted. "Let's look."

And so they looked. Every nook and cranny in those walls was carefully studied, every floorboard checked, and even the breaks that William had seen earlier were poked and prodded, but with no result.

William decided that, given that it was the only thing left in this vast room, the pedestal must hold the answer. So, while Ranson and Alayna were feeling their way round the walls, he walked over to the squat rock.

He noted every miniscule mark and shape that was on it. He used his fingers to map the curving, waving shapes all the way up it, and he pushed at anything that could possibly be a button or lever. But not a sign could he find; no clunk of machinery or whoosh of magic. He stood up and sighed; he was completely ready to give up.

But then a voice whispered inside his head, as if it were a person right next to him, muttering into his ear quietly, scared of whom else might hear.

I have waited many years for you, Cyfarwydd.

William looked around, but Ranson had not spoken the words nor heard them. He was still searching the walls with Alayna. He could not think of anything else to do but answer. In any case, he did not seem to be in any immediate danger.

Who are you? And what did you call me?

The voice spoke to him again.

All in good time. But first, bring your friends around the dais and place your hand on top of it; right in the centre.

The voice ended, and William realised that it would not reach him again unless he did what it said, so William called over to the others.

"I think I've found something."

The other two hurried over, and watched from a triangle around the stone podium as William reached out his hand and laid it on top.

A strange white mist curled up out of the stone and moved over his hand. It almost seemed to slither across his skin. Then, as if it had found what it was looking for, it retreated back into the rock.

Then the floor around them rotated ever-so-slightly but with an almighty click. It suddenly became obvious that the breaks in the wooden floor were arranged in a circle, and as they rotated they were offset from the rest of the floor. Tiny clouds of dust were disturbed by the movement, and they flew up into the air around them.

But then nothing happened. The trio looked at each other, confused.

"Was that it?" asked Alayna.

No-one had a chance to reply however, as the circle of wooden flooring suddenly fell rapidly down. They could barely breathe due to the sheer force of the wind whipping past their faces.

The hall was already high above them, and the circle of light that indicated its position was getting smaller by the second. The walls that were speeding past them were so completely smooth and flawless that it looked like they weren't moving at all.

William heard the voice in his head once more; somehow clear over the loud rush of air. It told him what they had to do, and he relayed it to the others.

"We're nearly at the bottom!" he yelled over the noise. I'll need you to jump and I can hold you up, so we don't break our legs."

The other two nodded, looking at him insistently, waiting for their cue.

William listened, hoping for some kind of countdown, but he just suddenly heard:

Now!

"Now!" he hollered, and the three jumped.

While in the air, William concentrated, closed his eyes and stretched out his arms towards the others, holding them and himself up with invisible strings.

He opened his eyes, and the trio saw exactly how painfully close they had come to an accident. The platform had landed in a cloud of dust and dirt, and must have been protected by some kind of magic because it was still in one piece. They were only about ten metres above the impact site; in the perfect tube that ran all the way up to the surface. How far away it looked.

They were all quite out of breath, and Alayna looked at Ranson.

"Are you telling me that a group of old men did this more than once and survived?"

Ranson glanced at her.

"I'm as surprised as you. But they were powerful practitioners."

William cleared his throat.

"Do you think we could continue the history lesson at ground level?"

Ranson smirked and nodded.

Their feet soon touched the wooden flooring of the platform, and they stepped off it onto the stone-flagged floor of the cave.

"This is an ancient chamber and place brimming with magic," Ranson informed them, almost solemnly. "I had no idea that this was what was meant by the Vaults."

They looked around them, and although they were far below the hall, light still streamed out from the vertical tunnel and lit up the entire room. And they were glad that it did so.

The room was thin but long. They had landed at one end, and they saw that it was flanked on both sides by pedestals; the same size and design to the dais in the centre of the platform. But on top of these were curious glowing shapes; some beautiful, flowing, sleek objects, and some angular, sharp, almost ugly items. But they were all possessed of an aurous dignity; they shone with bright gold in the semi-darkness, vividly lighting the way.

William wondered if any of these was the Stone, but the he looked to the other end of the room, and saw an archway, out of which flowed a pale light. It wasn't particularly bright, but it immediately caught the attention of both Ranson and William.

Alayna, however, did not seem to see anything, and she expressed this as she did everything else.

"What are you looking at?" she asked impatiently.

"It's some kind of light. I think it's the Stone."

"It must be something magic if we can see it and you can't."

Ranson and William both walked, utterly calmly, towards the source of the light, however Alayna, still feeling a bit uneasy, drew her sword and walked forward more cautiously.

The trio came to the top of a small flight of stairs, and they descended carefully. Their surroundings were certainly striking.

The room was completely round, and the great expanse of it all was awe-inspiring. It was made up of two levels; one higher, and one lower. The lower level was bordered by water, which almost seemed to glow in its own luminescence. It also occupied the space underneath the higher level, which was somehow held up by one single, shallow stairway. This was basically just a wide, circular platform, but it was dark marble; flawless and smooth, and looked so elegant in its battle against the shadows.

Alayna had just stepped down off the first set of stairs, when she put her hand to her head, and collapsed. William turned around just in time and caught her using his powers. He laid her gently on the ground, and drew his sword, his whole body suddenly bristling with furious energy.

"What have you done to her?!" he shouted, looking around the room, sure that the voice could hear him.

She is simply sleeping. The power of this hallowed hall was too much for her to bear. She will be fine once she is removed from this place.

William looked round at Ranson, but he was looking around as well, searching for the source of the sound. This time he had heard it too.

But you cannot leave yet. Not without what you seek.

"And what's that?" Ranson asked. He looked purposefully at William, and the younger Caster realised that it was a signal to calm down and think. And then the obvious struck him.

Ranson was testing it.

You have come for answers. Answers that you need to win the war against the Three.

"And you can give it to us?"

Of course.

While Ranson was talking to it, William had pinpointed the exact source of the sound. With the many echoes and reverberations it had been difficult, but he was sure that the source was on the high platform, just out of sight. He crept up the stairs and peered over the lip of the precipice.

And what he saw made him wonder how he had not realised straight away.

Of course I can give you the answers, for I am from the source of all knowledge; the source of all magic.

In front of him, on a pedestal identical to all the rest, was an object that simply oozed light. It seemed to flow from it like hair from a head while underwater. The bands of pure luminescence swam out from it, and lit up the entire room.

There was no doubting what it was.

It was the Stone of Draoidh.

Ranson joined William on the platform and saw the Stone. He immediately knew what had to happen next.

"I'll take Alayna to recover in the Outer Vault."

William turned to face him.

"But I can't do this by myself," he protested.

"Yes you can. You were meant to. This is your destiny, not mine. I just have the privilege to come along for the ride. But you can do this. I know you can."

William nodded, even if a bit unsurely, and Ranson turned away. Once he was on the lower level he picked up Alayna, like a baby in his arms, and climbed the stairs.

The young Caster turned back to the Stone. It was not what he had expected it to be. It was not a cut diamond, nor was it smooth and round; it was somewhere between the two. It just looked normal; like any other rock in this ruined palace.

Apart from when it caught the light. It was curiously slightly transparent, so that William could see the water behind it, and from it came the occasional flash of gold. It was so normal, but so abnormal all the same.

The voice came from the Stone once more.

What is it you wish to know?

"Why did you call me Cyfarwydd? My name is William."

Cyfarwydd is an ancient name for 'story'. I call you this because your story it so important; above so many others. But the start is so sad, and the end will be too. Your story does not last forever.

William was taken aback, but somehow he knew not to ask about his own future. So he put it out of his mind.

"I have to find all of those who are like me; Children of Casters. Together I believe we would have the power to defeat the ArchCasters. But I need to know where to find them. Can you show me?"

Yes. Put your hand on the Stone.

William reached out his hand, and as soon as his first finger brushed the Stone, he was transported to what looked like another world.

Stars wheeled overhead, and thousands of colours blurred into one as they whirled past. The voice appeared once again in his mind, and seemed to guide him through this wondrous abyss of colour and light.

To defeat your enemies you must harness the powers of the elements: Earth, water, air and fire. But you cannot do this alone. The powers you possess are not enough. A Child was born to each element. The Earth gave up its power to them so that it may once again be free.

An image of the Torridon appeared, but there was a vast battle raging around and above it.

When the Casters were defeated, the Three sent soldiers to kill every bloodline. Hundreds if not thousands of children were hunted down and slaughtered. None were old enough to use their powers, so they perished.

But William saw four children, hiding in different parts of the world. He felt their fear and their pain as his own, and his heart nearly broke to hear their screams and their cries.

The Earth protected them. Their powers masked themselves from the eyes of the Three, and protected the children from harm. They guided them to food, water and shelter. They survived because they needed to. Now they are older than you, and are living normal lives, scattered across the four winds, their powers hidden until the day when they are needed.

"How do I find them?" William asked, but his voice was so different in this world that he barely recognised himself speaking.

This I cannot tell you. You must use your own powers and reach out to them. I will amplify your abilities. You must quiet and control your mind. Concentrate.

William summoned up a map of the Three Realms in his head. It was completely black. But then he saw the Torridon in the centre, and the massive white aura that himself and Ranson were emitting.

Then, suddenly, he felt a power surge through him; the likes of which he had never felt before. The power of the Stone was his to command.

He noticed on the map that where there had been a white glow, there was now a golden light. He reached out all around the Torridon in his mind, covering more and more ground with each second.

On the map it looked like a ripple tearing out from the centre of the Three Realms in a perfect circle, and it slowly passed over the earth.

Eventually it began to pass over the places where people dwelled; Macros, Tursus, anywhere with people registered as faint grey auras. But then a bright white glow showed up, and then another, and then another, and then finally the last one.

Four small points of light on a map. These were the locations of the Children of the Casters.

Suddenly he let go of the Stone, and he was back in the dark Vault underneath the Torridon. But his eyes were closed, and beneath them was a brilliantly bright light. He was containing the power of the Stone.

Blindly, he scrabbled about in the bag strapped at his waist and pulled out a rolled up piece of paper fastened with a length of string. He untied the fastening, still with his eyes closed, and unrolled the paper, holding it front of his face.

Then he opened his eyes, and golden energy shot from his eyes onto the paper, each speck of aurous power finding its mark; singeing the material black.

William regained his sight, and ended up looking straight at a map. He had translated the map in his mind onto the parchment, and, using the intense energy of the Stone, had blackened the parts that needed to be darkened: The map-lines, the borders, the rivers, but most importantly the four points where he would find his allies.

He was told to harness the elements, and that was exactly what he was going to do because now he knew where to find them.

Alayna's eyes fluttered open, and she awoke on the hard floor underneath the low ceiling. She was looking up at Ranson who was standing over her, staring at something to her right.

She sat up and Ranson registered the movement. He knelt down beside her and helped her to sit up.

"What happened?" she asked, putting a hand to her forehead.

"You fainted," Ranson answered. "The power of the Stone was too much for you to cope with."

"Where's William?"

Ranson put his hand on her shoulder.

"He's fine," he said comfortingly. "He's using the Stone."

Then his whole body jolted and he put his hand to his head.

"I just felt a massive surge of power tear through me. It must have been William. He has become incredibly powerful."

As if on cue, a few moments later the young Caster appeared in the archway. Alayna scrambled to her feet and ran to him, gathering him up in a tight embrace.

But Ranson noticed that his face was drawn and his eyes were dark, and he realised that something bad had happened.

"What's wrong?" he asked.

Alayna looked at his face, and she noticed too. "William?"

He was looking at the floor, but he was staring into nothingness.

"The Stone..." His voice was quiet and somehow empty. "It showed me my future."

Ranson cut him off, suddenly deathly serious.

"William. What did you see?"

"If I do beat the ArchCasters, if we win, then..."

Ranson stood up, and Alayna's hand was clamped on his shoulder.

"Then I die."

Ranson's face fell, and his ran his fingers through his hair, trying not to accept what he had just heard.

"No..." Alayna said, but her voice broke as a tear ran down her face. "There must be another way."

"There isn't." William's voice grew in strength, as if he had accepted his fate. "But there are more important things to deal with than my life. The ArchCasters know we're here, and they know we have found the Stone. We have to get out of here, but first we have to destroy it. We cannot let it fall into their hands, and we cannot take it with us. If we do, the ArchCasters will find us and kill us."

"But how do we destroy something that has more power than us?" Ranson asked.

William shook his head.

"I don't know," he admitted.

"Couldn't we use its own power against it?" suggested Alayna.

Ranson and William smiled, and knew that she was right.

"It cannot defend against its own power," agreed Ranson.

William went back through the archway, down the stairs, and within a few moments he returned with the Stone. He beckoned the others over to the platform that had brought them down, and placed the Stone onto the pedestal. Then he laid his hands on top of it, and the platform suddenly shot up.

The trio was pressed down to the floor by the speed of the air, and they were forced to stoop, however William still managed to keep his hand on the Stone, so the platform was still rising rapidly.

Once again the smooth walls rushed past them, and all the time the tiny circle of light above them grew and grew, until it began to fill their vision.

They then began to slow down, and the trio were able to stand up straight. But they had slowed down enough so that when they got to the level of the hall, the platform slowly rose and clicked, and then rotated slightly to lock into place.

They were back at ground level.

The windows blew outwards, and broken glass was scattered across the battlefield. The trio stepped out over the threshold of the empty frames and down onto the dusty ground. They walked towards the massive circular pile of stone, and were about to leave when dual voices boomed through the air. They were not only audible in the minds of Ranson and William, but also to Alayna. They spoke together and their synchronisation added a further chill to their words.

Casters!

The trio jumped and looked around for the source of the voices.

Alayna looked south, and saw the barrier around the citadel smashed outwards and a figure, glowing red, floating ominously through the gap. Ranson and William looked to the west and saw the same thing.

Kelthane and Solaxe had come.

They spoke as one over the scene.

Surrender the Stone to us, and we will let you live. There is no way that you can escape. You will submit or you will die.

William told Ranson and Alayna to both put their hands on the Stone, over his, and he concentrated.

Then everything happened at once.

The two ArchCaster cast massive fireballs at them, but William used the power of the Stone to transport them to another place; the trio seemed to be surrounded by a bright, golden aura and they disappeared in an instant. However, because the Stone's power had been drained massively by the teleportation, it had little power left in that one moment so the fireballs smashed straight into it and destroyed it completely. All that was left in the space it used to be was a glittering cloud of dust, caught by the wind.

The two ArchCasters burned with a furious energy; they had been searching for the stone for decades and it would have meant the complete destruction of their enemies, and they had destroyed it with their own hands. They turned wrathfully away and began to fly back to their own fortresses in the South and West Realms. What they didn't see was the dust catch the wind and blow across the horrific sight of the battlefield, finally coming to rest on a small wooden cross, standing alone, having been raised as a memorial by the one who fled a coward and returned a hero.

Lettering across the horizontal arms simply read:

BROTHERS IN BLOOD
BROTHERS IN ARMS

Chapter 16 - Shark-Bait

William, Ranson and Alayna suddenly fell down onto a wooden floor from a golden blast. This had faded as soon as the trio had appeared.

The young Caster had landed on his back, and his father landed on top of him, knocking all of the breath from the two men. Alayna, being lighter and more nimble, caught herself with her hands, so that when she landed she was in a cat-like position.

The ground underneath her seemed to rock and sway, and she told herself that it must have been the teleportation that had made her feel so giddy.

However, she heard the fluttering of fabric above her, and the clump, clump, clump of heavy boots on the wooden floorboards.

William and Ranson were already looking upwards, and therefore realised their location sooner than she. She followed their gaze, and what she saw made her eyes grow wide in surprise.

Above them was a giant canvas sail, rippling violently, as if it was angry with their arrival. Sea-birds screeched high up in the sky, and the smell of salt exploded into their noses.

The mystery of their location had evaporated into emptiness, and Ranson suddenly seemed to panic. He drew his sword while still on the ground, but it was kicked out of his hands by muscles of iron wrapped in leather boots. All three were dragged to their feet and relieved of their weapons, and were then forced to turn and face a slanted wooden door.

As it did not open for a moment, the trio drank in their surroundings. They were standing on the spacious deck of a vast ship, and they were surrounded by ocean. There was a vague, misty outline of a shore over to one side, but none of them were able to identify any of it before the wooden door was thrown open.

A man stepped out, and immediately commanded absolute attention and authority over everyone on the deck. He wasn't a tall man, but he was broad-shouldered and extremely tough-looking. There could be no mistaking the muscles underneath his thin shirt.

His face was very unforgiving. It was criss-crossed with scars and his nose had been broken. At his side hung a very wide sword that had a long, viciously curved blade.

As he walked over to them, William saw that he was on the balls of his feet, perfectly balanced; ready for anything.

It was obvious that this man was born to kill.

A few metres away from them he drew his sword, and it was so quick that the point was pressing against Ranson's neck before he could blink.

"Who are you?" he asked, in a surprisingly quite voice.

Ranson did not answer.

"Our affairs are our concern," said William, making no attempt to hide his curtness.

The man lowered his sword from Ranson's neck and looked at William with a mixture of surprise and distain.

"Really?" he growled, raising his blade once more until it was level with William's eye. "Well I say that it's my damn business if you're on my ship!"

William smiled, and a bright white light flashed in his eye. But then Ranson gripped his arm, hard.

Don't!

The word coursed through William's mind, and he was shocked at how much fear it contained.

Really?

William's reply did not encourage a verbal or mental response, but Ranson nodded, deathly serious.

Fine.

The young Caster's muscles relaxed and his composure became entirely submissive.

"My deepest apologies," the young man offered. William could see that he had annoyed the man severely, but now that he was surrendering he was sure that he was in little danger.

Sure enough, the scarred man broke eye contact and sheathed his sword. As he walked over to one of his men and barked out orders, William heard his father exhale shakily, and saw him relax.

But then his attention was grabbed back to the scarred man, as he turned back towards the trio. But now he looked far more threatening because a crooked leer was etched from one battered ear to the other, and he was flanked by two tall, thick-set, scowling men.

As the horrific trio strode menacingly towards them, William took Alayna's hand in his, and held it tight.

Alayna, Ranson and William were practically dragged down into the belly of the ship. They passed through small corridors that were flanked almost entirely by doors; there was barely a square foot of the wooden wall that was free. If William had been anything but worried, he would have been impressed that the men knew their way so flawlessly through the identical passageways.

Eventually they must have reached the right door, because the scarred man threw it open and led the party down a shallow flight of stairs. William's feet banged down onto each step, but he ignored the negligible pain.

They were in the brig; the ship's prison. It was nothing but dank and dark. The floor was invisible through a murky film of water, and the only source of light was the grey streaks that crept through the gaps between the roughly hewn planks that made up the hull of the ship.

Due to the damp nature of the entire atmosphere, everything was being conquered by the water. The planks were practically dripping with moss and fungus, and even the bars of the cells, as strong as they were, were slowly being eaten away by the patient rust.

It was behind these bars that the trio was thrown. Their feet splashed as they entered, as the water was surprisingly ankle-deep. The room was on a slant and they had been cast into the deepest part. Their only saving grace was that they had all been imprisoned in one cell.

Inevitably, the cell door clanged behind them, the key clicked the lock shut, and the men walked back up the stairs, laughing between themselves.

Only the scarred man remained, and he spoke to the group in the now familiar low growl.

"This is my ship. If you three cause me any more trouble I'll strap anchors around your necks and throw you over the side myself."

Apparently this was the end of the conversation because the captain turned and walked away up the stairs. They heard him momentarily shout at some of his crew at the top; something about "eavesdropping" and "severe punishment". Then the door was shut and they were alone, cut off from the lights and sounds of the rest of the ship.

They stood in silence for a few moments, before Alayna spoke.

"Well he's a pleasant man," she said, making no effort to disguise her sarcasm. This lightened the mood a little, but a question still burned in William's mind.

"Why didn't you let me kill him?" he asked.

"Because we are on a ship, and the only ships that exist now are owned by the ArchCasters. All others were destroyed years ago. If we had used our powers, we would have been detected straight away.

We would have been hunted down and killed, as we would have been if we had tried to fight."

"But wouldn't they have felt the teleport? And wouldn't the men report us?" asked William.

"If the power of the Stone was masked from them in the past, there is no reason that it shouldn't have been then. And from the point of view of the men, we just appeared from nowhere. It is the same as when Alayna couldn't see the light in the chamber underneath the Torridon. They have nothing to report apart from finding a few stowaways on board. We just have to hope that they won't kill us for it."

Alayna tried to change the subject away from their imminent deaths.

"So how do we get out of here?"

"I don't know..." replied Ranson, trailing off and looking down into the water.

They stood in silence for a while, and William leant against the bars, not caring that his hair, which was now quite long for a boy's, was trailing on the rusty bars.

However, as he stared into the darkness, he had an idea.

"We all saw the way the captain treated his men. They obviously hate it. Could we... I don't know... turn his men against him?"

"You mean a mutiny?" asked Ranson.

William nodded.

But then a voice from the blackness made them turn in surprise.

"Mutiny," it said, coming from somewhere in the shadows on the other side of the dark room. "What could possess you so, for you to think that it is a good idea?" The voice was definitely a man's voice; low and gruff.

William whispered to Ranson.

"Do you think that if I used my power in a small way it would not be detected?"

"Do it," Ranson replied. "Just be careful."

William nodded and reached out his hand, through the bars, towards the shadowy area the voice had come from. Then he sent a tiny sliver of white flame out from the tip of his index finger.

It moved slowly, and glided almost elegantly towards the shadows. But because it was such a small flame, it gave off very little light. The trio were just about able to make out the outline of a figure hunched against the wall.

However, the tiny sliver moved up, above the very vague outline, until it lit up a small plinth that was help up by four chains. On top of this tiny shelf was a candle, and the flame moved up onto the wick. After a few seconds, the candle lit, and the entire room was bathed in light. The light seemed blinding, even though they had only been in the dark for a few minutes.

The man that had spoken was lit up instantly from the candle above as if it was as bright as daylight. His wrists and ankles were bound in grimy shackles. He looked thin and was clearly underfed, and his hair and beard had not been trimmed for days.

"Who are you?" asked Alayna, quietly.

"I was First Mate on this ship before I tried to arrange a mutiny. But the Captain found out, and the night before we had arranged it he dragged me down here as an example for everyone else. None of them now dare to act out against him, or his two new First Mates."

"Do you mean those brutes that dragged us down here?"

"Well I hope so; otherwise there are more of those thugs around here. They do anything that he says, and they are incredibly strong and incredibly merciless. But if we take them, we pretty much take the ship. Then we just have to deal with the Captain, but if we have beaten his men he would be powerless."

"How is the attitude on board? Would we be able to arrange another rebellion?" asked William.

"It is a powder-keg. The men are at breaking point, but they have no spirit left to do anything about their anger."

Ranson smiled.

"Then all they need is a spark."

The air in the ship's galley was choked with steam, and it was difficult to see more than two metres in any direction. But even through the haze, the mess was evident. Pots and pans were piled up in every free space not taken up by stored food. Even though the room had ample space, the floor was barely visible.

Like a spider in the middle of its web, a man stood in the midst of the disorganisation. He stood over a pot that was practically gushing steam, heated by a fierce fire. It barely had to be controlled, because the air was so full of water vapour that nothing in that room would light.

Suddenly, a rectangle of orange light appeared through the mist, and a shadowy figure stepped into the room with an empty tray in his hands. The man navigated his way through the treacherous mountains of crockery and balanced the tray precariously on a smaller pile next to the cook.

"Three more prisoners were caught today. The swine always seem to get better food than us," he said.

The cook didn't move from his hunched position over the steaming pot, but just grunted his reply.

"If you don't want it, then you can starve."

The man didn't retort. He knew that this was the cook on a good day, and that if he upset him he may end up in the pot himself. So he roughly placed four bowls onto the tray, being careful not to overbalance it, and waited as the other man ladled some kind of brown broth into each one.

Despite the overspill that almost coated the tray, the man picked it up and walked out. Closing the door behind him, he walked down three passageways and two flights of stairs, wondering along the way why he had to make this journey every day.

Finally, he reached the door to the brig, and walked down the stairs. However, as he descended, he heard the sounds of fighting and pained cries. The cells came into view, and he noticed the candle lighting the scene. He realised it must have been lit by another crew member, as none of the prisoners could reach it.

He looked back to the cell, and registered the problem at hand. At the back of the small cell, a young and an older man were fighting savagely; they were punching and wrestling, and kicking up gallons of water as they did so. Almost splayed against the bars was a girl. She looked terrified as she called out to the man.

"Please help me! These savages are going to kill me!"

The man dropped the tray, which hit the water with a dull splash, and he rushed towards the cell fumbling with the ring of keys on one side of his waist. As he reached the bars, the girl suddenly stuck her arms through the gaps, grabbed the knife on the man's belt and used one arm to hold him still while the other held the blade to his neck.

The men immediately stopped fighting, and the girl grinned.

"Open the door," she said in an almost sickeningly sweet voice.

With shaking hands, the man chose the right key and turned it in the rusty lock. As the door slowly swung open, Alayna still had the man locked between the knife and the bars, and William and Ranson walked out of the cell to relieve him of his keys. They were talking calmly together as they unlocked the shackles of the man in the corner, so they were clearly only feigning the fight.

"That was one Hell of a right hook," said Ranson, rubbing his jaw.

"It was meant to look real," replied William, smirking at his father.

Then he looked at Alayna.

"I think calling us savages was a bit extreme," he said.

"I don't," she said, utterly focused on keeping the man from escaping or calling out.

Eventually, the chained man was chained no longer, and the two Casters began to secure the jailer using those very chains.

"You don't want to be allied with him," protested the jailer, gesturing towards the freed man. "He's a traitor and a mutineer."

"Exactly the kind of man we need to overthrow the captain and get off this ship," replied William bluntly.

"Are you really going to relieve him of command?"

"I'll relieve him of his head if I get the chance," joked the young Caster, but there was some violent edge to the jest.

"Then I shall not say a word. I don't like him any more than you do. There is no need to tie me down; I will keep your secret."

William looked at Ranson, who nodded, and then release the man from his bonds.

"If you are truly with us, you will know when to rise up."

"I will make sure that no-one knows of your escape, but I will need my knife and keys back."

Alayna threw him his effects which he caught and stood up.

"What will you do now Drustan?" he said, and for a moment the group was confused, but when the previously imprisoned man answered they realised that must have been his name.

"We will hide with Bevyn. He is young but he always supported our plight. He will hide us for a day or so."

"That is all we will need," said Ranson.

"Apart from our weapons," Alayna said, turning towards the jailer. "After the captain took them, where would they have gone?"

"They will be in the armoury, but it is guarded all day, every day. There is no way you could retrieve them."

"We can work out how to get our weapons later. Right now we need to hide."

"Come on then," said Drustan with a final nod of thanks to the jailer.

The group followed him up the stairs and into the long passageway of doors. They suddenly all realised the danger; any one of those doors could open at any time to reveal anyone, if anyone saw prisoners trying to escape they would all be killed.

Slowly, silently, the group crept through the halls, turning one way then the other, hoping above all hope that they would not be seen. The utter lack of noise practically smothered them, but they eventually reached a flight of stairs leading upwards.

Drustan signalled for them all to wait and ascended carefully, looking in every direction before disappearing onto the deck above their heads.

They heard creaking and faint whispering, and then silence again. The tension was practically unbearable as the trio just stood, stock still, and waiting for something to happen.

Alayna started as Drustan appeared at the top of the stairs. He was smiling so they assumed it was good news.

"Bevyn will hide us, and the rest of the men on this deck are with us. We will hide you up here, and disguise you in case you have to leave this room."

"Thank you, friend," said Ranson, and they walked up the stairs.

As they reached the top they took in their surroundings. The first thing they noticed was the hammocks. They seemed to take up every free space in the air like some dense cloud of fabric, and the floor was just as choked with clothes, baskets and other various objects and belongings. William saw that there would be no end of places for them to hide without being seen at all.

They were soon busy meeting all of the different men, all of who seemed extremely excited about meeting them, as if they all had some kind of celebrity status.

"As long as they're on our side," William thought.

After a few too many minutes of shaking hands and slightly forced smiles, a man bolted up the stairs but tripped up the top step in his haste, tumbled into a pile of clothes and got tangled up in a hammock. A couple of men went over to help him, and he was soon steady on his feet.

"What is it Seth?" asked Drustan, realising from the young man's unfortunate entrance that it was something important.

"The captain demands that everyone must come up onto the deck, now."

The men immediately burst into life, grabbing clothes and weapons; one even brushing his hair.

Drustan beckoned them over to the side of the busy scene and threw clothes at each of them.

"Get changed," he said. "We have almost no time and you each have to look like one of the crew."

"Is this an eye-patch?" asked William, understandably sceptical.

"You need to cover as much of your face as possible so no-one recognises you."

William tossed the small piece of fabric away all the same and removed his leather armour, replacing it with a loose, ill-fitting shirt made from rough, itchy fabric.

Ranson and Alayna were in similar attire, and they began to walk out with the milling multitude that was making its way to the top deck. Just before she left the room Alayna grabbed a piece of fabric and wound it round her head, tying it at the back. Her long hair was now completely hidden, and the badly-fitting clothes hid anything that would give her gender away.

They walked hurriedly through the passageways and passed the door to the brig. William noticed that it was slightly ajar and no candlelight emanated from within, but the figures around him jostled him away before he had a chance to investigate.

As their journey to the surface neared its end the dank, musky smell began to fade away and fresher, cleaner smelling aromas danced into their nostrils. The air also seemed less dense; down in the belly of the ship the atmosphere pressed down on them, but here it began to lift like a weight rising from their shoulders.

Finally they burst out into the open air, and the sunlight was dazzlingly bright. They were still in the midst of unending water; even the faintest glimpse of a shoreline was gone. The sea was calm, and there was no wind so the sails were tied up to the mast.

A semi-circle had formed around two figures, but the trio stayed towards the back of the group to avoid detection.

Murmurings emanated around the half-circle, and as the men shifted uncomfortably a view of the scene presented itself to William. The other two were still blocked by figures.

The captain was pacing in a circle around the other man, who was kneeling with his hands tied behind his back. He was swaying on his knees as if he was too weak to stay upright.

His face could not be seen; it was pointed down towards the floor, and it was masked by his hair which hung down over his face. However there were spots of blood on his shirt and on the floor beneath him, so it was clear he was in a bad way.

Still pacing, the captain called out. His voice wasn't loud but it was surprisingly captivating.

"This man," he began, "is a traitor. He is a dog and conspirator and a mutineer. He has defied me and broken my trust."

The group silently scanned their peers, trying to see who was missing.

Meanwhile the captain slowly moved himself behind the man and grabbed him by the hair, making his face visible to the group.

The man had clearly been beaten. One of his eyes was dark and swollen. His nose was caked in drying blood and he was barely conscious. But even so, William recognised him.

While the mutterings grew loud once again William told Ranson and Alayna what he had seen.

"It's the jailor," he whispered. "The one who helped us."

"If he gives us away, we're dead," replied Ranson quietly, but the worry was evident in his voice.

William looked back to the scene as the voices died back down.

"So you helped four prisoners escape," said the captain to the kneeling man. It was somewhere between a question and a statement of fact. "Three highly dangerous stowaways and one mutineer."

"I… I," stuttered the man, too dazed to even formulate words.

The captain became impatient at his bumbling.

"Where are they?!" he demanded.

"I… I don't know where they went," the man replied.

William realised that the man had revealed the truth, and his face fell as he saw the captain smile unpleasantly.

Then, suddenly, without warning, the captain produced a knife and cut the man's throat. The body fell forwards with a thump and a pool of red spread rapidly out from under him, mixing with the puddles of water on the deck.

Alayna turned away and buried her face into William's shoulder, but she had not looked away quickly enough to miss the blood splatter out onto the deck, nor the last look of surprise in the man's eyes.

The captain stood up and sheathed his knife; the deed was so quick that the blade had not been dirtied at all.

"This is what becomes of those on this ship who oppose me!"

The statement was brief but there was no mistaking its message.

Suddenly William and Alayna were pushed aside, and the two beefy First Mates made their way to the front of the crowd.

"No sign of them, sir. We searched every room," reported one of them.

The captain nodded, and then addressed the crowd.

"The fugitives have not been found below deck. I'm sure one of you knows something about this. You must do. Come to me by the end of the day and you will be rewarded. Fail to report, and the punishments will be..." He paused, trying to find the right word, and when he had he almost growled it. "Severe."

He turned his back on the crowd, most of who were still transfixed by the bloody spectacle before them, and walked towards the door of his cabin, followed by his First Mates.

His last words before the door slammed shut behind him were:

"And someone clear up that mess."

So Bevyn and another man picked up the body and tossed it overboard and got to work scrubbing the blood-stains on the wooden boards of the deck.

Below them the corpse hit the water, as sharks wheeled beneath, sensing the arrival of a fresh meal.

Chapter 17 - Mutiny

Night drew in.

William, Ranson and Alayna, and dozens of others were crowded around a table, and a single candle lit up all of their engrossed faces. Besides the candle, the table was all but empty.

The young Caster was addressing the group, and Ranson was impressed at how easily he took up the role of leader.

"Now that the captain knows we are free he will begin inspections and searches to find us, which he eventually will. And that will mean that you are all in danger too because you have all helped us, so now we have to fight to stay alive."

Murmurs of agreement rippled around the table.

"We will need weapons," said one of the crew.

William nodded.

"Drustan tells me that they are all locked up in the armoury, so we have to get in somehow."

The young man they now knew as Bevyn perked up.

"I have an idea."

With his head covered with a hat and his face masked by an eye-patch, William strolled along the gloomy passageway with as much confidence as he could muster. The light was so bad that there was little chance he would be noticed.

A single man was standing outside a single door; at the end of a long, blank passageway. The man was not stood stock still to attention as William had expected; he was slumped against the wall, fiddling with the loose fibres of his shirt, looking extremely bored. It shouldn't be hard to get him to leave his post.

"Good news!" he said, calling out to the man. "You get the rest of the night off."

"Really?" asked the man, obviously sceptical.

William nodded.

"Captain's orders. He wants shorter shifts so we're more alert; you know, with these escaped prisoners running around."

The other man looked quizzically at him for a second.

"Great," he said, smirking. "I'm barely awake anyway."

William pretended to share his relief, and the man stood up fully; away from the wall. As he walked past, the young Caster swiped the keys from a hook on the man's belt.

"I'll sleep for both of us," said the man as he walked down the passageway. Even if he had turned, He would only have seen William facing him with his hands behind his back.

Once he was sure that the man was far enough away, William tried the various shapes of keys and the door was soon wide open.

He went in, and as he looked around he saw rows upon rows of swords in racks; they were single-handed, short and slightly curved. Leant up against one of these racks were three different-sized blades, plus a bow and quiver. All of their weapons were here.

William smiled, and by stamping twice on the floorboards, he put the next phase of the plan into action.

Directly beneath him, Ranson heard the signal and prepared the men with him. There were about ten in total, and they were standing silently in the pantry. It was very close to the crew's quarters, so they weren't in too much danger.

Ranson reached up and knocked quietly on two adjacent floorboards that made up the ceiling above him.

Above him, William noted which floorboards had been knocked on and painted two lines of pitch over two floorboards using a rag and a small pot of pitch Drustan had given him. Ranson had done the same underneath in exactly the same place, and all the men involved tied pieces of cloth over their faces that covered their noses and mouths.

Once this was done, Ranson held a candle-flame to the black liquid and it suddenly ignited, enveloping the line of pitch in flame. He lit the other line and stood well back, because the smoke was beginning to fill both rooms.

William was bearing the brunt of the smoke as it rose. The mask was allowing him to breathe, but his eyes were beginning to sting.

However he held on, and a few minutes later, just as the fire began to spread, William put all of his weight into one precisely-aimed kick. It knocked the pieces of the floorboard that had been weakened by the fire into the room below where they were smothered by wet pieces of cloth almost before they hit the floor.

Luckily for William, the smoke was beginning to dissipate through the walls, so he was able to remove his mask. He also took off the eye-patch and the itchy hat and threw them all away into the corner of the room.

As soon as he could see clearly enough through his stinging eyes, William wasted no time in to passing down the first weapons through the gap in the floor. He had strapped on his own sword, and has passed down Triscant and Alayna's bow and blade, and after that sword after sword was passed down.

Once each man below had a few blades in their arms they carried them into the crew's quarters, and once they had given them to someone else they rushed back to get more. It was not a particularly quick process, and they were all completely aware that they could be found out at any second.

William had picked up yet another pair of swords, and as he was passing the first one through the gap in the floor he heard a voice.

"We saw smoke coming from this room. Is anyone hur..." The man's voice trailed off as he reached the doorway and saw what was going on.

"Who are you? What's going on?" Another man appeared behind.

No answer, so the men drew their long knives. They approached menacingly, and William dropped the other sword through the floorboards. While still crouched, he drew his own knife, stood up, twisted round and threw it in one smooth movement. It flew straight into the chest of the first man, who fell forwards into the room. Then, taking advantage of the second man's surprise, he drew Melnhir.

Having seen the fate of his counterpart, this man knew that this opponent was young but not to be trifled with. He picked up one of the many swords that were left and swung it at William, who parried the strike and launched his own attack. This was blocked too; this man had excellent technique and deadly ability, not to mention a massive weight difference and considerably more height.

The two men were soon lost in a flurry of thrusts, slices and parries from both sides, but Melnhir was heavy and awkward; it was difficult to swing between the low ceiling and the tall racks of swords. Eventually it slammed into one of the wooden frames, and before William could dislodge it the man kicked him backwards away from it. He pulled the blade out of the rack and threw it aside, advancing with utter confidence on William.

The young Caster was about to use his powers to save himself despite the consequences, when an arrowhead stuck itself out of the front of the man's chest. As he fell forwards like his ally before him, William saw that a long arrow was sticking out of his back. He saw Ranson lower a bow, and he realised that he must have shot the man through the hole in the floor.

"Thanks," William said, picking up Melnhir and talking to Ranson through the hole. "But I don't have time to get down there before you start the mutiny. You have to get it going, and then join me on deck. Our swords will be pretty useless in the passageways, and we need to take out the captain and the First Mates."

"I'll get Alayna and meet you up there."

"Stay safe."

"I know that it's ridiculous to say on a ship in the middle of a mutiny, but you too."

William sheathed Melnhir and dragged both dead men over into the corner of the room. Then he retrieved his knife from the first man's chest and picked up one of the short swords from the rack.

He was soon walking calmly down busy passageways, but no-one tried to stop him. As far as those he passed were concerned, he was just one of the crew. He thought he might actually be able to get away with this and re-join the others before it started.

But then his pleasant thoughts were shattered by a voice crying out from behind him.

"Stop him!"

William was running almost before the shout had ended, and as he sped along the corridor he sent a message to Ranson.

It's begun.

As he ran he heard the thumping of boots and shouting behind him, but he didn't turn to look.

He skidded as he practically flew round a corner, and just as he was regaining his speed, he saw a man standing in the middle of the passageway. He wasn't particularly big, but he would be enough to slow

William down enough for others wielding weapons to reach him.

Maintaining his speed, he drew Melnhir and as he got to him the man reached out to grab the young Caster. William ducked under the man's arms and swung the two swords downwards together.

They slammed into the man's shins, breaking them with a considerable noise, and the man flipped onto the floor, landing on his back with loud cries of pain.

He kept on running, and soon the fallen man was far behind him. He ran for a long time, and the size of the ship became painfully obvious, but he eventually burst through the doors into the early morning sunlight. Just before they shut, William looked behind from the first time since the race began.

In some ways he wished he hadn't.

Dozens of men were thundering down the passageway only about twenty metres behind him; some with long knives, some with swords and even a couple with spears and vicious-looking harpoons.

The doors clunked together again, shielding William from the murderous hordes for enough time for him to think.

The rumbling vibrations under his feet were becoming very noticeable when he had an idea. He stuck the short sword between the handles of the door and began to scale the rope ladder on the mast. No sooner than when he reached the first yard did the doors on the opposite side of the deck burst open and the captain walked through, flanked as usual by the two First Mates.

William knew he had to slow them down, so he looked around for something he could use.

There was net-like metal rigging right above the three men secured by two ropes. One was right next to him and he cut it immediately, causing one side to sag a bit, but the other rope was holding up the four corners so the net remained relatively flat.

He drew his long knife, balanced it in his hand for a moment, and threw it. The knife sliced about half-way through the rope, but it held strong and the knife flew into the ocean below. William's face fell as the men below heard the banging on the jammed door.

Then he looked up and saw that the rope he had hit was still quivering. The movement had carried through up the rope, through the pivot at the top, and back down to where it was tied off, less than ten metres over William's head.

The young Caster drew Melnhir and sprang into action, leaping from horizontal arm to rigging and back again. He landed on the yard-arm next to the rope rather unsteadily and nearly over-balanced forwards off the smooth wood. Knowing that this was his last chance, he threw Melnhir at the rope.

The blade sliced through a few ropes, the desired one included, and thudded into the wooden mast behind. The recoil from the force of the throw also pushed William backwards and he regained his balance on the arm.

The metal net fell incredibly fast and pinned all three men to the deck. Not only this, but the edges of net were bordered by thick heavy chains and massive balls of lead at each corner. These all plunged into the deck and some even went through, however even if they hadn't they would have been too heavy to lift.

The three men obviously weren't going anywhere, and William grinned, wondering how the others were doing.

It's begun.

As soon as Ranson heard William's voice, he gathered all of the mutineers together and rallied them against the rest of the ship.

They charged out of the crew's quarters and bundled into the rooms around them. They found nobody, so they kept looking. Still nothing.

Everyone seemed to have vanished from the lower decks. Then they heard the rumbling of dozens of men running over their heads. They hadn't noticed it so far because they had been almost roaring themselves.

"They're all in the passageways above us," cried Drustan. "Let's go!"

Ranson and Alayna we less keen for the killing to start. Because they were both experienced warriors, they knew that battles in a small space were usually a bloodbath. They followed Drustan and Bevyn anyway, keeping towards the front so they could find William as soon as possible.

They reached the stairs and ascended in ordered silence, but everyone knew that a battle was just around the corner, and under their calm exteriors was a raw, primal energy just waiting to leap out.

They reached a set of double-doors at the top of the shallow stairs, and Ranson held a finger to his lips. It was obvious that they were near their target, as they could hear the banging and shouting from the other side of the door.

Slowly, silently, Ranson began to count down on his fingers.

Three... Two... One...

Now!

With a deep-throated roar the men charged through the door and their enemy turned to look at them. It was obvious what was happening; that they weren't on the same side.

Ranson's men had the advantage of numbers, but there were still dozens against them; whether they were acting under loyalty or fear of the captain, they held their ground. They had been trying to open another set of double-doors at the other end of the passageway. It seemed to be blocked, but no-one was bothering with it now; they were fully focused on their approaching enemy.

Ranson, Alayna, Drustan and Bevyn made up the first line, with others three or four abreast behind them.

Suddenly, from the other line of men appeared a man holding a crossbow. He fired and it whistled through the air, finding its mark in a fraction of a second.

Ranson turned in horror to see Bevyn fall backwards with a crossbow bolt in his chest. The young man's body was caught by Drustan, but he knew that he was already dead. The rest of the men stopped and looked down at the body; the boy's short, spiky hair and his grey eyes still open in surprise.

There was no mistaking the division then. This could no longer be settled by words. A young man had been shot and killed at point-blank range. One side lives, one side dies.

The rebels charged once more at their enemy, but they had to go around Ranson, Alayna and Drustan who were knelt around the boy. However, their opponents were now prepared. A barrage of knives, spears, bolts and arrows cut the first couple of lines down immediately, and then the next, and the next.

Ranson's men faltered and ran back the way they came, disappearing into doors along the passageway and down the stairs at the far end.

In the midst of this, Ranson and Alayna had to all but drag Drustan away from the body of his fallen comrade and into one of the rooms. They knew that they would not make it to the stairs alive.

The rest of the men were re-grouping. Some were trapped in certain rooms, and they were slain on the spot by the advancing enemy, but the majority had gathered on the stairs. Knowing that their adversaries' missiles were all but spent, they formed into lines and marched up the stairs to fight. Soon the entire passageway was a battlefield.

Ranson and Alayna were sitting on a bed in the cabin they were hiding in, trying to comfort Drustan.

"He was so young…"

Ranson replied.

"Then you must fight in his memory."

Drustan did not respond; he just kept looking at the floor.

Then something thudded down hard onto the boards above their head. They were already rather shoddy, but the movement had knocked them enough to allow Ranson to see sunlight through the gaps.

"That must be the top deck," he said, standing and walking over to the streams of light. He peered through one of the gaps and looked up to see William standing on one of the arms of the mast, looking very pleased with himself.

"It's William. We have to get up there and help him."

He moved Drustan respectfully off the bed and, with Alayna's help, wedged it against the door.

"Nothing's going to get though that," he told the other man. "You'll be safe here."

Still no response, so they led him to the bed, sat him down, and then got to work on removing the ceiling.

William was admiring his handiwork, when he noticed that the men had got over the initial shock and were working together to get free.

At that point, he heard a series of loud cracks and Ranson and Alayna appeared out of the deck close to the bow. They were fully armed and ready, and just as they began to walk towards him, the captain was free.

The two First Mates had somehow managed to achieve a kneeling position, and had lifted the chain enough on one side for him to crawl through. Then they took it in turns to hold the chain up for the other man to crawl through. Within a few seconds they were all free.

The three sailors looked at the two others, and then up at William.

Deciding not to disappoint them, William had retrieved Melnhir, and he ran along a yard-arm parallel to the ship but high above it. Once he got to the end he leapt onto the foremost sail, stabbed his blade into it and held on tight with both hands. As the sword sliced through the material the resistance was enough to slow him down considerably, so he landed just in front of his two allies, rolled onto his shoulder and was back on his feet completely unscathed.

The captain grinned, vaguely impressed. Perhaps this boy was a worthy adversary after all. The man was not aware of the fate of the last captain to underestimate this young man, but William was determined that he would share it.

The trio descended a few very shallow steps, and walked towards their opponents, swords raised, ready for anything. Alayna shot an arrow at the First Mate opposite her, and it hit him in the shoulder. However the man barely seemed to notice it. He pulled it out very calmly and dropped it onto the deck. Alayna saw that she would not have time for another shot so she released the quiver from her back and threw it, and the bow, backwards towards the hole in the floor. She drew her slim, curved sword and a long dagger of a similar design.

The First Mates both held swords very like Melnhir, but their edges were viciously serrated; they were blades designed to inflict as much pain as possible to their victims before they died.

As they walked closer, each combatant chose their opponent. So, as it turned out, William was facing the captain and the other two were facing the First Mates. They stood five metres apart, each soldier waiting for the other to make a move.

Instead, the captain began talking.

"I assume it was you absconders that started the rebellion."

Ranson nodded.

"As with any battle, it has come down to a fight between the best and most important few," continued the captain.

"Soon there will be three fewer," replied Alayna.

The captain simply laughed; a horrible noise that turned William's stomach.

"You're a feisty bitch, I'll give you that," he said.

William's body bristled with thunderous anger.

"You'll die for that," he said, and then suddenly launched forward. Ranson and Alayna followed suit, and they were soon all lost in combat.

William had to utterly focus on the captain. He was almost super-humanly fast, and the power of his strikes was like nothing William had felt before. But he could feel his powers guiding him, controlling every ounce of his being and giving him strength.

As a result of this, he was the first to draw blood. The captain and he locked swords and were putting all of their weight into pushing each other's blade back, when William kicked him hard in the solar plexus, winding him and knocking him back. And he stumbled, William swung Melnhir at the man's neck, but the captain was too quick and managed to manoeuvre out of the way just in time. However, he did not move enough to stop the blade cutting a gash into his cheek.

Alayna was doing just as well with her opponent. She was quick and agile, and he was heavy and slow, but he was still deadly. One hit from that hideous blade and she would be dead in seconds. Her sword was also a lot shorter, so having the extra blade was extremely helpful. It allowed her to split the power of his strikes in half, so his extra strength meant very little. It also let her get the occasional strike in, but although he was bleeding quite considerably, it did not seem to affect him.

Ranson was also doing incredibly well. This was no surprise; although his opponent was tough, he had been in many battles and he knew exactly how to beat every kind of opponent. For now he was tiring his enemy out; he was heavy and had a heavy sword, so this was happening quickly. Soon he would be so tired that Ranson could achieve an easy victory.

Alayna unleashed a flurry of thrusts and slices against her opponent, and he simply couldn't block every hit. First, a slice tore the bicep in his right arm, then a stab into the stomach, and then a glancing blow to the left knee. He fell to his knees and dropped his sword, and Alayna picked it up and skewered him upon it where he kneeled. The blood that flowed from under him as he fell forwards was incredible.

Next to her, Ranson's opponent was tiring, and Ranson took his opportunity. He twisted his sword in barely noticeable way, but the result was the other man's sword flying out of his hands and into the sea. The First Mate looked at his empty hands and his ally's blood pooling across the deck. He broke combat with Ranson and jumped head-first after his sword.

However, he hit one of the rigging supports sticking out of the hull, which his head smashed into and he died in an instant. His body was left floating on the surface of the water, motionless, and pink stuff came out of his head.

Back on deck, the captain realised the fight was over when Ranson and Alayna joined William and they all pointed their swords towards his chest pinning him to the back railing at the stern of the ship. He dropped his sword.

"This ship is ours now. We should run you through here and now," hissed Alayna, still rippling with murderous energy.

"No!" Ranson said. "No matter what he has done, he must have a fair trial."

For the first time, the captain looked almost grateful. That was until an arrow thudded between his eyes, and he fell backwards over the railing and into the blue waters below.

The trio turned, surprised, to see Drustan lowering Alayna's bow.

"That was for Bevyn," he said.

Down below the surface of the water the captain's body sunk like a stone. A cloud of translucent crimson billowed from his punctured forehead into the sapphire-blue water.

If he had been conscious, he would have noticed a circling shark as it turned its attention to this new delight.

Chapter 18 - Insomnia

Another night had fallen.

William lay awake on a hammock in the crew's quarters. He was surrounded by other sleeping shadows, suspended by the same thin pieces of fabric, but apart from the occasional grunt or snore they did not break the loud silence that encompassed him.

Staring at the ceiling, William was fiddling absently with a loose fibre of the fabric bed letting thoughts and memories play out in the air around him.

Out of the darkness came a quiet laugh, and William turned towards the source of the sound. The hammock tilted slightly as he sat up and scanned his murky surroundings. Nothing moved and nothing seemed out of the ordinary; just the dark shapes of hammocks hanging around him.

He heard the same laugh again, this time from the other side of the room, but once again he saw nothing when he looked in that direction.

William felt genuinely scared, but lay back down. Just in case, he drew a short knife from a concealed scabbard in his boot and held it close, looking back up at the ceiling.

Suddenly a knife sliced down from nowhere and stuck into his bare chest. William tried to cry out, but his mouth refused to make any kind of sound. He couldn't breathe, but he just about managed to move his head and look towards his attacker.

Standing less than a metre away was the captain; the man who had torn his life apart by killing his mother and taking the man William now knew as his step-father. But he was laughing maniacally and blood was pouring out from the man's open mouth.

William's eyes were glazing over, and the world around him began to blur and merge into one white smear. Everything faded into the white light, and he breathed his last breath.

His body went limp and he died.

William jolted awake and realised that he was brandishing Melnhir. Sweat was literally pouring down his face, and he grabbed at his chest with his free hand.

He sighed as he sheathed Melnhir, put on his shirt and walked up onto the deck.

The fresh air was a refreshing wake-up call, and as he leant against the deck railing he closed his eyes and savoured the crisp feeling and smell of the cool, salty sea air. A slight breeze ruffled his long hair and made him shiver, but it was a good feeling after the hot, humid atmosphere that the crew's quarters offered; especially after his horrible vision.

He cradled his face in his hands and began to cry; for everybody who had died around him. His parents, Bevyn, everyone in the Resistance had died because of the actions of a Caster. And how many more had he killed? The number was certainly into the hundreds, possibly into the thousands. How many of them had families; loved ones who were just waiting in vain for them to come home. Whether his enemies had acted under their own volition, under orders or out of fear the chances were that someone was now without a husband, brother, son or father. What he had done to those families was the same as what the captain had done to his. Whatever cause was being fought for, that was the true evil.

He couldn't stop the tears then. His whole body shook and convulsed as the horrors and sorrows of his journey were realised. He saw himself for what he was; a killer. He saw the last glint of life fade in every single face that he had encountered, and he abhorred himself. He decided that there was no difference between him and the ArchCasters.

A hand was laid on his shoulder and he turned to face Alayna.

"What's wrong?" she asked, noticing the obvious state he was in.

William didn't answer; he just shook his head and wiped his eyes on his sleeve. Alayna embraced him comfortingly and he buried his face into her shoulder.

"Thanks," he whispered softly into her ear.

She smiled.

"Even Casters are allowed to cry sometimes."

He chuckled, and realised how lucky he was to have Alayna. Still in each other's arms, they turned their heads and their lips met, and for a few seconds they were lost in a moment of love and compassion.

Alayna knew that William would not be able to get back to sleep so she stayed up with him, lying on the deck talking about everything and nothing until his eyes slowly closed and he drifted off peacefully into unconsciousness. She covered him with a blanket she had brought from the crew's quarters and sat down beside him, resting her back on a pile of crates and ropes and, watching over him, she wandered off to sleep herself.

From the other side of the deck, Ranson saw this and smiled sadly to himself.

William didn't need him anymore.

William woke up peacefully from his first full night's sleep in days.

He felt a warm, comfortable light on his eyelids and as he sat up he saw the sun seated low in the cloudless sky. As its light hit the calm water it made it burn a brilliant gold, and William was dazzled not only by the light but also by the beauty of his surroundings.

All of the feelings of sorrow from the past night seemed to melt away into nothingness, and the shadows in his mind were driven out by the light of this dawn.

Looking around, he saw that Alayna was still asleep so, not wanting to disturb her, he silently took off his shirt and boots and dived into the crystal water below.

In a matter of seconds if he was in another world.

If the scene above the surface had been beautiful, this was in another league entirely. The clear blue was absolute around him, and the warmth of the water was serenity itself. The sandy sea floor was about seven fathoms down, well below the keel of the ship which was sitting low in the water. Even so, he dived to the bottom with ease, and followed a line of coral that was the beginnings of a reef. In a few metres, the sea floor was teeming with life.

Various kinds and colours of fish darted this way and that, and retreated into the safety of the coral as William passed by. His heart skipped a beat when he saw the shark appear in front of him, but it barely seemed to notice him as it drifted lazily past. It must have been very placid as it swam close enough that William could have reached out and touched it.

William found that he could stay under the water for minutes at a time, and he supposed that it was an extra benefit of his powers, but inevitably he had to come up for air. After his third trip down he broke the skin of the water facing the ship and noticed Ranson beckoning him back. Having gone further away from the ship than he had meant to, William had quite a swim back. He climbed up using the rigging supports sticking out from the side of the ship, and soon he was on the deck. Ranson threw a thick cloth at him which he used to dry himself off.

"What's going on?" he asked the other man; he was not worried, but he was wondering why he had been called back.

"Fetch the map that you got from the Stone, and meet me in the captain's quarters."

William nodded, and on his journey across the deck he picked up his shirt. The warm sunlight and slight breeze meant that he was dry enough to put it on, moments before he disappeared through the large double doors that led down into the ship.

A few minutes later, William, Ranson, Alayna and Drustan were crowded around a circular desk. William placed his map flat on top of it and put a candlestick on each corner to stop it curling up.

In front of them, painted onto a wall, was a massive map of the entire world; all three Realms with borders painted black between the light brown earth and the vivid blue sea. There were various pins with painted heads scattered across the massive blue border, but they were all black except one. It was painted red, and it was obviously dictating the ship that they were on.

Ranson pressed his index finger on the same place but on the small map.

"We're here," he said. "About ten miles out from the coast."

The map showed that they were a good distance west of the top left-hand corner of the West Realm.

"If we head south and then east we could sail down the Nafar river system and end up less than a day's ride from our first potential ally."

As Ranson spoke, he traced the route with his finger until he reached a circular symbol. This dictated the first location of the first Child.

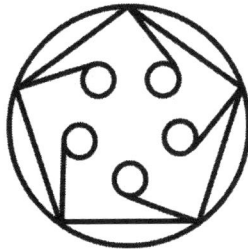

"This is the ancient symbol for Earth, so this must be the Caster with control of that element. It is also very close, so we will look for this Child first."

The others nodded in agreement, and went up onto the deck. The ship was soon slicing through the water at full speed towards the place where the vast river system opened out into the ocean.

Within an hour, the ship was encompassed in the shadow of the massive ridges that flanked the beginning of the river system. As William watched the colossal walls encompass the vast ship, he felt slightly like he was riding into the Valley of Death.

As they ventured up the main waterway the wind died down and the tide was against them, so the majority of the men went below and began to row with gigantic oars. William and Alayna both helped while Ranson took the wheel. He had obviously been on a ship before, but when William asked him about it he didn't say when.

With a repeating yell of "Row!" the men pulled on the thick oars and the ship was propelled forwards.

William and Alayna were rowing together on the same oar, and grinned at each other as outside the world flew past; the rocks on each side of the waterway had given way to mangrove swamps. The trees themselves were giant, and their roots dived deep into the river-bed more than fifteen metres below the surface of the water. They were travelling down the main waterway which was vastly wide as well as deep. Occasionally an oar would hit a mangrove root, but such was the force of the lever action that the wooden blade sliced straight through.

Various branches of the river split from the main flow at right-angles, heading either heading northeast or southwest from the main flow that flowed northwest against them.

After a few hard hours of rowing, Ranson called out.

"Halt all!"

Every rower stopped their oars instantly and drew them into the ship, closing the holes in the hull with tar-lined flaps.

William and Alayna went up onto the deck and stood behind Ranson who was at the wheel.

The ship was still moving under its own momentum, and William noticed that they were approaching a particularly wide exit, off to the right.

Ranson told William to go to the front of the ship and stand by a lever. The bow had just started to pass the mouth of the water-way when Ranson called over to him.

"Now!"

William pulled the lever towards him, heard a clank and a scraping sound, and a massive anchor slid out from a track in the right side of the bow.

It smashed through the water and hit the river bed in a matter of seconds, catching immediately.

Ranson shouted again, this time addressing the entire ship.

"Brace!"

Each man dropped whatever they were holding and grabbed the nearest solid structure just in time.

The ship juddered violently and William was thrown off his feet. If the wooden rail hadn't been there he would have tumbled into the water below.

Slowly, the ship began to turn towards the smaller waterway, and Ranson nodded to Drustan who was clinging for dear life onto the mast. He pulled another lever attached to it and a series of pulleys loosed thick ropes.

The main sail tumbled down, and caught the wind just as the ship was facing the right way. As a result, the ship was propelled forward at surprising speed. In the bow of the ship a man smashed the chain bracket apart with a massive metal hammer, separating the hull from the anchor and leaving it behind on the river bed.

Once they were heading in the desired direction, Ranson let one of the crew take the wheel. The man seemed very glad to take the control of the ship away from the Caster, as he walked down the shallow steps towards William.

"We seem to have lost an anchor," said the younger man. "Why didn't we just turn using the oars?"

"The current was top strong; we never would have made the turn," replied Ranson, and then he smirked. "Anyway, that was more fun."

Alayna joined them.

"How much longer until we get to the Child?"

"A good few hours yet," Ranson replied. "And the ship can't take us the whole way. The swamps get too shallow so we will have to walk the rest of the way. Ideally, we should get to our 'friend' at dusk tomorrow. We might as well get to sleep now, as we will have to begin walking at nightfall."

William stood abruptly.

"Not me," he said, and walked away, leaving Ranson and Alayna behind him.

The older man looked at the girl, obviously none the wiser.

"What was that about?" he asked.

"He doesn't sleep well," she replied. "He has nightmares about the battles that he's been in."

Ranson nodded, understanding completely. After all, he had been in the same position, if not worse.

"I think I'll go after him," Alayna said, getting up.

"No," interjected Ranson, grabbing her arm. "He just needs some time alone."

Alayna watched longingly as William walked out of sight behind the main mast.

"I hope you're right."

William was leaning back on the mast on the highest platform on the ship. He was sitting with his knees up close to his chest and his arms resting upon them.

He knew that he would not get any sleep that night, but when he was in prison he found another way to replenish his body's energy. If he relaxed his limbs and stared at something relaxing, he was able to go into a dreamless trance.

And so, staring out over the shining, golden river and the setting sun, William was lost in an overwhelming sense of calming peace. What he didn't know was that many miles away, the two ArchCasters rallied at the ruins of the Torridon.

There was only one subject matter;

The destruction of the Casters.

Chapter 19 - Child of Earth

Solaxe landed from his long flight, and bones shattered beneath his feet.

Sitting on a rock in the ruins of the Torridon, he saw that Kelthane was waiting for him.

"I got your message. What do you want?" asked Solaxe with a tone that held no evidence that they had once been as close as brothers.

Kelthane seemed just as reluctant to be there.

"This Caster has managed to kill Vanyol and harnessed the power of the Stone. Even though he has Ranson's help, he is clearly becoming incredibly powerful. We have to get rid of him."

"How? I have felt his power of late, but I cannot locate him."

"We have to be ready," the other ArchCaster replied. "We have to work together!

"No," said Solaxe. "The only time you watch my back is when you're working out where to stick the knife. I'll deal with this imp myself. Meanwhile, you watch your borders and I'll take care of mine."

"Then can we stop the petty fight for the borders?"

"No chance," the venom evident as he almost hissed his reply. No alliance, no nothing. I don't trust you for a second; there is no way that I'm standing down my men."

"If this is your final word, then this is war."

Solaxe looked grave, but nodded.

"War it is then."

Without another word, the ArchCasters turned their backs on each other and shot into the sky; one went to the west, the other to the south.

And so the alliance of the Three was ended.

The world was at war.

The first thing that William knew of the following morning was a loud thud and a juddering that ran through the entire ship.

The main sail had been lifted and the port anchor had thumped down into the stones of the river-bed. The ship stopped quite smoothly, as there was barely any momentum; the ship had been travelling very slowly for quite a few minutes.

It took William but a few moments to descend from the mast, and he headed towards the slanted double doors that led into the bowels of the ship.

However, they slammed open before he could reach them, and Ranson and Alayna emerged followed closely by Drustan. Ranson was carrying two packs, and Alayna was carrying one. The older Caster threw one of the bundles at him and said:

"Here's your armour. Get changed; we leave as soon as you're ready."

A few minutes later, William emerged from the captain's quarters. Curiously, he was not wearing all the clothes that Ranson had thrown him. William had decided that travelling through largely civilian populations with full armour on would be too conspicuous, so he had modified it. Gone was all the metal, so he was wearing the thick leather armour that was underneath it. It was dark and fitted him well, and was tough enough to stop the average enemy knife.

He had also strapped Melnhir to his back as opposed to his waist, and in its old place were two long daggers; one on either side. A strap was tight across his chest, and this was attached to a curious cylindrical pack that contained a blanket, a water-skin and some food. Ranson and Alayna shouldered identical packs and a few moments later the gangway groaned slightly as they descended onto the shore.

When they were about a dozen metres from the ship William turned back and waved, and Drustan waved back from the deck. He had a strange feeling that this was not the last time he would see the man, but he buried it deep and turned away, following his counterparts.

The trio journeyed through the day, and continued as the sun began to lower in the sky.

As they walked, they talked about everything and nothing; old tales, and new tales, and tales of no time at all. And all the time, as they walked and talked, the lands around them changed. They had left the swamps far behind them, and now they were travelling through more familiar landscapes; wide, flat areas covered with trees in some areas. But these were not like the tilled fields of Tursus. The lands around them were grasslands; vast expanses of lush grass that stained the horizon green. All around them nature's beauty conquered their vision.

A line of trees enveloped them, but it was thin and they soon broke out. The low sun dazzled them, and as their eyes adjusted to the glare they saw a collection of curious building; they were about forty in total, and they were all short and round with squat, conical, thatched roofs. The trio walked slowly between them, but everyone who saw them ran inside the nearest house, closing doors and shutters noisily.

Once they reached a clearing in the middle of the houses, William turned on the spot, only to be greeted by the slam of another door.

"Charming," he muttered, not entirely to himself.

Ranson noticed a man who seemed to be dressed in little more than rags, standing in dark corner, shaking. It was not clear whether it was fear, the cold, or just his age, but Ranson edged towards him, hands held up in surrender to reassure the old man.

As he got closer, the man picked up his walking stick and held it out, but Ranson gently lowered the trembling stick with his hand and helped the man to sit down against the wall behind him.

"We're not here to hurt you," the older Caster asked in a voice so gentle that it did not fit his face. "What's going on?"

The other man seemed to calm down a bit, and answered.

"We just want to be left alone. They're coming for us."

Ranson looked concerned.

"Who's coming for you?"

"The ArchCasters. They've declared war."

The man began trembling again, and Ranson stood up. When he turned, the other two saw that his face was grave.

"What's the problem? They've always been at war," said William, but Ranson shook his head.

"So far, it has just been a petty grudge. This is full scale war."

"A petty grudge?" replied Alayna. "Men have been dying on the border in their hundreds."

"Exactly," Ranson explained. "That was just the overture. Now it will be millions of lives, and it will be everywhere; not just the borders. Imagine; the entire world a battlefield of blood and mire as far as the eye can see. It's just unthinkable. We have to find all the Children by then."

"Let's just start with this one."

William walked back over to the old man.

"We're looking for someone," he said. "He should be about my age, or a bit older."

The older man became more responsive, hearing insistence in William's voice.

"All of the young men are up in the crags. They're clearing a rock-slide that happened yesterday."

"Which way?" William asked.

The old man told him.

The journey was short; just a few minutes from the village, but as soon as they got there, the trio found themselves on the outskirts of a sizeable crowd.

When they pushed their way through the throng they found that the front lines were on the edge of a gulf, and on the other side was a wide, flat area. It was split from the rocks around it by the circular fissure, and the only way off it seemed to be a thin, natural bridge made of rock. When the trio saw two figures scrabbling at each other they realised that this was an arena.

As they watched, they saw that one figure was dominating the other in the fight. From him came swift punches, ferocious kicks and brutal knee jabs. He was completely balanced on the balls of his feet, and he seemed almost relaxed as he and his opponent danced around one-another. Suddenly the figure spun and put all his strength into a high, sideways kick. He caught his opponent full in his chest and he was propelled backwards a full few metres. Once he had regained his composure and what little breath he had left, the floored figure got shakily to his feet and limped away. The other figure followed him, but stopped as he crossed the small bridge to safety. Only now did the trio realise that the two figures were both young men; about the same age as William.

As the victor raised his arms and cheered in triumph, something caught William's eye. On his right wrist, as his sleeve fell away, was a circular symbol that was very familiar.

William glanced over at Ranson. Had he seen it too?

Yes, his father was looking forcibly at him. He must have seen it! Then Ranson jerked his head towards the young man, and William got the message. He took off his pack and weaponry and walked across the chasm into the arena. The young man stood aside to let him past.

"I take it that you're here to fight me too?"

"No," William assured him. "I just want to talk."

The other man smiled.

"Oh, I don't think so," he said, moving in front of the bridge.

Now he was between William and his only way out.

"I saw your wrist." William began, causing the other man to roll up his sleeve. "I know that you may not know what it means, but I can help you. We can help you."

"That suggests that I need any help."

The young man stood up straight, and for the first time William got a good look at him.

He was almost exactly the same height and build as William, but his hair was a striking blonde and his eyes were a profound blue. He was not particularly attractive, but he wasn't ugly either; he was just normal. However, his body was not. His limbs were long and lean, that meant speed. His had a lot of muscle, which meant power, and purely by the way he was speaking William could tell that he had a mind to match. Even if he had not seen his demonstration of skill earlier, William would have realised that this was a boy who had spent his whole life fighting.

"My name is William. What's yours?"

"Ræl," the other man replied.

"Ræl, I know that will be hard for you to understand, but you're a Caster. Your father was too, and you have extraordinary power."

Ræl walked towards him, a confused look on his face.

"I always knew that I was different." He was face to face with William now. "There's only one problem."

"What?"

"I know I'm a Caster, and believe me, I'm not going to be easily killed."

Suddenly, a lump of rock flew up and hit William in the face, knocking him back with blood running from his nose and a cut on his already swelling lip.

William had only just recovered when Ræl slammed his foot into the ground. A massive crack shot from the ground under his feet straight at William, and from about two metres away great pillars of rock shot out of the earth and hit the Caster in the chest.

This time William went flying backwards, and he landed with a thud, winded, on his back, many metres away from the other man. Ræl didn't even take a second to relish the hit. He had already begun running towards the other Caster.

But William was faster. He was already on his feet, and hurled a mighty stream of flame right at his opponent. Ræl raised his arm as it to cover his eyes, and a shield of rock shot out of the ground and shielded him from the blaze. As the fire continued, the rock began to change, and William summoned ice-cold water and launched it at the barrier. The heat had turned it to glass, and the water suddenly cooled it, causing it to shatter violently and fire razor-sharp shards out in every direction. Ræl only just ducked in time to avoid being cut to ribbons, and summoned a long, thick piece of shiny, translucent quartz out of the ground. Ranson threw Melnhir to William just in time to block a stab from this bafflingly beautiful spear. Ræl swung and spun the spear effortless in his hands, and drove William back with a flurry of translucent points.

The younger Caster was now nearly at the edge of the precipice over-looking the fissure and he was being driven back so furiously that he would soon plummet to his death. Just as his foot was slipping over the edge and just as Ræl raised the spear, William closed his eyes and concentrated.

The ground underneath Ræl's feet moved; just a few inches, but it was enough. He lost his balance, and William seized his chance. Just as Ræl's arms became level in order to right himself the younger Caster swung Melnhir upwards and sliced through the middle of the spear, completely shattering it.

Ræl over-balanced backwards, and William summoned white shackles to pin him down as he held his blade to the other man's throat.

"First lesson about using your powers. If you use them all at once it drains you and you die."

Ræl looked at him with eyes full of contempt, but even he did not take the risk of antagonising the man with the sword at his neck.

The floored man sighed.

"What do you want from me?"

"I want you to become my ally. I want you to help me find others like us, and when the time comes I want you to fight with me against the leaders of the world."

Ræl just looked at him, genuinely astounded.

"Is that all?" he asked, making no attempt to disguise his flippancy.

"You will probably end up dying before we get ten miles away."

The other man considered for a moment, and then spoke.

"Fine," he said, nodding. "I'll do it."

William released his restraints and stood back to let him get up. He offered Ræl a hand up, but he ignored it and got to his feet on his own.

"But on one condition."

"Go on," William replied.

"You let me do my own thing. You don't give me orders and you don't try to control me. Just point me in the right direction and get the Hell out of my way."

"Sounds good to me," said William, offering his hands once again.

But Ræl ignored him for the second time, and walked straight past towards the stunned crowd. They had just witnessed a battle quite a bit more surprising than any of them had anticipated, but eventually began dissipate away from the trio; four including Ræl.

As William approached, Ranson threw him his blades and his pack, and patted him on the back.

"Well done," he said.

"One down, three to go," said Alayna, as reassuringly as she could.

"I suppose," replied William, sceptically. "But why do get the feeling that this was the easy bit."

As if on some hideous cue, they heard a blood-curdling scream from behind them. The trio immediately began running towards the sound, closely preceded by Ræl.

Being high on a hill, they reached a precipice and stared at the scene below them.

The village was being ransacked. Houses were burning, woman and children were being struck down by men on horseback, and the men were being collected and tied together in long lines with chains.

William reached out to grab Ræl's arm, but he was a second too late to stop the other man charging down the sheer rock-face. The stone was completely vertical, but Ræl's feet were somehow clinging to it by some unseen power. At the bottom of the cliff were two armoured men on horseback and as he was a few metres above them Ræl jumped at them, grabbed them both by the neck, and slammed them onto the dusty ground below. They lay there unconscious, and Ræl moved on into the fray, taking out man after man as he ran.

William turned to Ranson.

"Get her out of here," he said, gesturing to Alayna. "Take her to the forest on the outskirts. I'll deal with him."

Ranson grabbed Alayna's arm and William's pack, and began to run. William strapped on his weapons and jumped down from the precipice himself. As he landed he went down into one knee, and the ground beneath him cracked as dust flew up into the air around him. Then he drew the two long daggers strapped to his waist and ran after Ræl as fast as he could.

The other man was overwhelmed with anger, and a fierce blood-lust had claimed him. He struck down as many of the enemy as he could as if in a blind rage, but his unarmed skills were lethally accurate. As he went, he picked up a blade, and was just as deadly with that. The swings and thrusts of the sword were so accurate and fluid that the blade might well have been one of his own limbs as opposed to a separate, metal object.

William was slowly catching up with Ræl. It was quite easy; all he had to do was follow the trail of armoured corpses. But as he was only a few metres away William noticed dozens of men following him and flanking him, drawing blades or fitting arrows into bows. He knew that if they reached Ræl before he did, they were both dead, so he quickened his pace and reached out his hand to the other man. As soon as he felt his fingers came into contact with Ræl's arm William closed his eyes and concentrated.

There was an almighty flash of bright, white light and the two men disappeared. A fraction of a second later, dozens of arrows tore through the space where they used to be.

A flash of light appeared in a clearing nearly half a mile from the ransacked village. William nearly collapsed and fell to one knee. The transportation had drained him almost to unconsciousness, and Ræl took a few moments to collect his thoughts and break out of his bewilderment.

As William slowly stood up Ræl realised what had happened and was bristling with anger.

"Why the bloody Hell did you do that?" he shouted at William.

"You were going to get yourself killed! I saved your life!" William shouted back.

"They attacked my home! They were killing everyone; destroying everything that I've ever known! I had to do something!"

"Believe me, I understand. But if you charge in blinded with anger all you'll be doing is giving worms food and the ground fertiliser!"

Ræl stopped shouting, but he was still seething.

"Look," he said, slightly calmer. "You are not my father. You're younger than me; you shouldn't be giving me orders. If you try, you can take that fancy sword of yours and shove it up your..."

"William!" Alayna called to him from the other side of the clearing.

The two men turned to see her and Ranson running over to them. The high tension and testosterone level suddenly dissipated, but Ræl still had something to say.

"Listen, I've known you less than an hour, and I already can't stand your merry little band. As we teleported I felt your plan. When we get to the next Child, you won't need me so I'm staying there. I'll fight in the final battle, but not for any of you. Those bastards destroyed my home, and that's all I care about now."

"So you've filled you heart with hate," said Ranson. "That's good. Just focus your temper on someone who deserves it."

Ræl nodded, half smiling, but then shook his head to clear the smirk and pushed past them. As he began to walk out of the clearing, William called out to him.

"The next Child is that way," he said, pointing in the opposite direction. Ræl turned silently and walked off.

The trio chuckled and headed onto the same path.

The first Child had been found.

Three more were left.

Chapter 20 - Child of Fire

Solaxe landed from his second long flight in the last week, but he was none too happy about having to come so far from his palace again. The threat of direct attack from either Kelthane or William was pressing hard into his mind, and his paranoia was growing. After all, he was technically the one who had declared war, and he wanted to be as safe as possible inside his fortress behind hundreds of his own personal guards.

He smashed into the ground and suddenly disappeared in cloud of dust and dirt. As he emerged from the shroud he was striding towards the soldiers that awaited him.

"Captain!" he demanded at the group.

A man stepped forward and knelt on one knee before the ArchCaster, not daring to look him in the eye.

"My Lord, I'm afraid that Captain Stenzan was killed in the attack."

"Killed?" Solaxe's tone was anything but forgiving.

"Two young men took out nearly a third of our troops including the captain and the lieutenant who were on horseback. When we found them their necks were broken. By then the two men had vanished into thin air; they disappeared right in front of me."

Solaxe knew immediately what he was talking about, but the identity of the second young man truly was a mystery.

"My Lord!" called a soldier from behind the group. The lined-up soldiers moved aside to let them through, and they saw that two soldiers were dragging an old man between them.

"This man knows who the rebels are," the man informed the ArchCaster.

Solaxe knelt down in front of the frail, old man talking quietly to him.

"Tell me," he demanded.

The old man seemed only just conscious; there was a dull, bloody wound on his forehead and it seemed to take all of his effort merely to speak.

"Three people... came to find another..."

"Who?"

"A young man called... called Ræl. Three travellers were looking for him. Up in the... in the crags, north of here."

Solaxe stood up away from the old man, and without a second look incinerated him where he knelt. The ArchCaster shot up into the air and landed on the flat, wide arena where William and Ræl had their first fight. He looked around at the ground that had been ripped up and the towers of rock protruding from it. I was obvious that this was not only caused by magic, but that this was a battle between two powerful practitioners.

Solaxe muttered to himself, and then re-opened a psychic channel between his mind and Kelthane's; a link that had long since been broken.

He has found other Casters.

In his palace, Kelthane's anger manifested into a pulse that smashed into the walls of his throne-room and caused them to topple into rubble.

Solaxe received a message back; he was not expecting it, but he nodded in agreement.

He must die.

William was actually quite enjoying the journey to the next Child. The sun was shining and the grass was very green. The leaves on the trees around them were dancing in the warm sunlight, and birds twittered as they soared on high or sat together amongst the branches. The group was not surrounded by trees, but they grew out of the ground in a loose formation around them.

As they walked along, William and Alayna walked arm in arm, talking and laughing, and Ranson chuckled as he walked in front of them, occasionally turning to share in the mirth. Even Ræl smirked as he strolled along behind. For a day or two, they walked nearly carefree with nothing to suggest the horrors that each of them had witnessed. Ræl did on occasion think about his village and everything that he had lost, but it was hard to keep ill thoughts in his mind. They disappeared so easily in his beautiful surroundings and the mirth of his present company that they seldom bothered him.

The Child that they were now heading for was indicated by another circular symbol on the map.

This was the ancient symbol for the element of Fire, and the group continued on their way towards this Child who controlled it. But soon they began to notice changes around them.

They began to walk past settlements and dwellings, but the houses and homesteads were merely skeletons; most of the thatching and wood had been burned away to leave the bare bones of the buildings standing as horrific monuments of the pillaging by Solaxe's soldiers. More often than not, the skeletal structures were surrounded by the lifeless bodies of their previous owners; the aged, the woman and the children, but not the men. They had been taken to fight in Solaxe's army.

Still they walked on, and day after day they found bodies next to destroyed or abandoned buildings, and whole patches of forests and crop-fields had been razed to the ground.

They headed almost directly south, and slightly east, and within four days they were just north of the border between the West Realm and the South Realm.

As they went south, the landscape became more and more bleak and the horizon became gradually emptier. There were fewer and fewer trees, the number of buildings decreased and the number of bodies increased. But these bodies were clad in armour and had weapons in their cold hands. The ground became a mire of mud and crimson, and for the last few hours of their journey the group began to feel uncomfortable.

Ranson had already told of a future of mire as far as the eye could see, and William was getting an uneasy feeling that he was right.

But still they pressed on, walking and walking for a few more hours. The silence that had taken hold of them was lacerated by Ræl.

"How long is it until we get to…"

He didn't even get to finish that sentence before his foot stepped into thin air. He had been walking and was not expecting to step into nothingness, and he toppled forwards. William grabbed the back of his belt and pulled him back suddenly, landing of top of Alayna and Ranson who were standing behind them. All four collapsed in a heap, and as silence descended they heard the clanking of armour and metal, and the shuffling of feet.

Staying low, the group poked their heads out over the precipice and looked at the scene below them.

A platoon of soldiers was marching along the narrow chasm, and as they reached a widened section they slowed down. The man who seemed to be in charged shouted something, and the soldiers broke formation. Some sat, some leant against the rocky walls, but all were slightly out of breath and were trying to have a brief respite. The group moved away from the ledge, and Ranson spoke.

"I've seen this type of men before. They are grouped assassins; mercenaries who go through settlements and kill as many civilians as they like. They tend to kill over half of a town at night, before the army gets there and takes over. We would be doing to world a favour to get rid of them while we have the chance."

Ræl stood up.

"Leave this to me."

The others didn't have time to say a single word before he jumped down into the middle of the soldiers. They grabbed their weapons and encircled him, and as Alayna strung her bow William stopped her.

"Let's see what he's capable of," he said.

Ranson looked concerned.

"They're professional killers," he replied.

"And he's a Caster. He needs to be tested," came the reply.

Ranson and Alayna were uneasy about it, but they all watched from the ridge.

Ræl just seemed to be standing in the middle of the circle, with about a metre between him and the closest man. His head was bowed, and his expression was blank. He didn't seem to be in any kind of stance; his arms hung lazily at his sides and his feet were flat on the ground.

One of the men, wielding a war hammer, lunged at him, and Ræl smiled. Then everything happened at once.

Ræl sidestepped out of the way of the blow and grabbed the man's wrist, twisting the weapon out of his hand and snapping the man's forearm at the same time. Another man stabbed at him from behind, but Ræl leant backwards so the blade missed and plunged into the chest of the disarmed man. Ræl then knocked the blade out of the other man's hand and felled him with a fatally precise blow with the war hammer. Then he reached behind him and pulled the sword out of the first man as he fell.

The others all charged in at once, but Ræl fought them off expertly, changing stances nearly every second to counter every blow and return one himself with both weapons. Man after man fell, until all but one were lying, lifeless and bloody, on the dusty floor of the canyon.

William, Ranson and Alayna jumped down to join him, and William was about to express his surprise as a voice made them all turn sharply.

"Lay down your weapons, and turn around slowly!" ordered an armoured man, standing a bit further along the gorge.

Bowmen appeared over the edges of the cliffs on either side, and caused the group's smiles to vanish in an instant. Ranson looked surprised for a second like the others, but then he seemed to register the voice. Without following either of the commands, he replied.

"I really am very attached to this sword!" he shouted, causing the man who shouted first to draw his blade and run towards Ranson. The older Caster drew Triscant and whipped round. The two men both ended up with the tip of their swords pressed against the other man's throat. Then they both started laughing, and everybody relaxed.

"Not bad for an old man," said Ranson, lowering his sword.

"I'm only a few years older than you, and you know it!" replied the other man. He too lowered his blade and the two men embraced each other warmly.

Then Ranson turned to the others who seemed a bit dumbfounded.

"This is Styron. He joined Raimos' Resistance at the same time as me. After a few years, he left, and joined the branch in the West Realm."

"That's when he stole Triscant from me."

"I didn't steal it. We had a duel and we were fighting for blades. I won, so I got your sword fair and square."

"I still think you cheated," said Styron, slightly quieter.

Ranson clarified.

"He was the only one in the Resistance who knew about my powers."

"That's enough reminiscing for now. What are you doing in these parts?" Styron asked.

"We're looking for someone. Another Caster," William told him. To counter his obvious confusion about the existence of Casters, he added, "It's complicated."

"Well there aren't any Casters around here; not that I know about anyway. To be honest we could do with some extra help. Solaxe's army has been fighting relentlessly, both with us and Kelthane's men."

"We can't use our powers to any measureable degree, or they'll find us," said Ranson, "but if you take us to your base we can help as best we can."

Styron nodded.

"It's much appreciated," he said, and looked up towards the bowmen. "Continue towards the border, and report back when your mission is completed."

One man nodded, and they all disappeared at once.

Meanwhile, the two old friends walked off together, talking about days gone by. William turned to see what Ræl was doing, and he was swinging round the war hammer that he had taken from one of the men earlier.

"You know, I think that I'll keep this. It's got almost perfect balance and it's more versatile than a blade."

"Try this too," said Alayna, throwing him a round shield.

Ræl caught it by the handle in his left hand. It was about fifty centimetres in diameter, it had a domed, metal hand guard and although it was wooden it was encased by a metal skin. It also had a decorative pattern on the front, and carvings around the edge. There were two leather loops on the back, and Ræl put an arm through each one so that he could carry it on his back. Then he fitted the lean hammer through a loop in his belt so that the head was sideways against his waist and the metal handle hung down parallel to his leg.

"Not bad", said William, nodding approvingly. "But you might want something to use at longer range."

At which point, a sharp sliver of rock flew up from the ground into Ræl's hand and he threw it. It whistled through the air and smashed into the cliff face millimetres from William's head, causing the rock-face to splinter in every direction.

"I think that I'll be okay," said Ræl, walking off behind the other men.

William was still in a stunned silence as he walked off, but Alayna patted him on the shoulder.

"Come on," she said, giggling at him before placing a kiss on his cheek and guiding him by the hand in the same direction as the others.

They walked for a while; nearly an hour, before they were back in the mire, and Ræl was having to walk in front and bring up stepping stones for them to get across.

Suddenly, the three Casters whipped round, and formed up side by side, shielding Styron and Alayna behind them.

Solaxe had appeared in the air behind them in a flash of light, and he suddenly unleashed blankets of crimson flame and fireballs at the group. Within seconds of turning, the three Casters formed up as a trinity of power.

Ranson deflected each of the attacks while William launched his own. Ræl summoned dozens of fist-sized rocks into the air around him, and after they had hovered in the air for a second they flew directly at Solaxe.

However, Solaxe deflected the path of William's fireballs and the let out a pulse that atomised the stone missiles far before they reached him. Ræl, not wanting to be outdone, summoned a quartz javelin and threw it, its flight enhanced by his powers. Solaxe stopped it in the air, flipped it round and launched it straight at William. Such was its speed that he did not have time to get out of the way, but at the last moment Styron pulled William back and out of the path of the missile. Instead it plunged through Styron's breastplate and he fell backwards.

Ranson looked from his dead friend to Solaxe, and he suddenly bristled with something that surpassed rage and hurt. As one, the two men launched streams of energy at each other. Ranson's was blindingly white, and Solaxe's was a striking crimson. The two torrents met in the middle and a shockwave boomed out perpendicular to the onslaughts that split the ground and knocked a fissure in the clouds high above them.

William shouted to Ræl.

"We need to get out of here! I can take Alayna, and you take Styron's body. We were heading West. Keep going until you see a valley with a lake at the bottom, and wait for us there."

Ræl nodded and stood next to Styron's body. He made the spear disappear, lifted up the round area of rock that they were both on, and sped off into the distance a dozen metres off the ground.

William grabbed Alayna, but she protested.

"We can't just leave him," she said, meaning Ranson.

"Trust me," William said.

Albeit reluctantly, Alayna allowed him to hold her tightly, and the two rose into the air and sped after Ræl.

Meanwhile, Ranson was holding off Solaxe's attack perfectly. He was matching him for power and force, and because he held such hate in his heart, in his attack were tiny flickers of crimson. Inevitably, his hate was less than his enemy's, and his power began to wane.

Sensing that Ranson was weakening, Solaxe increased the power of his attack, and the point at which the two streams met retreated towards Ranson as his enemy got the upper hand. Soon Solaxe's stream of energy was only two metres away from Ranson, and the force pushed him down to one knee.

Solaxe released a final pulse the knocked Ranson clean off his feet and he was unconscious before he even hit the dusty ground. It used to be thick mud, but the scorching heat of the battle had dried it completely.

Solaxe held his hands above his head, and between them formed a massive fireball that was ready to incinerate Ranson in an instant. Just before Solaxe was able to throw it however, he heard a deep booming sound. A fraction of a second later William, having just reached super-sonic speed, smashed into his side in a glorious blaze of fire. The fireball vaporized in an instant, and the ArchCaster was catapulted for miles, landing head-first into a river many kilometres away. But such was his momentum that his head smacked hard on the hard, rock bed, and he was out cold for a good few minutes.

William picked up Ranson's unconscious body, and carried him like a baby. He flew to the valley in which Ræl and Alayna were waiting.

Once they had landed, William laid Ranson down beside Styron's body.

"He's just unconscious," he said, before the others had time to worry.

He looked around at his surroundings.

"How did you know to bring us here?" asked Ræl. "I know that you've never been here before, but you described this place very well."

William nodded to Styron's body.

"He showed me. As he pulled me back he must have known he was going to die, so he opened his mind and envisioned this valley. Because I had just used my powers, my mind was open too, and he must have known that."

Ræl nodded.

"It would make sense that once a door is unlocked it can be opened from either side, no matter who has the key," he said.

"But why bring us here?" asked Alayna. "I mean, it must be important otherwise he wouldn't have used his last thought to get to this place."

As she finished speaking, dozens of figures in hoods and cloaks appeared from the crags and caves around them, and knocked first Ræl then Ranson, and then Alayna unconscious with well-aimed blows to the back of their heads. William panicked and ran towards them wielding Melnhir, but an arrow thudded into his back, and he was down. He watched as the hooded figures dragged his friends, including Ranson, into the caverns from whence they came, until one of them noticed that he was still awake and aimed a precise kick.

The last thing that William saw was the sole of a boot, a sudden pain, and then darkness claimed him.

The blurred image of the corridors and rooms around him swam lazily across his vision like paint being swept across a canvas. He couldn't feel anything except the fact that he felt cold. His hearing was blurred, he couldn't speak, and in his mouth he tasted the sharp tang of blood. He appeared to be moving, but he was not walking. He vaguely felt his feet being scraped across the floor, and his arms were out beside him as if he were flying. But he felt what he thought were hands gripping both of his arms, dragging him along, taking him God knows where.

After a while, he gave up and loosened his grip on consciousness, and the black surrounded him once more.

Alayna awoke, and Ranson was standing over her.

She tried to get up quickly, but before she was stable a sudden pain throbbed through her and she overbalanced forwards. Ranson caught her and sat her carefully back down onto the stone slab that she had been sleeping on.

"Don't stand up too fast," he said. "You've got a mild concussion. It'll wear off soon.

"Where are we?" she asked.

"I don't know," he replied. "I'm guessing some kind of prison. We got knocked out and taken, I'm not sure where."

Alayna looked around the small, stone cell. Apart from them and the stone slab, it was completely empty.

"Where's William?" she demanded.

"I don't know," he said. He was trying to be comforting, but he was obviously quite worried himself.

Even so, it seemed to calm her down a lot.

"Any ideas on how to escape?" she asked.

Ranson shook his head.

"This cell is very well built. The door is solid; no rotting and no window. It's damp so we can't burn it down. No weakness in the walls either, I can't seem to manipulate the stone, and the grate that is our only light source is twenty metres above us and fixed well to the same material as the walls. I can't blast it open, and because of the wind on the outside, I can't get it to melt without cooking us as well. "

"Great…"

They heard a clinking sound, and the turning of levers inside the door.

Alayna sprang up and got ready to fight, but Ranson shook his head. He knew that whoever built this jail was very serious about containing Casters. They knew exactly what they were doing. He couldn't imagine that they'd make it out or to William alive.

The door opened and a body was bundled through. It landed facedown, and the guards threw a tight package of bandages into the cell as well.

"Sort him out. You have one hour."

The door closed with a slam, and once again they heard the clink and clank of the door being locked.

Alayna crouched down beside the figure. A deep, bloody wound was in the centre of their back, and they barely seemed to be breathing. Alayna turned them carefully, and looked straight into the screaming face of William. He was crying out in pain, and blood was dripping down from his mouth.

"Get him onto the slab, now!" said Ranson, forcibly.

Together they lifted him onto the platform, with back facing up. For the whole time, he was crying out, and tears seemed to erupt from his eyes.

"Hold him down," Ranson instructed Alayna, who held his hand, and caressed his face while Ranson opened his armour at the back and exposed the wound.

"He's bleeding heavily, inside and out. I have to cauterize the wound." Ranson laid his hand over the wound, making William squirm. "This will hurt him massively. Prepare him and yourself."

Alayna nodded. She heard a scorching noise, and William suddenly convulsed, screaming louder than before. She took his face with both hands and put her face close to his.

"William, look at me," she said. "Just focus on me."

He opened his eyes and looked into hers, and it did seem to help a bit. But he was only just clinging to consciousness, and because of the immense pain he was in, he let go and drifted into a troubled sleep.

"He's out cold," Alayna told Ranson, her eyes overflowing with worry.

"I reached inside the wound with my mind and saw the damage. The arrow went through his spine and punctured one of his lungs. The idiot guards pulled it out. I stopped most of the bleeding, but he will lose control of most of his body, and won't be able to breathe if we can't do something."

"What can we do?"

"I do have an idea, but there's no guarantee that it will work."

Alayna looked down at William's pained face.

"Just do it," she said.

Ranson closed his eyes and concentrated on the wound. First, he focused on his punctured lung. He saw the exact damage in his mind, and as if using an invisible needle and thread, he brought the fleshy fibres together and fused them together, closing the wound. Then he focused on his spine. One of the vertebrae had been split nearly in half, knocked out of place, and most of the nerves had torn away. Again, Ranson began fixing his son's body; firstly reattaching the nerves, then knitting bone, until it looked like nothing had happened. Finally, he closed up the outer wound and reached up for the bandages. He wrapped one side around William's side and the other over his shoulder, until it went all the way across his chest and back diagonally.

Alayna noticed something.

"He not breathing," she said.

Ranson swiftly tied off the bandage in a knot under his arm, and put two fingers on William's neck, just under his jaw-bone.

"His heart's stopped. It couldn't take the trauma." He got up, and told Alayna to stand away. He then rubbed his hands together until sparks shot off them and bolts of electricity covered his palms.

"I saw the Elders do this once. It's a last resort but I can't think of anything else that will work."

He shoved his palms onto William; one on the left side of his back, and one of the right side of his chest, just above the bandage. William's body jolted, and started coughing violently. Ranson grinned in relief, and Alayna cried out on joy, seconds before nearly jumping on William and hugging him tight.

William sat up and looked at his father, who was leaning with his back on the opposite wall. He looked understandably drained, and although his son didn't say anything, the pure appreciation was obvious in his eyes.

The younger Caster looked around him.

"Where are we?"

"I'm not sure, but I don't think that we've moved all that far. Why would they inconvenience themselves by knocking us out and carrying us any great distance instead of making us walk ourselves?"

"And I take it we can't reach out with our powers."

"Not unless we want the ArchCasters to find us."

"Okay, well how do we escape?"

"We don't," said Ranson, much to the other two's surprise, so he clarified. "Even if we were all in top shape, it would take all of our power to get out of this place, and we will have learned nothing. But Styron led us here for a reason, and I'm going to find out what it is. Besides, using our powers could attract the ArchCasters, and William's in no fit state to fight just yet."

"I'm fine," he said, but as he stood up he visibly winced.

"No, you're not," replied Ranson, with all the compassion of a concerned father. "The guards said that they would check on us in an hour, so we're going to calm down, use our heads, and wait until we know what's going on."

"Fine," replied William sitting back down, and Alayna lovingly draped her arm around his shoulders, being careful to avoid the wound.

Ranson smiled.

"Why do I get the feeling that you're going to be the death of me?"

It had been an hour to the second when the guards came through the door. The trio allowed them to clap them in irons and march them out of the cell. They marched down the cavernous corridor lit only with torches, and they were flanked on either side by well-armoured men. William, determined to have a backup plan despite what Ranson had said, made a full summary of the troupe; how many soldiers there were, their exact positions, what weapons they had and how many, even the locations of the torches on the walls because they could be potential weapons. Nothing was missed, especially not the most troubling factor; the mysterious absence of Ræl.

Eventually, they reached the destination, but the trio were confused.

"It's just a wall," said Alayna, staring at the wide, smooth, featureless rock-face.

One of the soldiers walked forward and pressed a section of the wall. It gave way slightly, and sunk into the wall, and they all heard the sound of splitting stone and grinding gears. A portion of the wall slid up, and they saw that it was a cleverly disguised wooden panel. They were all pushed into the room beyond, which was circular with crossbowmen aiming at them as soon as they crossed the threshold, after which the door closed behind them. Although it was wooden, it had been painted with a type of resin that made it fire-proof. Ironically, it had been Styron who had introduced these security measures in order to keep any rogue Casters from assaulting the Resistance settlement.

The trio were forced forwards with their hands bound in front of them, and a women who looked about the same age as Alayna stood up from a raised, decorated chair, and walked through the crossbowmen. She seemed to be in charge.

"The thing that I find most curious..." she began, automatically assuming that everyone in the room was immediately paying attention."...is that the ArchCasters have begun bringing their enemy's dead to the door of the enemy's base, and are so easy to capture."

William would have been bemused if he didn't felt so insulted.

"ArchCasters?!" he said. "We aren't ArchCasters, nor any of their lackeys. We are Casters, and friends of the Resistance."

In response, the woman laughed in disbelief at William's pure audacity, but Ranson continued.

"It's true. My name is Ranson. I knew your father, Styron, when he was part of the Resistance in the East Realm." William and Alayna both stared in disbelief at this revelation, but he continued regardless. "I also met your mother briefly, God rest her soul. But we are not ArchCasters nor your enemies; we are here to help you, and also to find someone."

The girl's bright blue eyes widened.

"Ranson?" He nodded. "My father brought me up on tales of the brave Ranson; the last Caster and a shining example of everything a Caster should be."

William stifled a snigger.

Just then, a figure was bundled through a back door that none of them had noticed. The soldier that followed him held a knife to his back, and forced him to kneel. This would have been easier if he wasn't clapped in irons on both his wrists and ankles, which were joined by another chain. It was Ræl.

"We found him trying to break into the armoury. He escaped his cell and subdued all four of his guards without a weapon and without spilling a drop of blood."

The girl turned back to Ranson.

"You see? How do I know that you are Ranson? You could be a spy, here with other traitors to infiltrate our ranks."

"I am no spy, and nor are they. Release just one of my hands, and I can show you."

She looked reluctant.

"Put a crossbow at each of their backs and stay ready," she said to her men. "If he tries anything or if they move, cut us all down."

The men looked shocked, but did as they were told, and one who had a key released the iron from one of his wrists, keeping tight hold of the other.

"I'm going to show you something. I cannot affect your mind, just show you things."

Again reluctantly, she nodded and walked slowly towards Ranson. He carefully reached out his hand, and gently cupped her cheek as if she were fine china, and would break at the smallest touch.

He asked if she was ready, and when she said yes he closed his eyes and reached out with his mind.

Within a fraction of a second, he had showed her everything; from the first moment in his life that he remembered, all the way to when they met. He showed her things about her father that no ArchCaster could ever know, and showed her the battle in which he got the scar on his face as he stood beside Styron in what seemed an impossible battle. Few stood against many, but together band of rebels drew victory from the jaws of defeat and won with very few casualties. Of course, at the end, he showed her the fateful and terrible moment when her father was killed, and the pure pain in Ranson's mind was far too strong to be fake. When they opened their eyes, the girl understood everything, and she only had one thing to say. Her voice was quiet and heavy with emotion.

"Thank you for bringing him back to me."

"It was the least I could do," he said back, his voice as soft as hers. "After everything he did for me."

The girl regained her authoritative composure and put her hand up to her men.

"Stand down; release them."

"But ma'am..." one of the soldiers protested, clearly unsure, but she glared him down. They then proceeded to unclasp all of the irons. Before they got to William however, his arms burst into flame, the metal melted in a flash, and he shrugged them off while the man holding the key looked on awe.

The girl returned to her throne-like chair and took off her helmet releasing her long, curly, red hair. She seemed a bit unsteady, but she shrugged it off.

"I'm sorry for the way you were treated. If we had known it was you, things would have been different."

"Yes, but forget it. No harm done," said Ranson.

William said nothing but just shifted his bandage slightly.

"Let us start over. I am Eithne, and since my father died I am the leader of the Last Resistance. You're looking for Casters, but I'm afraid there are no settlements anywhere near here. Therefore they must be somewhere in my ranks."

"In that case, they are probably not aware of their powers, however we can assume that they bear a mark on their right wrists."

Eithne nodded, but the action seemed to hurt her. She put a hand to her head, and collapsed out of the chair. The armour took most of the impact, but she was out cold. The trio ran over to her, but when Alayna tried to take off her gauntlet to take her pulse it was scalding hot. William, able to control the heat, took it off instead and her hand was giving off enough warmth to bend the air around it.

"She's having some kind of unconscious fit. William, reach into her mind and bring her round."

William nodded and put his hand to her forehead and concentrated. He saw her mind in an image of greys but the lights were fading fast. He waded through her mind, searching desperately until, deep in the middle, he saw one tiny area that was glowing bright in an almost scorching white light. In his mind he reached out to it, but as soon as he touched the tiny nub of light it suddenly spread throughout her entire mind, and

William was forced out. He barely had time to open his eyes, he was thrown into the far-away wall in a blast of fire. Ranson and Alayna watched him fly through the air, and then looked down in surprise; only to see a circular symbol fade onto Eithne's wrist in a flurry of sparks. They looked at each other in disbelief because they knew the mark.

Two Children found, two Children to go.

William winced slightly as he lifted his shirt over his head. The wound on his back was healing fast, but it was still painful. He looked at himself in the circle of polished metal that functioned as a mirror, and he barely recognised the image staring back at him. He had filled out a lot, and his muscles were growing day by day; far more than was natural for the majority of people. But the most evident things were the scars; the pale mementos of the battles he had seen. Most obvious was the deep gash in his side, but small slices and cuts crisscrossed his body, and his face seemed drawn and far too grave for someone of his age. He knew that war changed people, but he was starting to think that he was looking more and more like his father every day.

The door behind him opened suddenly and Eithne walked in. William turned to look, and she flushed a deep shade of crimson before spinning round sharply.

"I'm sorry, I should have knocked," she said, still looking at the door she had just come through.

"It's fine," he said, picking up his shirt from the end of the bed and putting it on, still with a slight twinge of pain. Her back was still turned, so he spoke.

"You can turn round now," he said with a grin.

She turned, but she was clearly still feeling awkward. She was cradling one arm in another and she was still blushing, so William sat down on the bed and gestured for her to do the same.

"What did you want to talk to me about?" he asked.

She sat down carefully, and stared out into space as she summoned the right words. Her demeanour was a polar opposite to the way she spoke to her men. After a few seconds of silence she answered him, and William was taken aback by her words.

"I'm sorry about your mother."

He didn't know how to respond.

"Ranson showed me," she said, almost apologetically. "I'm sorry to bring it up, but I just need someone to talk to."

He realised immediately that this was about her father.

"Go ahead," he prompted.

"When I was growing up, it was just me and him. I never knew my mother; she died giving birth to me. Every night, he would tell me stories of his adventures. I always wanted to have some of my own, so when I was about seven I ran away from home. I got lost in the woods, and I had no idea where I was. I was scared and alone, and I didn't know what to do, so I just sat down and cried. It was so loud that a wolf pack heard it and began to circle in. But then suddenly my father appeared and fought them off, picked me up, and took me back home. He laid me down in my bed and said:

"Don't ever be scared, Eithne. Wherever you are, whatever is in my way, I will find you and I will keep you safe. Whether you're in the middle of the ocean, or deep in a forest, or down in the deepest cave, you can't be afraid because I am always coming to find you." "

A single tear fell from her eye, and William, slightly awkwardly, put his arm around her. She buried her face into his shoulder, and he was on the verge of tears himself.

"He died saving my life," he said softly. "I never really knew him, but I saw him at his best."

Eithne broke the embrace and sniffed back any more tears, before leaning up and kissing William lightly on the lips. He recoiled slightly and broke the kiss, and her face suddenly fell with a look of regret and guilt.

"I know you're hurting..." he said kindly, so she wouldn't be upset. "... but I cannot give you what you want."

Eithne choked back the lump in her throat.

"I just want a friend," she said.

"And you've got one," he said, embracing her once more. Using one hand, he sent out a blast of fire that lit up the logs in the fireplace, and bathed in the light of the flames he listened to her talk about her loss. They connected in terms of loss of loved ones on a level that no-one else could match, so they stayed up talking about first that, and then their own journeys, and finally William showed her how to use her powers. Of course, because she was chosen by the earth she was a natural, and quickly picked up on how to focus her thoughts until they manifested into magic.

Eithne eventually fell asleep as William was talking while he was sitting on the floor and she was lying on the bed listening. William noticed, and pulled the covers over her carefully. It had been a hard day for her, so he didn't want to wake her.

He put on his armour and weapons which had been returned to him, and he made his way out of the room, through the halls of the Last Resistance, and eventually out into the moonlit night. As soon as he was outside he soared silently into the air, and he passed first trees, then mountains, then flocks of birds with the moon on their wings until he finally cleared the clouds.

As he floated on high, the stars blazed above him. The moon was bright; a new moon in its full splendour, and the silence was both overbearing and unendingly blissful. As he looked down, he saw dark green covering most of the ground, and crystal water reflected stars back at him. But the thing that caught his eye most was a single fire that had just been lit almost directly below him. He descended fast at first, and the slower as he got low, so his feet touched the ground with barely a sound.

He had landed about a dozen metres away from the pyre, for pyre it was, and saw a single figure holding a torch, watching the flames leap high. William saw a body in a coffin on top of the carefully arranged pile of wood, and recognised its face as Styron. As he walked closer, he saw that the figure was Ranson, but he was not weeping for his friend; he was just standing there, watching the fairy castles in the flames.

"He was my friend," he said, apparently aware that William was there. "During the dark times, he was the only one who was there for me. He saved my life and yet I couldn't save his."

"I know, I fought him, and even I had to concede a draw," said a voice that William had not heard before but knew instantly. Kelthane walked out of the shadows and approached Ranson, but as William was about to charge at him he simply laid a hand on his father's shoulder. "A one day truce," he offered Ranson, "As homage to a worthy adversary." He glanced at William, and then took off into the night sky.

Ranson turned, and saw William. He said nothing, and just walked away into the shadows. Before leaving, William summoned up a tall, flat stone in front of the pyre. It read:

A BRAVE AND NOBLE MAN
A LOVING FATHER
A GREAT FRIEND
A HEROIC SACRIFICE

William gave one last nod to the man who had saved his life, and set off back to his room deep underground.

Ranson looked on with a lifted heart, as a single tear fell from his eye.

Eithne woke to find herself in William's bed. He was asleep on the floor beside the bed, and she looked longingly at him; his perfect features, his slim, muscled figure and his softly waved hair. She had fallen for him fast ever since she had first seen him, and last night he had refused her advance. He had stayed with her, listened to her, cared for her, but that wasn't enough. Perhaps it was the grief, or perhaps it was the loneliness she now felt, but she needed someone to love and to love her. So, thinking about this all the while, she got up and walked out quietly out of his room.

She walked slowly through the halls that she knew so well. She imagined her father walking beside her, but after the long talk with William she felt not sorrow or loss, only a heightened sense of peace.

She turned a sharp corner and ran straight into Ræl. She was deep in thought and he was running through the halls. They collided hard and fell down onto the hard floor in a heap.

Ræl became very apologetic, and tried to help her up, but she smiled and said that it was fine.

Once they were both on their feet Ræl just froze, staring at her for a few awkward seconds. He suddenly seemed to realise that he was gawking at her, and he snapped out of it and walked backwards while gibbering. Unfortunately he failed to notice the flags attached to the wall behind him, his back hit the wooden poles and they fell down on top of him. The red fabric got tangled around his neck and he stood up, and Eithne sniggered.

"Nice cape," she said, and he smirked. He pulled the flag off his shoulders and hung it back on the wall, clearly embarrassed despite the smile.

"So where are you going in such a hurry?" she asked.

"I needed to talk to William about something," he said.

"What was it?" she asked, suddenly curious.

Ræl blushed slightly.

"It doesn't matter now," he replied, smiling. "Where were you going anyway?"

"Oh, nowhere," she said, slightly distant.

"Would you mind if I joined you?" he asked.

She smiled, and nodded.

"Not at all."

William was staring at the map on a table in his room. He was trying to plan their next move, but his head was swimming. He'd told Alayna about Eithne kissing him and she'd reacted badly, accusing him of more and in the end walking off angrily towards the exit of the base. William could sense that she wasn't too far away, but frankly he was too scared to read her thoughts. Anyway, she'd made most of them quite clear.

Ranson walked in behind him. He'd entered quickly, but when he saw his son hunched over something on the table, he slowed down.

"William, are you okay?" he asked.

The younger Caster heard, but didn't turn.

"Of course," he lied.

"So what happened with Alayna?"

William sighed, dropping any subterfuge.

"So you heard that?"

"I think most of the base heard it."

"Great..." William muttered.

"Do you want to talk about it?" Ranson asked, more like a friend than a father, but William shook his head.

Silence ensued for a while, and William returned to studying the map. After a short amount of time he spoke, and what he said was a shock to Ranson.

"I don't think that I can do this."

The older Caster replied.

"What do you mean?"

"I'm not strong enough to go up against Solaxe and Kelthane. We can't win."

Ranson paused. He wanted to respond, but he knew that he had to be careful.

"I mean, why was I chosen? I can barely fend off one ArchCaster, and it cost your friend his life."

"The Stone told you that you could win, so you can. And we always knew that victory would have a cost. Styron was willing to give his life for you because I told him that you were my son, and that I believed that you were the last hope for all of us. He died for the day in which you would defeat the ArchCasters and restore freedom and peace to the Three Realms."

"But I still don't understand. I mean, the Stone said that the four united elements would defeat the ArchCaster, but I am none of those elements. Ræl is Earth, Eithne is fire, and Air and Water are still to be found but neither of them are me. So why was I chosen?!"

Ranson didn't know what to say. He knew the words "I don't know" were the only honest answer he could give, but he also knew that they would do more harm than good. Instead, he drew himself up to his full height and said gave one clear, sharp command.

"Come with me."

As he walked out, William didn't move so Ranson addressed him again.

"William."

This time, there was no compassionate suggestion in his voice; only sharp demand, so after begrudgingly kicking the table-leg the young Caster followed.

After walking a little way, William saw Ranson open a gate, and soon followed him through it. William was a little way behind, so it had nearly closed as he passed through the gap.

However, by the time he was outside, for that was where the door led, his father had disappeared. He looked around, but there was no sign of him.

Suddenly, a voice made him look up.

"Caster!"

William's face rose just in time to see fire raining down from the heavens. The young Caster fired a torrent of ice-cold water at the flames, and each element doused the other until nothing remained, but when William looked past where the fire had come from the sky was blue and clear, and empty.

Suddenly, a boulder smashed into his side, sending him reeling. He'd only just got back on his feet when another rock, as big as he was, came hurtling through the air at him. The power of its flight was such that it had no arc; its path through the air was fast, straight and pin-point accurate. Purely by instinct, William raised his fist into the rock's path and as it hit his knuckles it fractured into hundreds of sharp pieces. Some of the slivers scraped the skin off his face in shallow but painful stripes. One particular piercing and fast shard thudded into his shoulder, penetrating through the seams of his leather armour at the weakest point. William recoiled heavily from the stone missiles flying around him, but once again when he looked over from where the rocks had come from, the only evidence were two large holes in the earth from which they had been pulled from the earth.

William winced as he pulled the shard from his shoulder, but it had missed the bone and the main muscles in his arm and shoulder so it was neither bleeding badly nor overly painful. But as he continued to scan his surroundings and reach out with his mind, he drew Melnhir from the scabbard on his back. He was standing in the middle of a flat area of dry ground, with trees off to one side, mountains in the distance, and the mound of earth that the gate was so cleverly blending into was the only rise in the ground for a few miles.

William's heart thudded in his chest, but his breathing was steady and his mind was clear. Because his eyes were open, the image of the auras of living things appeared to be laid over his conventional vision, but he could not see any attacker anywhere around or above him; no flash of crimson that indicated an ArchCaster.

The young Caster whipped round at the sound of a twig cracking, but all he found was the body of a pitch-black crow, which had clearly just fallen from the sky. William relaxed slightly, but then he noticed a tiny sliver of rock embedded into its chest.

Suddenly he felt a twinge in the back of his mind and once again he spun round, but this time he was right to do so. Ranson had run up the mound towards William and abruptly appeared as he launched himself off the top with Triscant upside down in his hands. William spun round at astounding speed and dodged the blade, which slammed into the ground with a bright shockwave that sent dust hurtling up into the air. However, while he knew that the younger Caster was blind, Ranson swung his feet around as soon as they touched the floor and took William's out from under him. As he hit the floor, Ranson drew his blade from the ground and flipped it around in his hands, but before he could land a blow William launched more ice-cold water into his face, knocking him back. He then coiled himself up and flipped onto his feet. Ranson recovered and swung his sword and Triscant and Melnhir collided, biting and scrabbling. The impacts were so tremendous that sparks exploded and flew off the blades.

Ranson drove William back relentlessly, showing no compassion or mercy; the younger Caster felt like he was fighting for his life.

Suddenly, Ranson disengaged and swung Triscant high and fast. William had no time to block, so he leaned out of the way. The blade's path was so close to his face that it sliced cleanly through the strands of his now long fringe, and a handful of hairs fell past the younger Caster's eyes. There was no mistaking the message now. This was not play-fighting or training; his father was pushing him as far as he could, and if he could not push back he would die.

These thoughts stormed through his head in a fragment of a second, and he immediately retaliated with a reply of sharp stabs and thrusts. Ranson beat these off easily and spun sharply as William lunged forwards. Melnhir went straight past its target into thin air and the older Caster was suddenly behind him. The heavy, metal pommel of Triscant connected hard with the newly acquired scar in centre of William's back, and a current of pain surged through his body, nearly flooring him. Ranson hesitated for a second, but it was enough. Under the pretence of steadying himself, William put a hand to the ground, but then a sudden jet of sand and dust flew from the ground underneath it, straight into Ranson's face. William ignored the intense pain radiating from his back and whipped round, knocking Triscant out of his father's hands before he could react. Ranson recovered quickly and shot a small stream of fire onto William's hand as he swung his own sword, causing the second blade to hit the ground.

While William was occupied with putting out the fire on the wrist of his shirt, Ranson threw what looked like two spheres of light into the ground and then flew backwards a few metres, but as William was about to follow a rocky hand burst out of the ground and grabbed hold of his leg, causing him to fall onto his face.

As he turned his head sharply, he saw an arm rise up from the ground attached to the hand, then a shoulder, then another arm, all seemingly made of rock, dirt and sand. Then, finally the head and the face seemed to be crudely assembled from rock fragments; it was a truly horrific looking being. William drew one of his long daggers and slashed at the wrist of the creature, being shocked how easily he could cut through them and make his escape. However, another hand simply grew from the sandy stump and the creature continued to climb out of the earth, closely followed by another.

William looked around for Ranson, but he had completely disappeared, and the distraction almost caused the younger Caster's death. The creatures were out of the ground completely, and ran straight towards him. Their hands morphed and elongated into short blades of rock and William only just had time to draw the other dagger before they were slashing away at him with such lethal vivacity that was only just able to block them.

After a short while, William saw a weakness in their defence and he took the chance. He kicked one of them back and plunged both daggers into the other's chest. However, the sand just gave way and the blades went straight through, followed by his hands. Before he could pull them out again the sand went as hard as rock around them, and no matter how much he wrenched and pulled he was stuck. The other creature approached slowly, and the blade on his right arm melted away to form a spiked mace on a chain of quartz. William ducked as it suddenly swung at his head, and it carried on through the air until it collided with the face of the other creature.

Briefly.

The head exploded in a shower of rock fragments and sand, and the hold on William's hands was suddenly loosened. He pulled his arms clear of the creature and raised them, shortly before throwing them both at the shins of the other with the mace. The sandy structure fragmented and gave way immediately, causing the rest of the legs to fall downwards through what was left of the shins and feet and the creature was pinned to the ground.

The decapitated figure's head was growing back rapidly so William turned and bathed first one, then the other figure in white flame, freezing them where they stood and lay into clear glass. Then William just knocked the one standing onto the other and they both shattered into thousands of tiny shards. The younger

Caster bent down, picked up and sheathed the two knives, and then Melnhir too. Triscant had disappeared at some point during the fight, and he was under no illusions of whose hands it was in.

Nevertheless, he could not see Ranson anywhere. He had just decided that this was some warped training exercise and that he should return to the base to try and find Alayna, when the ground he was standing on suddenly rose up into the air. William stayed standing on the small disk of rock, but he held his sword tight and was constantly looking around him to try and spot his enemy. Then the disk stopped, and just hovered in the air, and it was only then, one hundred metres up, that he noticed another platform rise to the same altitude a few dozen metres to his left.

And Ranson was standing on it.

They both launched a barrage at each other, and both platforms dropped away from them as all of their concentration was on their opponent. They kept flying simply because they had no intention of doing anything else. William was sending a broad barrage of white lightning, which Ranson was launching a constant stream of flame. The two streams met in the middle of the Casters, and the electricity scythed through the flame, towards Ranson. He dropped closer to the ground to avoid the obviously prevailing bolts, and instead fired a beam of pure, pale energy at his son, knocking him upwards into the sky. But William kept going, clearly under his own power now, and Ranson had to follow.

Higher and higher they went, with William away in front until Ranson stopped. The one rule that he had never broken from the Order of the Casters was that he should never go higher than the highest cloud, as the air was so thin and the temperature so low that they could end up passing out and falling to their deaths. William looked down at him, and instead decided to turn around, heading straight back down; towards Ranson. Son collided with father with a blaze of fiery glory, and William pushed him down, faster and faster, lower and lower. Soon, they were going so fast that red flame began to appear around them, heating them up considerably, but neither really cared.

The ground suddenly rushed up and Ranson collided with the earth with such tremendous force that he smashed through it into a disused tunnel of the base below it, and then another, and then another. He went through a total of five before he came to a halt, smoking and groaning. He looked up and saw his son in the sky above, shining with luminous energy, in a blaze of triumph and victory. From his eyes flowed fire, and his skin was as bright as the Sun. The raw power that burst from him and coursed around him in a dazzling aura was incomprehensible.

Ranson winced, but smiled all the same.

"I never doubted you for a second."

Chapter 21 - Child of Water

My name is Dawyr, and if you're reading this then I may not be alive.

Because recently I've been having bad dreams, and in those dreams I do not survive.

They started a few years ago, and since then the things that I have seen happen have come to pass. I can tell when some will die, when a flood or an earthquake will happen, which building will fall and when. Everything I see happens, and last night I dreamt that everything ends - that the eternal blackness is not just my future but everyone else's as well.

And I have been given one word throughout these dream - one word that curses my nights and haunts my days. One word that ripples back through the ages and on to decide the future of this world.

*This word is **Story**.*

William had nearly finished packing up the last of his things into his pack when the door opened and Ranson walked in.

"Have you worked out which way we should go?" the older Caster asked.

"I was thinking through the Kracian Pass. I would cut our journey time in half, but we would have to sneak through the most highly fortified area in the whole of the Three Realms."

"With four Casters it shouldn't be a problem," he replied.

"No," said William simply. "Kelthane offered us a one-day truce; we're not killing any of his men."

"William…"

"That's my final word."

Ranson smiled inside that William was taking charge the way he was.

"I agree," he said. "It's more of a challenge that way anyway. But good luck convincing Ræl."

William sighed and dropped his pack.

"I knew that I'd forgotten something."

He opened the door and walked out, trying to remember where Ræl's room was, when he passed a familiar door that led to Eithne's room. He stopped, knocked tentatively, and then when there was no reply he opened the door carefully and looked inside.

Across the floor was strewn amour and clothing. William's eyes travelled up to the bed, and he saw Eithne asleep, her head resting on Ræl's shoulder and her arm across his bare chest. One of his arms cradled her protectively, as if even while he dreamed she would be stolen away from him. He was a bit taken aback, but then he smiled fondly and closed the door.

As he walked back to his room, he felt happy for his two friends and that they had found each other in such a way, but he couldn't help but feel a deep longing for Alayna. He had no idea where she was at that moment, and he had even less than that on how she was feeling; specifically about him.

Even as he entered his room to finish packing he hoped that she would be there waiting, but he wasn't surprised when he found the room empty.

He finished packing quickly and walked hurriedly towards the throne room where he knew that Ranson would be. On his way past a familiar door he thumped it loudly with three echoing smacks. He was sure that a moment later he heard the thud of someone falling out of bed. He smirked and carried on towards Ranson.

Their course had been mapped precisely, and journey times had been worked out. Ranson nodded one last time in agreement, and William rolled up the map. As he was fastening it with a leather strap, Eithne and Ræl walked into the room hand in hand.

Ranson, clearly understanding the situation, chose not to pursue it.

"Good, I'm glad that you two are here," he said. "We're nearly ready to leave for the South Realm, so pack whatever you need."

Ræl shifted slightly.

"Actually, I was thinking of staying here. I have my father's people to take care of," said Eithne.

"And I... Well we... were thinking..." Ræl stammered.

William smiled, and nodded.

"It's fine," he said, and Ræl was clearly glad that he didn't have to say any more. "Just be there when we call."

Ræl nodded awkwardly, and he and Eithne turned to leave. Just before they could, Ranson grabbed his arm and whispered something in his ear, too quick and quiet for William to understand. Ræl looked surprised, and he looked quizzically at Ranson as if to confirm what he had heard. Ranson nodded very slightly and the two left the room.

"What did you tell him?" William asked, suddenly curious.

"You'll know when the time is right," came the un-expositional reply.

William knew Ranson well enough to know that he would not be told anything else however hard he pushed. He decided that everyone was entitled to their own secrets, so he left it alone. After all, there was plenty that he hadn't told his father, and he had no intention to either.

After a short silence, Ranson announced that he was going to get his pack and weapons from his room and that he would meet William, and, he stressed, Alayna, at the lake at which they were ambushed a few days ago. William groaned but didn't disagree, and as Ranson left, the younger Caster reached out with his mind and searched for her aura.

Alayna swung her sword and a thick branch fell from the large oak with a crunch of dry leaves. In fact, the tree that was taking the punishment had precious little bark or leaves left on it.

She had begun her carpentry as a way to vent her anger with William, but now she was simply feeling low. The constant voices were chattering in her head, and fighting anything, even inanimate objects, seemed to be the only way to quiet them.

He never loved you. You don't have powers like she does. He'll stay with her and you'll be alone. This is your fault.

This last troubled her most, because she knew that is was at least partially right. Eithne had kissed him, not the other way around, and if he had wanted anything else he wouldn't have admitted anything to her. She had a right to be angry, just not with him, or at the very least not as much. She loved him so much, and she'd pushed him away.

Her blade slammed into the solid trunk and stuck fast. How could she be so unfocused? She'd barely miss-hit since she'd first been trained.

She shook her head to try in vain to clear the many thoughts coursing through it, and tried to dislodge the blade; but to no avail with either.

She just slumped down to the ground with her back against the tree and took a deep breath, trying to hold back the hot tears.

A soft voice made her swallow the lump in her throat and look up.

"Hello," said William. He was looking worriedly and concernedly at her, and he'd brought both of their packs with him. She didn't reply, so, laying them on the ground, he came and sat next to her against the tree.

She was wrong; she was still angry with him.

He reached into a pouch that was tied to his belt and took out a small loaf of bread.

"Here," he said simply.

Alayna looked up, and William saw that the only clean parts of her face were the tear-stained streaks where the evidence of her misery had coursed down to the ground.

She looked at the bread, then into his eyes, and smiled slightly. Then she reached out her hand, and took the bread, just as she had done when they first met.

"Thanks," she said softly, and leaned her head on his shoulder. He lifted his arm and put it around her, squeezing her warmly, and he linked his free hand with one of hers.

She looked up into his eyes.

"William... I, I'm..." she began.

Before she could say another word, he planted a deep kiss on her lips, and her fears and worries evaporated in an instant. He pulled away and she held him tighter.

William smiled lovingly.

"It's forgotten."

She looked up at him as if she could barely believe it.

"Agreed?" he asked with a grin.

She nodded, smiling too, but she was too busy holding back tears to reply.

Ranson, Alayna and William eventually met up at the lake, and they set off on their journey towards the South Realm; three wanderers on the march once again, as before.

The sun was beginning to climb in the sky, and they were all conscious that the best way of crossing the Pass through the mountains was to use their one day truce with Kelthane, and that day was fading fast. So much had happened in the last six hours, and so much journey time had disappeared so easily that they would have to move quickly to cross the Pass by dawn the next day.

The mountains that they were trying to cross were the Peaks of Kracia. They were high, treacherous heights that cut off the entire South Realm from the northern ones. The West and East Realms were almost square with no solid border between them, but the South was long and thin, and stretched along the bottom of both of them. This meant that the mountains spanned the length of the Clas Muîr, and cut off the Southlanders from the Westlanders and Eastlanders.

As a result of this, the Southlanders had developed separately to the rest of Clas Muîr and became a very advanced Realm. The cities advanced very quickly, creating soldiers and weapons far beyond their time, and the people were peaceful. But then came the Fall of the Casters, and Kelthane took over the land. The Casters had been using their magic to hold back the Sandwinds that came across the ocean, and when they died the sands rose up from the sea and swept across the land, burying and desolating everything in their path until the Realm was mostly desert, and the cities were empty ruins in a matter of days. Millions of people died and hundreds of years of knowledge and technology were lost, leaving the

Southlander settlements just occasional groups of basic villages dotted around.

As the three walked, the mountain loomed over them, more with every passing minute. They were heading uphill towards a place where the ridges stopped in a tall, thin gap. Although it wasn't dark, the hundreds of fires and torches that lined the floor of the pass were blazingly obvious, as was the presence of thousands of soldiers milling around, ready to defend that place from anyone who tried to get through. It was taken by the other side on a regular basis, and then retaken, but right now the men that were holding it were Kelthane's. Because of the truce, they weren't allowed to kill any of the three travellers, but whether they knew that was uncertain. News didn't exactly travel fast over those kinds of distances, and the soldiers would also have no clue who they were.

They all decided that it was in their best interest to use stealth, so they half walked half crouched through the long, dry grass until they got to the edge of the camp. This fanned out from the narrow valley in a semi-circle, and was very much fortified. Wooden palisades encircled the entire camp, and archers and pikemen patrolled the battlements, marching along the parapet; the platform that allowed them to see, and shoot over the top of the palisade.

The gate looked temporary but still very tough, and they wouldn't be able to force their way in without using enough force to kill many of the people on the wall, and in the small wooden gatehouse above it.

William looked on dismayed. He was torn between his honour in keeping the truce and his duty to their mission. Crouching behind a pile of small rocks, he surveyed the scene and tried to think of a way in. Suddenly a horn blew and they heard shouts. Feeling sure that they had been caught, they each drew their weapons and prepared to fight, but then they heard another horn blast from behind them. As their heads whipped round, they saw a small party, twenty at most, bearing spears, coming along the dusty path towards the camp. Their faces were covered by wraps of dark cloth so that only their eyes were visible, and their clothes were mainly just the same loose fabric. They had black leather plates on top of this; a single large one covering their torso, and then one on each section of their limbs. Almost insanely curved swords hung at their sides, and on the back of each man was a recurved bow, complete with arrows, in a quiver.

Hidden from view of the camp in the shadows of the rocks, and far enough away from the patrol that the long grass masked them, William and the others let them pass by. The gate was opened from the inside with an almighty creak, and closed behind them with an almighty crack.

Another horn blast sounded behind them, this time from far further away. William looked down the hill that they had climbed to get here, and then he looked back at the wooden wall, and he smiled.

"Okay," he said, turning to the others. "This is what we do."

William and Alayna were now clothed, head to foot, in the same black armour that they had seen earlier, and Ranson was in front of them with his hands tied behind his back and blood running from a dull wound on the side of his head, done by William because he wanted it to look like a realistic capture. They had ambushed the ten-strong second patrol and knocked everyone out, taking their armour and tying and gagging them all in the long grass to the side of the road. They would be found, just probably not before the truce would end.

As they came up over the lip of the hill and the camp came into view, William took the horn that he had taken from one of the unconscious men and blew a loud, clear note. After a few seconds, the camp replied and they heard the gates beginning to creak open.

"This is never going to work," whispered Alayna.

"It will," William whispered back.

"And when it doesn't you know what to do," said Ranson without turning.

William sighed exasperatedly, and they continued marching. They could almost feel the arrows being trained on them from the palisade, and as they passed under the gate they were stopped by a man without a head-covering and with light brown skin. He looked about middle aged, and seemed to have that impalpable air of authority about him. Two men with spears flanked him, and he put his gloved hand up to stop them.

"Who is this?" he asked, with a heavy accent.

William froze. They would both be immediately caught if, or rather when, they could not do the accent.

"My name is Ranson," the older Caster said loudly before either could answer for him. "I have a one day truce with your master, Kelthane. You cannot hurt me, and I do not appreciate this treatment in any way."

The man smiled unpleasantly, and spoke.

"Ranson. There's a bounty on your head. I may not be able to do anything about it today, but I'm sure I can send you to him tomorrow. Just your head; nothing attached to it."

William handed Ranson to the man's guards and he and Alayna walked behind as an escort. They marched through the camp, passing many men who were armed to the teeth and looked very on edge.

The way narrowed as they passed through the valley, and the sheer walls of rock only offered a path four men wide. As they began to reach the other end, Ranson opened one of his hands and counted down from three fingers.

Three.

William and Alayna counted and took note of every man around them.

Two.

They began to draw their weapons.

One.

Alayna discretely took out a dagger and got ready to cut Ranson's bonds.

Zero.

Ranson put his hands together into a hard lump of fingers and flesh, and smashed them first into the head of one spearmen and then the side of the other. Both men collapsed, and William and Alayna both drew their swords and defended Ranson's back, holding off any of the men from passing through the valley. William sent out a pulse and knocked the men back a few metres, and then closed his eyes, concentrated on the wall of rock, and brought massive boulders crashing down, blocking the valley completely but not hurting any of them.

On the other side, Ranson was busy disarming and knocking out the small unit of guards. There were so few because they had little need to defend against their own Realm.

They stripped off the foreign clothes and weapons, and Ranson took Triscant from William's back. Alayna was about to take off the quiver, when she unclipped the bow and held it in one hand. She'd lost her bow somewhere when they had been knocked out and taken prisoner by the Last Resistance, so she was in need of a new one. It seemed perfectly balanced, but it was lighter and more compact than the long-bow. It would be more easily concealed, and would also be able to be shot from a horse. She fitted an arrow, aimed upwards and shot, and a few seconds later a bird fell from the sky, dead.

Alayna smiled to herself, and refitted the quiver to her back.

"So where do we go now?" she asked after turning around.

William took out the map, and checked. Two symbols were left; those of water and air, and both were in the South Realm. But the one for water seemed to be in the middle of one of the great deserts, only a few dozen miles to the south of the Pass. The smaller camp on this side of the mountains was now empty of conscious soldiers, so they walked through it fairly calmly. When they got to the gate, it needed to be opened so Alayna walked into the gatehouse to find any kind of mechanism, but the small wooden room was empty apart from some tables, a few half-empty cups and some mouldy bread scattered around. The lack of mechanisms wasn't surprising; it was a fairly makeshift camp. She was about to walk to the window to tell the others, when she heard a thump and then a clatter, and she turned sharply. By the time she was facing the other way, she had grabbed the bow from her back with one hand, and arrow with the other, fitted it onto the string and drawn it. The sharp tip of the arrow was now pointing directly at a crouching soldier, who's eyes were wide in fear.

"Please... please..." he said, with an accent that was even stronger than the man that they had met earlier. It could very well be that this was the only word he knew.

Alayna tried anyway.

"Where are the horses?" she asked. It would be a long trip across deserts, and it was worth trying to commandeer some if they could.

The man didn't move.

"Hozzers?" he replied, clearly not understanding.

She sighed and looked around the room, noticing a wiry image of a horse had been carved into the wall, along with various other animals that she didn't recognise. She lowered the bow and, still watching him, went over to the carving and pointed to it.

He seemed to understand, and nodded, getting up and gesturing for her to follow. They walked out of the gatehouse and onto the wall, and then back down to ground level; the same way that Alayna had walked up. William and Ranson watched slightly bemused as they passed them.

"I see that you're making new friends," said William, and she jabbed him playfully in the stomach with her elbow as she went by.

A short time later, Alayna came back to them from behind some tents and had three horses in tow. The man that had shown her to them was with her, and William walked up, ready to knock him out like the rest, but he pulled off the head-covering and put his hands up to defend himself. William stopped; he was only a boy, no more than sixteen, and that was a maximum.

"Please.. I no tell… I no tell…" he said.

William lowered his hands, and gestured with his head towards the gate. The boy ran to it, unlocked it by pushing a cleverly concealed panel to the side, opened it, and ran out across the desert. He could only have been running for thirty seconds before three figures on horseback thundered past, sending sand flying up into the air.

Dawyr took off his shirt and dived into the lake. Everyone had been constantly arguing today, and he just had to get away from them. The water, although warm, felt so refreshingly cool compared with the scorching heat of the bright sun and the scalding sand. He kicked his legs upwards and swam to the bottom, as he had done many times before; he could hold his breath for large amounts of time, sometimes minutes on end.

The floor of the lake was mainly sand, but towards the centre it gave way to what looked like stone-flagging. Dawyr had often tried to lift or break some of it, but he had never been able to, despite there being a looped metal handle of curious design and a rusty hole that may once have taken a key. But he had no mental energy to spend time thinking about it, so he went to an area of soft sand and sat, cross legged on the bottom. Feeling finally relaxed, and due to the lack of sleep he had had recently, his eyelids fluttered and he closed his eyes.

Images suddenly flashed in front of his eyes. *People were screaming and shouting and fighting, blood and the dead were everywhere, pierced by blade and arrow, motionless in their final act, and fire rained from the heavens like a torrent. Perishing, spiralling winds threw people around like ragdolls, chasms opened in the earth and swallowed up the dead and the living alike, and veins of water rose up around people, swallowing them and suffocating them until they fell down onto the piles of the already dead. Above them, in the dark sky devastated by lightning, three suns blazed; two crimson, one gold. As he watched and could not look away, a sphere of golden light suddenly appeared around them, growing metres with every microsecond, and consumed everything in its path. More and more men were swallowed up as it stretched across the ground, until the light consumed his vision, and then everything was black and silent.*

He opened his eyes in a panic, and all the breath suddenly escaped from his lungs at once. His heart was thundering in his ears, and he scrambled, terrified, upwards until his head broke the surface of the water and he gulped in crucial air. His eyes took a second to adjust to the bright desert and sky because he had had them closed only a few seconds earlier, but as he looked around and saw the oasis, his home, his village, other people milling around like everything was normal, he breathed a heavy sigh of relief and calmed himself down. He had to go and write this down, as he did with all similar thoughts in hope that someone would find it and be able to help him.

"It's not real," he thought to himself. "It's only a dream."

He so wanted to believe that, but that's the problem with talking to yourself. You know when you are lying.

The going had become tough, as the smooth, flat salt-plains had given way to massive dunes of sand, some rising higher than any castles or towers that William had ever seen.

The Pass was in the centre of the north border of the South Realm, and they had travelled south east since there, so they were nearly directly south from the Torridon. Then they started going south, but they hadn't gone more than a couple of miles before Ranson stopped them and pointed off to the left.

The ruined wall was appearing out of the sand; the wind just happened to be blowing in that direction and the sand had been swept away just enough for them to see it. They dismounted, and William used his mind to sweep away the sand to reveal more and more of the building while Ranson brought up walls of rock to hold back the sand surrounding them that was trying to pour back into the now eight-foot deep hole. Finally, the building was released from the tiny granules, as was the dirt that it was founded upon. It was only one storey now; the top was only a corner of a wall that was previously sticking out of the sand. It was a square, squat room, with no windows and a thick wooden door.

William put his hand on the lock for a few seconds, and when he took it away the metal came away in his hand as the wood around it had burned away completely. The lock contained incredibly advanced and precise lever and spring systems, and it was decorated with a metal that would once have shone like silver. He handed it to Ranson and reached for the curved, metal handle, turning it and pulled the door open. It was completely dark, so William lit a flame in the palm of his hand; it was small but surprisingly bright, and illuminated the scene before them.

Leaning against the walls, and scattered across the floor, were small skeletons. Most of the rags of clothing that were still wrapped around them were in tatters, and every inch of flesh had been eaten away by time itself, but they were obviously children when they died. Ranson walked in with a sombre look on his face, while William lit up one of the torches on the wall. Alayna just stood in the doorway, wide eyes staring at the horrific sight.

The older Caster was bent down over the one corpse that was full size. It had plates of armour and chainmail still strapped on it, and a sword in its bony hand. His breastplate had a hole in the centre that had been punched by an arrow, but it had clearly been pulled out. Ranson lifted the empty hand and removed a ring from it, holding in his palm.

"Galawaine," he muttered, but it was nearly a sigh, and his voice was full of pity.

William walked towards him.

"Who was he?" he asked.

Ranson closed his hand around the ring.

"His name was Galawaine," he replied. "He was my mentor and for many others too. The last thing he ever said to me was that he was going to get the Novices out, but I thought he had died in the battle. They must have escaped and ran away south, hiding in here, waiting for it to end. But the Sandwinds must have trapped them; the door opens outwards, and he must have been too weak to use his powers or his strength to open it against the weight of the sand, and the children would not have any great control of their powers. They must have starved."

Ranson cleared his throat and stood up.

"Let's go, we need to reach the next Child," he said. William let him walk past and out into the sunshine, and a moment later he followed.

The older Caster then lifted up into the air, and William held Alayna and did the same, and Ranson took away the rock barrier, allowing the sand to flow back into the pit and cover the building once again, until not even the wall on top was visible.

William heard his father mutter, "we brothers in arms," just before he turned away, mounted his horse and began to ride further south, with William and Alayna close on his heels.

Dawyr checked no-one was around, and closed the door to his shelter and put a chair across it so no-one could enter. He then went to the holes in the walls that acted as windows and rolled down an opaque piece of fabric over them so no-one could see in.

He then went over to his bed, and lifted up the long-flat bag of rushes that functioned as his mattress and took out a worn, leather-bound book. He had found this one day while fetching water, just poking out of the sand. No-one had used books in the South Realm since before the Sandwinds, so it was a lucky find. He had picked it up and taken it home, but when he read through it the book was full of strange symbols and runes that he couldn't decipher and some words that he could read but didn't understand. He'd spoken them aloud anyway, and had felt a wave of energy surge through him. Suddenly he could understand the symbols; they hadn't changed, but they just suddenly made sense to him.

And so he read.

He read about the forming of the Order of the Casters and the discovery of the Stone of Draoidh. He read about the way that the Order organised Clas Muîr into the Three Realms, and how they policed and structured it from the fortress they built in the centre of those Realms. The final entry was about what little the author had heard about the fall of the Casters, and that Kelthane now ruled over them, but then it suddenly changed from elegant, neat runes to fast, scribbled, panicky writing about the Sandwinds, and how the author and his family were trapped in their fortress by the Sandwinds. Then it said that the sand was coming in through the broken windows, and about his family's plan to escape by diving out as the sand built up enough to be level with their highest window.

And that's where it ended.

Dawyr had seen that this person had written all of this down in the hope that someone would find it and save him.

But then all manner of curious things happened in his life. The oasis formed in the middle of the village, and it never seemed to run out, no matter how much that they took for drinking or washing. They used to have to capture the rains that came every few months and store it underground to keep it cool, but now they seemed to have an endless supply. Also, one person that had always tormented Dawyr about various things, but mainly his isolation, was found dead in underground water supply. He seemed to have been dragged in, but there was no trace of any animal or human tracks; only damp gorges in the sand where water had flown over it. But the curious thing was that the water had flown uphill. It was also about that time that he began to have bad dreams; vision of battle and death that he had no understanding of. He couldn't sleep well and he had to take a special herb that he stole from the elders of the village to knock him out every night. He still had bad dreams, but at least he was able to maintain his energy for the next day.

Something in the back of his mind told him to keep these things secret, but he had to tell someone so as not to forget. So Dawyr began to write those things down using thin lumps of charcoal from his fire, as he was doing now with this latest vision. The visions varied a lot, but one thing was always constant through all of them; he always saw a golden light battling against two crimson lights. He had no idea what this meant, so he wrote it down and then closed and buckled up the book, putting it back under the mattress and walking back out of his hut.

As he opened the door quickly, he ran straight into Greia, a girl that lived a few huts down. She was about the same age as Dawyr, and she had fairly short, jet black hair and blue eyes. He had had feelings for her since they were children together, but he had thought that it was not reciprocated so he had never acted on it. Instead, they were friends, and she was always getting him into trouble.

She stepped backwards to avoid the swing of the door but she fell backwards as Dawyr hit into her. They fell onto the sand in a heap, and he was apologising from the moment they hit the ground to the second he helped her back onto her feet.

She just laughed, and pretended to dust herself off. Her mirth was contagious; just like always he found himself smiling too.

"What are you doing here," he asked, still grinning.

"Well I was going to show you something I found this morning, but now that you've been so rude..."

She was joking, obviously, but she still turned away from him. He grabbed her arm and she gave him a feigned punch in the stomach before running off. He laughed, surprised, but sprinted to catch up with her. She turned behind one of the wooden huts, and he lost sight of her for a moment. Then she appeared on the back of a horse and thundered at him, but he jumped out of the way just in time.

She laughed as she slowed the horse and turned to face him, and he whistled for his own mount. Soon he was chasing her across the dunes, upwards and downwards, until she began to slow at a small oasis surrounded by trees and even small patches of grass.

Dawyr whistled in amazement, and they both tied up their horses' bridles around one of the palm trunks. He had never seen another oasis before; the one in his village had appeared overnight and no-one knew how, but this is the first time he had seen flowers and grass. Clearly, the Realm was starting to recover since the last of the Sandwinds.

Greia wasted no time in diving in to the small lake, and as she surfaced she shook her hair so that the water showered over him even while he was on the bank. She gestured for him to join him but he shook his head, remembering what happened last time he was underwater.

"Killjoy," she yelled at him, a wide grin spread over her face. He'd always loved her smile.

He sat down on a patch of grass with his arms resting on his knees, and she got out of the water and joined him. The wide leaves of the palm trees shielded them from the sun, but she was already drying quickly.

"What's wrong," she asked.

He picked at blades of grass, but said nothing.

She shoved him with her shoulder and he nearly overbalanced.

"Come on, what is it?"

He threw the grass away.

"Nothing," he replied.

She looked at him, concerned, but chose not to push the issue. Instead, completely to his surprise, she laid back and pulled him down with her so their heads were together looking up at the crystal blue sky through the gaps between the leaves.

He so wanted to tell her how he felt, but he loved just being with her so much that he wasn't even sure that he wanted anything else. No, he decided. He had to tell her. He turned his head towards her and she did the same, so that he was looking into her beautiful blue eyes. They mirrored both the sky and the water in their infinite depth and beauty, and all words suddenly evaporated from his mouth.

"I was… Well I was thinking… If you don't want to… Then that's fine, but… Well… Maybe you, I mean we, could…"

His bumbling fluster of words was cut short when she stretched towards him and planted a light kiss on his lips. He just stared into her hopeful eyes for about ten seconds, before smiling and drawing her back into a kiss that lasted a lot longer and they drew closer to each other.

The moment was broken by the sound of hoof-beats, which even on the sand were considerably loud, and they both sat up sharply. Three horses and three riders had just cleared the crest of one of the dunes to the north of them and by the time they were descending Dawyr had unhooked his short spear from his horse and was pointing it towards the riders, putting himself between them and Greia. Only Kelthane's men were allowed to ride in these parts, so any horsemen they met meant trouble. They were already in trouble with them for stealing the horses.

The three riders got to the bottom of the dune towards the oasis and dismounted, and Dawyr saw that they were a boy and girl about his own age and one man who looked about middle aged. They were armed, but they did not draw their weapons, and the younger man walked towards him with his arms raised.

"We mean you no harm," he said. "We are not Kelthane's men; we are but travellers."

Dawyr didn't lower his spear.

"A bit heavily armed for travellers," he replied.

The young man looked at the spear being pointed straight at him, and then back to Dawyr.

"Point taken," he said, and lowered the weapon, but kept his hand tightly around it.

Meanwhile, the older man was filling up two water skins at the pool, while the girl filled another.

The younger man got closer and extended his hand.

"My name's William. What's yours'?"

"I'm Dawyr, and this is..."

He didn't finish his sentence, as the second his hand touched William's, images flashed over his open eyes.

A short, wide-bladed sword with curious runes running up its length met another, longer, thinner blade, and as they collided the first blade shattered explosively into a hundred pieces and the second continued on its journey, severing flesh from bone. A word was whispered to him in a voice he didn't recognise.

Story.

Story.

Story!

All of this happened in a fraction of a second, and Dawyr recoiled from William, unable to understand what he had just seen. This was the first time a vision had occurred while his eyes were open.

He suddenly realised that he hadn't finished his sentence, and William was looking at him curiously. His hand was no longer extended.

"And this is Greia," he concluded. "It was nice to meet you, but I really think that we should be going now." He gestured for Greia to get to the horses, when a shout ran out from above them, and a dozen of Kelthane's men, some on foot, and some on horseback, charged down the slopes on all sides. William and the other two drew their weapons and began to fight, and five men had reached the bottom of the dunes on Dawyr's side as well.

First came a man on horseback, which he dispatched quickly with a lightning-fast stab to the chest. He fell off the horse, dead before he hit the ground. Then three men ran at him with their curved swords, and he was ready.

He swung the spear high and fast, slicing through the first man's neck without even dirtying the blade, and then, using his own neck as a pivot for the shaft, Dawyr used the momentum of the swing to slide the wood through one of his hands until it thudded into the second man's chest. He then pulled it out just in time to parry a slice from the third man, before knocking the sword out of his grip and skewering him. As he retrieved his blade, he suddenly realised that five men had come down the slope.

He looked up just in time to see the last man draw his bowstring back to his ear and then release it. Dawyr leant sharply to the left to dodge the whistling arrow and then used the momentum of straightening up to throw the spear with all his might at the man.

The point flew true and straight through the air until it found its mark in the centre of the man's chest. As he dropped the bow and fell to the ground, Dawyr looked behind him to check on Greia, only to feel his stomach and his heart vanish inside of him as he saw her clutching her chest, her fingers wrapped around the arrow that had pierced the very centre of her torso.

She fell onto the sand without a word, and he was on his knees beside her in a second, gathering her up in his arms. The blood was spreading across her chemise in a horrific crimson encroach, and the light was fading from her deep blue eyes. He reached down and gave her a final kiss, but her body fell limp and a single tear fell from the corner of her eye.

Then Dawyr lost all control of his body and his emotions. He began to shake and convulse with her in his arms, and the tears flowed like waterfalls from his eyes. He cried out his wrenching pain to the sky and his eyes, already red with hot tears, suddenly flashed a scorching and aggressive white flame. The three watched as the small lake suddenly became a dark, seething entity, which rolled and swelled and broke its banks, rising up into the air, higher and higher, until dived at Dawyr, soaking him and Greia and engulfing them both. When the water suddenly became lifeless and formless and washed away from them, the body of the girl had gone, and Dawyr was left unconscious on his back. The water seemed to swirl round and round his right wrist, until it was all soaked up into a round symbol that they all recognised from the map.

It was the ancient symbol for Water.

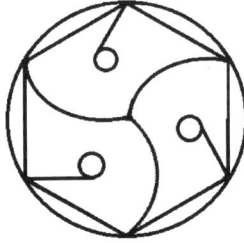

Three Children found, one Child to go.

Dawyr opened his eyes and sat up. For a moment, he couldn't be sure that he had opened them; the darkness around him was palpable, and the various colours of fluorescent light seemed to swim through the inky blackness like globules of oil through water.

As he studied his surroundings further, he realised that although he could feel a solid floor beneath him, the darkness just continued downwards.

"Where am I?" he asked, but his voice didn't seem like his own. It echoed and reverberated beyond anything he'd ever heard before.

A dark figure stepped forward out of the darkness, and he saw that it was the person that he had met earlier. What was his name? William? They'd met just before…

"I thought that it would be easier to do things like this," he said, and his voice was as echoing as Dawyr's own. "This is a between-space; the moment between reality and, well, everything else. Your mind travels here when you dream, like now."

"So I'm not awake?"

"No," William admitted, and he seemed almost apologetic. "You're asleep in the hidden oasis, where... Well, where we met."

Memories of what had happened flooded back into his mind and his heart filled with pain, but for some reason his mind didn't race; he felt strangely at peace.

"We wove a protective spell around you so you will not be seen until you wake."

"Spell?" asked Dawyr, standing up on the nothingness. "Who are you?"

"What do know of the Casters?" William replied.

"Enough to know who they are, but not much else."

William reached out his hand towards Dawyr.

"This will probably be easier."

Slightly doubtingly, Dawyr took his hand, and images suddenly flashed in the air around him; if air was the right word. William showed him images of the history of the Casters, and of the story of the Children of the Casters and their quest.

Dawyr suddenly understood and recoiled. The second he let go of William's hand the images disappeared from around him and he just stared into the palpable colours, trying to process what he had just learned.

After a few moments, he seemed to snap out of it, and he looked, suddenly confident, at William.

"When will you need me?" he asked.

William half-smiled.

"Just be there when we call."

Dawyr seemed to lose his focus for a moment, and William saw his eyes. Images were flashing across his eyeballs, but they were only blurs to the Caster.

They disappeared as suddenly as they had begun, and he looked surprised.

"What did you see," asked William.

Dawyr's eyes suddenly turned bright with white light, and his voice changed; it wasn't just echoing but it seemed completely different. William knew he'd heard the same whisper... From the Stone of Draoidh.

"The ruin of the world will be decided at the ruin from which both father and son ran from. The once traitors and the once hero will meet where the fragments of the world will come together as one, and there will be death; so much death. So much will be lost and so much will be saved, and gold will rain from the heavens at the end of the world."

The light faded from his eyes, and he looked at William.

"What does it mean?" said Dawyr in his normal voice, even if it contained a lot of surprise.

William looked just as surprised.

"The final battle; the place where everything is decided, is the Torridon."

The lights began to fade around him, and Dawyr asked William "When will you call?".

The Caster smiled, almost sadly.

"Before the end."

The images faded completely and Dawyr opened his eyes, the desert sun obscuring his vision. He sat up slowly, and noticed that the pain in his chest had returned. It burned as brightly as before.

He looked over at the small lagoon surrounded by the oasis, and noticed some soldiers refilling their water-skins and drinking from the crystal water. Suddenly, one of them noticed him and cried out in the strange language of Kelthane's men. They all drew their weapons, but he stood up calmly.

Smiling slightly to himself, Dawyr clenched his fist, the circular symbol on his wrist glowed white, and none of the soldiers noticed the water in the lagoon move.

Chapter 22 - Child of Air

The three wanderers were once more galloping across the vast deserts of the South Realm. After Dawyr had passed out Ranson wove around him spells of protection and, after checking the map, they mounted their horses and rode away to the most southern coast of Clas Muîr.

Their journey was surprisingly uneventful; they travelled under the heavy heat of the day, and at night they gathered together around a fire, lying on thin blankets, William and Alayna in each other's arms in order to keep warm.

After three days, Alayna assumed that they were going in circles, so she asked Ranson:

"How far do we have to go?"

Ranson stopped to join William in checking the map, but Alayna kept going, looking backwards at the two Casters.

Suddenly, the ground seemed to fall away under her horse's hooves and the two fell together, and then moved away from each other as they rolled. William saw her disappear and leapt off his horse as he went to the edge. They were tumbling at incredible speed down a sand dune that was at least forty five degrees downwards. He lit up with a palpable white energy and rose into the air, and then almost immediately shot down the slope, parallel to the sand and only about half a metre away from it. Dust flew up into the air behind him as he flew, and he noticed something.

Alayna was falling in front of the horse, but as the dune levelled out she would slow down but the horse wouldn't and she would be crushed. It began to flatten out only about twenty metres in front of them.

William sped up.

Fifteen metres.

Even faster, and a strange cloud seemed to form around him.

Ten metres.

William banked wide to the right.

Five metres.

He swung back in towards Alayna, and the cloud boomed as he reached supersonic speed. With less than a metre to go, William caught her and carried her off to the side. She was unconscious in his arms, her skin was scraped and raw, and her arm seemed misshapen.

His feet landed at the bottom of the slope a few hundred yards away, and although they dug in slightly sending sand flying, he remained perfectly steady and Alayna stayed stable in his arms. He checked her over and apart from the wrist, which seemed nothing more than a sprain.

Meanwhile, Ranson was careful edging the two remaining horses down the sloped sand, and when they were at the bottom he checked on the third. It had not been so lucky; two of its legs were broken and its breathing was heavily laboured. Ranson put his hand on the horses head and muttered some words, and the horse's breathing slowed down and its eyes closed. With one final exhalation of breath, the horse was still.

William, after carefully lifting Alayna onto his horse, looked around him. The sea began only a few miles away and stretched out to the horizon, and the sand stopped in an area around a small group of huts on the coast. Grass and trees were thriving around the village, and there were some crops. The young Caster beckoned Ranson over, and they rode up to the outskirts of the village, tying their horses off on a rack of hanging fish.

William was about to walk into the centre of the conglomeration, but Ranson put his arm across the young Caster's chest, stopping him.

"No," he said. "Look around you."

William did so.

"What?" he said, confused.

"There's no sand," he explained. "The Sandwinds haven't touched it. Something of great power dwells in this place." They checked the map, and the circular symbol for Water was exactly where the village was. "It'll be the last Child for definite, but I'm not going in blind."

William agreed, and he locked his right hand around Ranson's right wrist, and Ranson did the same. Then they both closed their eyes and as one they reached out with their minds, scanning the village. And they both opened them again with a look of surprise.

There was no hint of any kind of power. Just a few normal people. Even with Eithne, where her power was dormant, there was a tiny node of bright power deep in her subconscious. But here there was nothing.

William double checked the map. This was where the last Child was meant to be. What was going on?

Alayna grabbed the two men's shoulders as they were looking at the map, and as they turned to the same way she was looking their eyes both widened in shock.

With an almighty roar, a gargantuan cloud of sand tore over the ocean towards them. The wind was carrying the tonnes of granules over the waves, and they barely seemed to touch the water. The only thing between them and the Sandwinds was a tiny, rocky island a few hundred metres out from the land; there was no protection from the shards that were less than a minute away from tearing them apart.

William raised his right arm, ready to form a barrier to stop the sand. They would be buried in a matter of minutes, but they might be able to use their powers to dig themselves out.

But as they watched, the Sandwinds reached the island and parted obediently around it, stretching round further, avoiding the village by about twenty metres, and re-joining itself one it had passed all of the houses, and to everyone's relief after it had passed William and the others too. It finally slammed into the massive slope and flew up and over it. After about thirty seconds, the last of the sand has disappeared over the top crest.

Ranson brow furrowed.

"The Child of Air *must* be here somewhere," he said.

William, shocked that anyone could have that much power, ran into the village before Ranson could stop him. Even he, with all of his power, would only have been able to deflect most of the storm around him and possibly the others; whoever did this deflected every single grain of sand around an entire village.

The young Caster grabbed a man that was just walking down between a row of huts and spun him round to face him.

"What was that?" he asked. "How did it happen?"

The man had been unfazed by the sand, but he somehow seemed surprised when someone was asking about it.

"Where the Hell have you been recently?" he said, shrugging off William's hold. "We've been protected since just after the burial of the Realm."

"How?" William asked.

The man didn't answer; he just shifted uncomfortably and avoided William's gaze.

"How are you protected?" William insisted, an edge to his voice that the man picked up on; an edge that said "Do not mess".

"The island," he said. "I was against it, but…"

He trailed off, and William realised the conversation was over. The man walked away, and Ranson and Alayna approached him. She had woken up and Ranson had fashioned her a crude sling out of a piece of cloth.

"Stay here," he told them, and ran towards the beach. As he reached the edge, he jumped off the small cliff and lit up with the same white aura, launching himself onto the rock surface of the island in a matter of seconds. It was did not feel like solid rock; the surface was porous like a reef, but it wasn't organic. He saw a metre-wide hole in the surface, and jumped down into it, landing on a similar surface about ten feet down.

He was at one end of a corridor-like passage, and at the other end was a dull orange glow. Slowly drawing Melnhir from his back with a metallic, scraping sound, he walked carefully along the tunnel. It sloped downhill steeply, and the glow increased massively as he went down.

As he reached the end of the tunnel, it opened out suddenly into an underground hall. The ceiling was quite low but the room was almost circular, and the room was completely surrounded by bright lava, apart from where the tunnel led into the room and where another archway left the room on the opposite side. This left a circular section of rock in the middle, on which was a chair made of the same stone as the rest of the island. In this chair was a boy; a thin, dark-skinned boy with pale, milky, weak eyes. His hands and wrists were encased in iron, and the metal glowed with a white aura. William ran to him, and he immediately knew who he was; there was no mistaking it. This boy had magic.

Two men appeared at the entrance to the tunnel that he had come through a few moments ago, and they had farming tools in their hands; one was a large pitchfork, and the other was a sickle.

"Leave him alone," one of them said. "You can't be here."

The men were wet through and had clearly swum here. They looked out of breath, and they had just noticed the sword in William's hand and his leather armour. If William chose to fight them they would be no contest, but there was nothing that they could do to stop him anyway. Instead he embellished his blade with a blazing flame and raised it above his head with a murderous look on his face, and they fled back up the tunnel.

William then extinguished and sheathed his blade, and ripped off the manacles with each of his hands, softening them with heat as he did so. The boy seemed to convulse as the link was broken, but then he visibly relaxed and sighed out a breath of an obvious release from pain. His eyes faded from milky white to turquoise green, and the colour seemed to return to his skin.

"Thank you," was all he could muster out of his lips, and even that was a hoarse whisper.

Even as he watched, the boy's skeletal figure seemed to grow and tighten like a skin being filled slowly with water. After a few seconds, what was before him was a perfectly healthy-looking man. The skin on his wrist was now completely unwrinkled and William saw the same circular symbol as was on the map; the ancient symbol for Air.

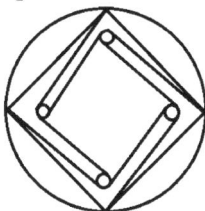

"What's your name?" William asked.

The young man stood up, still unsteadily.

"Èadhar," he said. "Who are you?"

"My name's William.

"And what do you want from me, William?"

William seemed a bit taken aback by his rudeness.

"Oh come on," said Èadhar. "Don't treat me like a fool. People only ever want something from me. How do you think I ended up in this place?"

William looked around.

"What *is* this place?"

"The Casters built in ancient times. The energy from the molten rock somehow amplified their powers and they were able to keep the Sandwinds from destroying the Realm. This is where I have been imprisoned for the last fifteen years, suffering endlessly to keep the village safe."

"What do you know of the Casters?"

"Enough to know what I am, and enough to sense what you are too. I sense great power and pain, but little evil. I don't think you're here to kill me, or I'd be dead already. So I'll ask again; what do you want from me?"

"I want to join me and a few others like us. I want you to fight with us because together we have enough power to destroy the ArchCasters and their armies and restore peace to the world."

Èadhar pondered for a moment, and then spoke.

"Prove yourself to me," he said to William.

The young Caster lifted up his arms and white flame engulfed his hands, burning bright but not harming him or his armour.

But Èadhar shook his head.

"I know that you have power, as I said before. That's not important. I want you to prove to me that you have a spirit strong enough to lead me into battle."

He pointed to the archway that was the opposite side of the room to the exit.

"That room has a curse upon it. The villagers took me there to scare me into doing what they wanted. Walk into it and stay for as long as you can. Your powers and weapons will be of no use to you."

William considered.

"How do I know that you'll still be here when I get back, and how do I know that you won't just try to trap me?"

The other young man shrugged.

"You don't, but where do I have to escape to."

He had a point, William had to admit, so he walked past the throne-like chair and through the archway. The light from the bright molten rock seemed to stop as he stepped through the doorway; one moment a brilliant orange light filled his vision, and the next he was in complete darkness.

Well, not complete; there was an ominous blue glow coming from somewhere. As his eyes adjusted, he was sure he saw some shadowy figure dart past him, and then disappear again, and then another from the opposite direction. He held out his hand and a bright white flame suddenly lit up two face that were standing only a metre away from him.

"Mother? Father?" he said, as he looked into the eyes of the people that raised him.

"Look at you," said his mother. "Who do you think you are? You're not special; you never were."

William just stood there, shocked at her words.

"I can't believe you thought we loved you," said his father, or his step-father as William now knew he was. "You're just a bastard child of a weak coward."

The flame on William's hand began to flicker and wane.

"You couldn't even save us," said his mother, looking down at her chest. William followed her gaze and saw blood spurting from a deep wound in the centre of her ribs. William reached out to her but the figures receded backwards into the shadows, consumed by the inky blackness.

"What do you think that you're doing here?" said a horrifyingly familiar voice from behind him. He spun around and found that he was staring into the face of Ranson.

"Are you so arrogant that you came here on your own?!" he shouted at William. "You're just a proud little boy pretending to be a Caster! You'll never defeat anyone!"

The flame on William's hand had shrunk into almost nothing, and Ranson stepped backwards into the darkness. Then William heard a quiet sobbing in the corner, and he ran over to the crouching figure. The light was just enough to make out wavy, brown hair and a beautiful face.

"Alayna?" he said. "What are you doing here? Did you follow me?"

She shook him off and stood up to face him.

"Of course not! Why would I follow you?"

His face showed the hurt that was tearing its way through his heart.

"Oh, did you think that I loved you?" She laughed at him dismissively. "I never loved you! The only reason I stayed with you was because I was using you to keep me safe and fed."

Another figure joined her and took her hand.

"I'm in love with Ræl," she said, as if it was a totally obvious fact.

William looked up at Ræl, and he spoke.

"Oh, by the way, I figured out how to control all the elements. I can't believe that it took you so long! You must be *so* weak!"

He held up his hand and lit up a flame, far brighter than the gaping Caster's had been since he had enter the room, while William's had completely gone out.

He spun around, and there was the captain, laughing maniacally with blood pouring from his mouth and Melnhir in his chest.

"No, not you," said William, but it was barely a whisper.

William stepped backwards, away from his enemy, and he tripped, falling onto his backside. Ræl's flame was now lighting up a circle of faces from his journey that were surrounding him, suffocating him with laughter, while words echoed through his head.

Weak.

Unloved.

Disappointment.

Stupid.

Disaster.

Pitiful.

Unimportant.

His hands were clamped tightly around his ears, but the voices only got louder. He managed to pull himself up to a kneeling position. Shouting with all of his might he slammed his first into the floor and a pulse of white energy ripped through the figures and the darkness, until it hit the wall, cracking them but not breaking them. Lumps of volcanic rock fell from the ceiling and sunlight streamed through, illuminating a gasping William as he collapsed onto his back, breathless, trying to forget what he had just experienced.

A few moments later, he emerged and Èadhar just looked him, amazed.

"How did you beat it?"

William smiled slightly, but it was a sad smile.

"You can never beat it, you can just choose not to listen."

Chapter 23 - An Deireadh

William and Èadhar emerged together from the entrance to the lava-caves, and Ranson and Alayna were waiting for them; the older Caster had flown over, carrying Alayna with him. The others were talking almost hurriedly about something.

"I think, well I was told, that the final battle will be at the Torridon. I would stay close to it so you'll be there when we need you. How long will it take you to get there?"

"Not long," he said. "I'll be there when you call."

And with that he summoned an almighty but severely localised wind, rose up into the air, and William thought that he would be flying off. Instead, he hovered over the village and raised his hands over his head. Another immense, rushing wind rushed from the north, causing the top of the massive slope of sand to cascade down. This triggered an avalanche of sand that buried the village, extending the coast a full fifty metres into the ocean.

After this, Èadhar flew off to the north and disappeared from view. William knew that every member of the village was dead, so there was no point in mounting a rescue. It was brutal, but in some way fair. Either way, he was still glad to have Èadhar on his side.

And then he heard Alayna scream.

He whipped round and saw Ranson convulsing, as if something was burning him from within. He put his hands to his head, and doubled up onto one knee. Then, as quickly as it had begun, he became strangely still. He stood up, but his eyes were closed.

"Oh thank God, he's okay," said Alayna, but William looked at him curiously. Then he opened his eyes.

And they were completely, terribly, bright red.

"No, I don't think that he is."

Ranson drew Triscant.

"Ranson?" said William.

Then he began to walk towards them.

"Father?"

And then he began to run.

William drew Melnhir from his back just in time to smash a stab from Triscant away from his chest. Ranson's flurries came thick and fast, and such was the force of each impact that sparks burst and flew off the metal. The surprise of the attack had thrown his defence off, and now he was trying hard catch up with his strokes. Suddenly, William noticed a gap in Ranson's defence, and took the chance. He drove his knee up into Ranson's stomach, and he immediately collapsed, dropping Triscant and taking a few steps back before collapsing onto the hard rock. The younger Caster slid Ranson's sword away with his foot, but didn't take his eyes off his father nor his hands of the hilt of his sword.

"What's happened to him?" asked Alayna, her voice full of worry.

William didn't have a chance to answer before he heard Ranson's voice in his head.

It's not... me.

The voice seemed very strained.

Mental... link... with... ArchCasters. Not strong enough to stop them... I'm about to fight you again. You have to kill me.

What?! replied William, but Ranson, or rather not Ranson, stood up. When he spoke, his speech had a duality two it, but he recognised both of the voices; Kelthane and Solaxe.

"Ranson is ours now. His heart is strong but his mind is weak. We are one in this body; We are Three once more. And we are strong!"

With this last, Ranson summoned Triscant to him and ran once more at the pair. Once more, William swung Melnhir into the other sword's path, but at the last second Triscant became embellished with crimson flame, and the two blades met.

And Melnhir shattered into pieces in a fraction of a second.

William's eyes opened wide in surprise and he leant back as far as he could to avoid the embellished metal, but he still felt the hot tip of Triscant slice through the skin of his cheek. The young Caster stepped backwards, and again, dodging and ducking past the vicious slices, ignoring the throbbing pain in his face and the blood streaming down past his mouth. Ranson lunged forward with one hand on Triscant and William launched freezing cold water into his face; Ranson flinched and the lunge went wide. William had time to sidestep away from the blade and summoned up a pillar of rock around his wrist, trapping it but leaving his sword sticking out horizontally into the air.

William!

The young Caster heard his father's voice in his head once again.

You can't restrain me. I'll never stop until I've killed you, and taken back the East Realm for the power of the ArchCasters.

But father... William replied.

I won't be a puppet of evil. You have to kill me!

The rocky restraint around Ranson's wrist was cracking and was about to break.

William heard his father's voice in his head one more time.

Goodbye.

The rock finally shattered in a burst of crimson flame, and Ranson swiped sideways with Triscant. William grabbed turned away sharply, grabbing the handle of Ranson's sword with one hand and bringing his other elbow down on his sword arm with the other. Still turning, William spun Triscant in his hands and plunged the blade into Ranson's chest, and as he did so lighting thundered across the sky and black clouds rolled over the crystal-clear blueness.

Ranson's glaring red eyes opened wide in surprise, but then the crimson faded and the sharp eyes that William knew so well returned. The old Caster just had time to smile contentedly before he fell backwards lifeless. His light faded from his eyes, and they rolled backwards as the lids closed. Bright blood ran across the rock below him, and a furious, terrible anger bristled across William's very being. A carpet of rain began to crash down over them, and the blood was washed away. With tears falling down his cheeks, William manipulated the rock underneath Ranson and it enveloped him, burying him forever, and then the young Caster stabbed his sword into the rock before him. Triscant stood as a wordless memorial to the last of the Order of the Casters, and the shards of Melnhir were washed into the ocean by the thrashing wind, where they sunk into the sand on the seabed.

Alayna put her hand on William's shoulder.

"William... I'm so sorry..."

He turned and drew her into a tight embrace.

"I love you."

Before she could even react, he closed his eyes and concentrated, and he teleported her away.

Now alone, he let his anger loose in a pained cry to the heavens.

"ArchCasters!"

The cry echoed across the entirety of the Three Realms, and in the minds of every man, woman and child as well as on their ears.

"You wanted a battle, and you've got one! Before the sun sets on this day, you and all of your followers will be destroyed. Meet me at the Torridon, and do not test me. If you fail to face me, I will hunt you down and you will be obliterated."

With a blaze of white fire, William shot up into the air, and without looking back towards his father's grave, he made his way towards the Torridon.

Alayna woke up on a wooden floor. She got up dozily, and nearly banged her head on a thick crossbeam; she was in the eaves of an oddly-shaped house. Suddenly memory of what had happened flooded back to her, and she ran down the stairs. She burst out of the door in a panic, and found that she was on the edge of a small, stone-flagged square in the centre of all of the houses, and in the middle was a large sundial.

She grabbed a short, dumpy woman who was walking past.

"Where am I," she almost shouted at the woman, who seemed taken aback.

"Blimey my dear, how much have you been drinking," she said with a slight smile.

Seeing nothing but panic in the girl's eyes, she answered bluntly.

"Tursus."

Alayna shook her head.

"William," she muttered to herself. "You clever boy."

"You know William?" asked the woman.

Alayna shrugged the question off.

"Which way to the Torridon?" she asked, and then thought of something.

"I'm going to need the fastest horse you have."

William smashed into the dusty ground at the site of the Torridon, sending bones flying up into the air around him. His anger was palpable in the fizzling air around him; he was ready to finish this, once and for all.

A few seconds later, Èadhar landed in front of him, the wind that was carrying him sending dust pluming up and away from him. Then Eithne hit the ground in a blaze of fire, and then Dawyr after being held aloft by a single wave of water that seemed to roll in the air. And finally Ræl arrived, surfing the air with a thin piece of black rock and landing with a smack on the dry ground.

They had all met, as Èadhar and Dawyr had been drawn to Ræl and Eithne at the Last Resistance, and Eithne had shared their plight and all of the information they had, including what she had received from Ranson, to each one of them. This meant that none of them needed a briefing or a speech; they all knew what they had to do, and their faces were all grave from knowing the price that would be paid by the end of the day.

Eithne scanned their surroundings, and then looked at William.

"Ranson?" she asked, as if fearing to know the answer.

William shook his head but said nothing.

Suddenly, they all felt a twinge in the backs of their minds that signalled only one thing.

The ArchCasters were on their way.

"They will be bringing their armies to destroy us," said William. "We are only five, so I'll deal with the ArchCasters; you deal with his armies."

Ræl smiled slightly.

"We're not just five."

As if on cue, William heard a deep roar of voices, and scores of people appeared over the large wall of rubble around ruined fortress and they began to flood through the gaps that Kelthane and Solaxe had made just before the Stone had been destroyed.

He was about to defend himself when he noticed some of the faces. Surely that was Aniik, the man who had helped him escape Vanyol's palace, and he recognised a few others from that escape, with Cedric leading them in charge. Then there was Arthur the barman, leading a rag-tag band of warriors with weapons that had clearly been cobbled together from farming tools and blacksmith hammers and the like. Next through the gap was Drustan, and all of the mutineers he had met on the ship. William smiled slightly to see the cook, still in his dirty apron, wielding a heavy-looking meat-cleaver in each hand. And then of course the most numerous company were the members of the Last Resistance; each one was armed to the teeth with bows, arrows, sword, daggers and spears. He even saw one carrying a gigantic hammer on his shoulder.

Every one of these men was armed with a dangerous look in their eye, and they numbered about five hundred in total. As they all came to a stop inside the circle of rubble, some men began to move through their allies to William until standing in front of him were the Children of the Casters, finally united, Annik wearing tribal, leather armour a brandishing a sleek spear, Arthur wearing clearly ancient pieces of armour

365

and an equally old sword, Drustan wearing his pirate gear and wielding a cutlass, and a man that William vaguely remembered as being appointed Eithne's second-in-command.

The Caster looked at Eithne

"How?" he asked.

"Ranson," Ræl answered for her. William remembered when his father had grabbed the Child of Earth's arm and whispered something in his ear.

"In a second when he took my arm he showed me your story and those you had met, and told me; "Find them, unite them." So when you three travelled into the South Realm, we retraced your steps and gathered all allies to the base of the Last Resistance, only a few miles away from this fortress. All we had to do then is wait for your call."

Eithne smiled.

"The United Resistance," she said.

"Okay," said William, with no smile and no hint of softness in his voice.

"This is what we do."

A short while later, the ground began to shake with the footfalls of what was clearly a surfeit of men marching in time.

The United Resistance was shaken but did not falter from their stations. The soldiers had taken their positions on what was left of the many battlements of the Torridon, but there was enough for every archer to stand there, bows strung and ready, arrows and blades eagerly waiting in their cases. The Children stood at equal distances apart in front of the fortress, with William at the very front; no sword and no knives. They faced south west; since Vanyol was dead and his forces destroyed, there would be no reason to defend the east border.

The rumble of footsteps got louder and louder, closer and closer, until with a blast of crimson the wall of rubble collapsed in a great plume of dust, and through the dust two bright red figures floated. William blazed white and rose too; he was directly between the ArchCasters and his own men at the Torridon.

"This ends here."

With no further words, the three sorcerers rose into the sky, a final trinity of immense power, and they each side launched a massive stream of fire at the other. The streams met in the middle and a battle between red and white began as the meeting-point of the flames exploded and blasted outwards, making the sky blaze with furious light. At this massive burst of scorching radiance the ArchCasters' armies charged from out of the smoke and dust. On one side there was Solaxe's men; loosely armoured, horde-like men with a great variation of weapons, and on the other were Solaxe's; men clothed head to foot in black fabric with curled shoes and curved swords.

Eithne lifted one of her hands above her head and every archer drew an arrow and fitted it into their bows, and then she snapped her arm down. Strings twanged and arrows whistled as hundreds of lethally sharp metal points screamed towards their targets. The Child of Fire held out her arms towards the charging enemy, closed her eyes and concentrated, and each of those fatal tips were suddenly embellished with white flame. The Child of Air then hurled a vaguely white wind to the backs of the arrows, propelling them forward at a mind-bending speed and causing the flame on their tips to stream back behind them like tails. The enhanced shafts tore into the first few ranks of their enemy, now bottlenecked slightly by the rubble, and they were very nearly torn apart. Like a wave, bright flame rippled out into the men behind the impact and dozens of men immediately caught alight; their hair, their clothes, none of it was able to withstand the unearthly fire and caught alight.

The United Resistance thought that this would break the enemy army's spirits, but they just ran forwards with renewed vigour. The fear that their masters invoked was powerful indeed. Eithne seemed unsteady and Èadhar put his hand to his head; concentration of power on this scale took its toll on the one who conjured it. It only took a couple of seconds for them to recover, and Eithne raised her arm and snapped it down once more.

The second wave of arrows thudded into their targets, and dozens more men fell dead staining the dusty ground with crimson. Ræl's weapons were on his belt, but he summoned up a dozen sleek, sharp rocks and launched them at a group of the enemy men. Then as the men fell to the floor he focused on the projectiles and they fractured and exploded, firing bullet-like slivers all around and instantly killing more men in a wide circle. He then unhooked his war hammer and his shield and prepared himself, as the enemy just kept coming; there must have been thousands of them.

Eithne shouted out to the Children in their minds.

Once more, together.

Ræl nodded, and he raised his hammer and smashed it into the ground, and through his power twenty great, nearly person-sized lumps of rock leapt into the air around him. Èadhar then summoned a swirling wind that lifted them swiftly into the air like they were feathers, and Eithne bathed them in blisteringly hot fire, turning them to burning glass in the air. Then Èadhar let the wind stop and the rocks began to fall towards the approaching enemies, and Dawyr launched freezing cold water at each of the scolding-hot lumps. They shattered into razor-sharp pieces but they only picked up more speed, and thousands of mortal shards rained down over a wide area. The slivers tore through shoulder and skull, clothes and flesh, skin and bone; the blood that flowed from where the shards fell was so plentiful that it slicked the ground and made other men fell on the lacerated corpses. But still they charged.

The United Resistance and the Children of the Casters readied their weapons and stole their hearts as the enemy plunged in,

Alayna was pushing the horse as far towards its limit as she could; she was flying over the earth towards the Torridon as fast as the horse was able. William had sent her away to protect her, but she was not going to stand by and let him fight the final battle. He was more powerful than anyone in Clas Muîr, but she couldn't get his words as they were in the Vaults below the Torridon.

If I do beat the ArchCasters, if we win, then I die.

She shook her head to clear the thought,

Whatever happened, and whatever the end, she wasn't going to let him face it alone.

She was skirting the edge of the forest of Delsus, between it and the mountains that marked the border of the East Realms. It was the most direct and fastest route to the ruined fortress of the Casters.

Some movement caught her attention to her right, and she didn't let up on speed but she looked over to the forest. Shadowy figures were running in and out between the trees, and she got a glimpse of shaggy, brown fur and long, wide claws. They weren't quite as fast as the horse was going but they were going in the same direction.

Alayna jabbed her heels into the flanks, willing it to continue on, to go faster, to get to the Torridon first; before the Scarra.

Before the end.

William's stream of fire seemed to be winning, and was pushing back both of the ArchCasters'. The second they noticed, they finished in a pulse that extinguished it all. William blocked a fireball from the left, then a blast of energy on his right, and then he launched his own attack of white fire.

He seemed to be more powerful than before, as if since his fight with Ranson, he had a new energy flowing through him.

Another blast from his right hit him a glancing blow in the shoulder, and he recoiled for a second of a second.

But it was enough.

The ArchCasters suddenly hammered him with a barrage of ruthless attacks, not letting up while battering the young Caster with fire and jets of sharp water and energy pulses. He was pushed down from his place in the sky and had to fight to stay in the air. All he could do was summon a force-field to protect himself, but it was waning fast.

As each attack rattled his arms to exhaustion, he thought:

I can't do this.

He was ready to give up, he was ready to just give in to stop all of this pain; to stop this war and to have peace.

A second before he was going to let down the protective barrier, he saw Èadhar take off from the ground and cast pieces of what had the effect of solid shards of air into Solaxe, knocking him back and stopping the attack. Solaxe tried to launch a fireball at his but roaring, hurricane winds extinguished the flame. Kelthane never stopped to help Solaxe; he just continued to batter William.

Solaxe finally summoned a metal blade out of thin air and launched it at Èadhar; the blade cut through the wind and then buried itself into Èadhar's shocked heart. He took one last look at William, and then the wind that was carrying him just stopped and he dropped like a stone only to crash onto the dusty ground below.

William shouted furiously.

"No!"

An anger built up in him like nothing he had ever felt before. He had been holding in his pain about Ranson, about his mother, and about his allies that had died along the way, but now they flowed like lava through his veins. His eyes were no longer white.

They were gold.

He felt the power of the Stone flow through him, as did Vanyol's, and now so did Ranson's. All of these had been destroyed by his hand, and now they were his to command.

He pushed the force-field, which was now aurous and shining, up and towards his combatants; it became suddenly fast and smashed into Kelthane. It was like being hit by a brick wall, and the ArchCaster was knocked back with astounding force. William then launched a torrent of bright, golden energy at Solaxc and nearly grilled him, but Solaxe dodged it and cast his own attack. Kelthane then soared back down to the pair and engaged William again.

The Children of Earth, Water and Fire had seen Èadhar fall, and they each felt a deep pain, right down in their very being. They hadn't known Èadhar well at all, but he was their kin, and now he was dead and their anger manifested into fierce, aggressive elemental attacks.

People were screaming and shouting and fighting, blood and the dead were everywhere, pierced by blade and arrow, motionless in their final act, and Eithne summoned fire that rained from the heavens like a torrent. Perishing, spiralling winds from Èadhar's still body threw people around like ragdolls, Ræl opened chasms in the earth and swallowed up the dead and the living alike, and Dawyr made veins of water rose up around people, swallowing them and suffocating them until they fell down onto the piles of the already dead.

The United Resistance were not doing so well; they had been driven back into the fortress' ruins, and were now fighting a close-quarters urban conflict. Most of them were hardened warriors so they had an advantage over the slaves and mindless puppets of the ArchCasters, but their enemy's numbers were vast. Although they were killing five or six men each before they were cut down, they had no chance of winning; only about three hundred of them were left, They fought in the hallways and they fought on the battlements; in hall or courtyard. The fortress seemed to go on forever and they never seemed to run out of new areas to battle in. Eithne's lieutenant had been felled by an arrow, but Aniik, Arthur, Drustan and Cedric were on the front line in a curious hall with a pedestal in the middle; it had become a battleground with blood slicking the floor and bodies piling higher and higher. The ship's cook was in the middle of the fray, cutting down man after man with wild swings with his axe-like knives, and he seemed to be rather enjoying himself before a thick broadsword was plunged into his stomach.

With the Children just outside, defending the main entrance to the citadel, the United Resistance managed a great push and drove out or killed every enemy within the walls, and they fought now to defend it.

Ræl, Eithne and Dawyr fought shoulder to shoulder; Ræl gave furious strikes with his war hammer and expertly dispatched enemies with perfectly timed finishing moves, Eithne fought with a long, slender sword embellished with fire and cut down enemies with even the thickest armour, and Dawyr had taken a spear from one of Solaxe's men and was slaying enemies in what was almost an elegant, flowing dance. Their weapons all seemed as much a part of them as their own limbs, and they defended the main gate successfully, using their powers when needs be. They all had enough battle experience to know that they wouldn't be able to hold out forever against so many foes, but they knew that they had to buy William as much time as necessary so they kept fighting.

Alayna had reached the Torridon, but the direction from which she was coming was still blocked with the tall pile of rubble. She could hear the terrible sounds of battle from beyond the rubble and she knew that she had to get to her allies before the Scarra arrived so she could warn and prepare them. Most of them had attacked and slaughtered the city that was built around the blow-out section of the wall of the Torridon, which had delayed them, but they would still be there soon. She began to hastily scramble up the rock pile, but as she did so she heard the sounds of falling rocks behind her. Looking back and down, she saw that the first of the Scarra had begun climbing up behind her; just a few of the fastest. She drew her sword and as one of them reached her it swung its arm, only to have it cut off at the wrist before it got close to her. The beast roared out its pain, and she kicked it hard, sending it tumbling back down the slope.

She began to climb again and heard more animalistic panting and rock-falls behind her, but she ignored them.

"You can do this," she thought, climbing faster.

William was winning, but he was weakening fast. The ArchCasters had been using, training and fighting with magic for years so that it was not taking as much of a toll on them, but with every expulsion of power he was becoming weaker. He was sure that it was affecting them too, but none of the three showed it or let up in their attack.

The Stone's terminal prophecy weighed heavily on his mind.

Your story does not last forever.

He had long since stopped trying to clear these thoughts; they had been plaguing him since they had left the Torridon the last time, and he had just learned to live with them.

A lightning bolt was cast at him but he put out his left hand and absorbed the crimson forks, only to throw out his right hand and launch a thicker, stronger golden bolt that hit Solaxe square in the chest. He was knocked back and his armour fizzled with smoke from where it had hit him, but it seemed to only slightly affect him. This was almost ridiculous. With all his power, William had no attack powerful enough to strike a fatal blow that would not leave him severely weak and therefore open to the other ArchCaster, and he was against two combatants that had spent decades studying magic and its lore.

The young Caster blocked another fireball, and held on; he had to think of something.

Alayna had reached the bottom of the slope on the other side of the wall of rubble, and she ran towards the Torridon. This wasn't just a battle between Casters; this was a full scale war. She saw the vague outline of William above the fortress, and he was glowing gold. She could see two other crimson figures, and between the three she saw flashes of fire. She tried to shout to him, but he was too far away and the battle too loud for him to hear her.

As she was about to plunge into the battle to try and reach him, she saw a face that she recognised though a familiar but empty window frame. Surely that was Aniik, and Drustan too. And wasn't that the man from the inn that they visited? They were using rocks and rubble to close up the window gaps, and before they could she ran over to them.

"Alayna?" asked Aniik, clearly both thrilled to see her and horrified that she was here.

"We don't have much time," she gasped, trying to catch her breath. "Scarra, hundreds of them, coming from the east."

Their faces looked grave at the news.

"We've only just got enough men to defend from two fronts."

"We don't need many. This half of the fortress is the least destroyed and is mainly still sealed. As long as you block this room off, we need only defend the room above. The walls were destroyed, but the door leads right into the main part of the palace. We can guard that against the Scarra."

With this last, she gestured to herself, Drustan, Aniik and a few of their men.

Drustan nodded and turned to the men.

"Don't barricade the windows; everyone should leave and barricade the door behind us."

And so they abandoned that room through the holes in the metal doors that William and Ranson had created what seemed a lifetime ago, and barricaded the holes with half a tonne of rubble and held it together with swords from the fallen men in the room. Then Aniik, Drustan, Arthur, Cedric and Alayna found a nearby staircase and ran up it, eventually coming out into a wide, flat, open area, about seven by five metres squared. The door was in the centre of the side attached to the fortress, and was only wide enough for two men to walk abreast, so they could defend it well if they stayed together. The Scarra weren't famed for their intelligence, so they would only run at them a few at a time.

After a few moments, they saw a shaggy, brown, hairy smear run down the inside edge of the rubble, and then the first monsters began to scale the walls. They appeared over the edge of the plateau, saw the door, and ran towards it in their all too familiar rabble-like fashion.

The five humans defending it drew their swords, and all too suddenly battle was joined.

William was suddenly hit in the face with a jet of boiling hot water; Solaxe had very little honour in battle. The young Caster couldn't stop himself recoiling, and the ArchCasters were now directly either side of him. They seemed to nod to each other, and then they released the same pulse that they had used to kill the leader of the Order of the Casters and his lieutenant, but William was not simply a creature of peace. He focused, lifted one arm towards each ArchCaster and created a sphere of golden energy that held back the pulse. William and the ArchCasters' focus was evident by their physical straining and the look of effort on their faces. William could feel his power abandoning him, and he looked down to the gate of the Torridon.

Enemies massed around the Children of Earth, Water and Fire, but they were seeing them away.

Suddenly, a man with a sword in one hand and a knife in the other ran at Dawyr, and Dawyr blocked the sword and plunged his spear right through the man, drawing their bodies close together. Then the Child of Water simply pushed him over and he fell backwards of the spear. He prepared himself for his next opponent, but his vision seemed to blur and sway, and all of the colour drained from the battle scene before him. He felt a thick, warm liquid is his mouth, and he looked down.

Only to see the knife handle sticking out from between his ribs.

Dawyr dropped his spear, and he fell to his knees, before closing his eyes and falling onto the body of the man that killed him, lifeless.

Ræl connected his war hammer hard with a man's skull, and as he fell the Child of Earth turned to see what the twinge in the back of his mind was about. He and Eithne watched Dawyr fall, and as she turned back to look at him, a crossbow bolt thudded into his chest. He didn't get a single word out as his pierced heart stopped, and he simply fell backwards.

Eithne turned to the men now surrounding her and cried out in a feeling of pain and loss that tore her soul in two. As she did so, a wave of fire shot out from her and barbecued the enemy men for many lines back in a wave of hungry flame that rippled out across a lot of the army. In silence, not noticing the men running around as they painfully burned to death. Her whole world seemed to run in slow motion as she knelt down beside Ræl moments before he closed his eyes, and the tears began to cascade down her face as she ran her fingers through his hair, unable to accept the terrible reality before her.

From on high, William felt her pain as his own. He looked down at her, and their eyes connected for a moment as she nodded once, and then closed her eyes and bent down to cradle Ræl's body in her arms.

The pain built up inside William, as he relived the moment when his mother had died, then his step-father, then Ranson, and now his allies too. He allowed the terrible emotions to fill his very being, until they awakened in him a power that he knew he could not control nor survive. Liquid gold flowed from his eyes as his very life-force was put into one final act.

The sphere of golden energy expanded as if the ArchCaster's pulse wasn't even there. William's enemies didn't scream; they only had time to open their eyes wide in surprise before they were enveloped by the golden light. It ripped through their very beings, and tore fibre from fibre, and then they were just clouds of dust, falling from their place in the sky.

But the sphere of energy kept expanding and expanding, growing metres with every microsecond. The base of the sphere reached the earth and it began to expand across the ground, consuming every living thing in its path and turning it to dust. It stretched across the armies of the ArchCasters and the soldiers were atomised without a sound. More and more men, living and dead, were swallowed up as it stretched across the battlefield. It reached the main gate and Eithne was consumed along with the bodies of Dawyr and Ræl, and then it washed over the Torridon, rattling the stones and some of the weaker walls collapsed.

All of the Scarra that were still alive had been drawn to the site of the Torridon, so they were completely wiped out when the golden wave of energy consumed their scared, roaring bodies.

Once the edges of the sphere crossed the pile of rubble, the heaps of rock collapsed and the sphere suddenly faded as if it had never existed.

Right in the centre, the golden light had faded from William and he fell from the sky, landing with a thud on the dusty ground.

All was silent across the dusty ground around the fortress, and the wind blew dirt across the battlefield.

Then suddenly there was movement at the gate of the Torridon. Alayna and Drustan pushed some of the rubble out of the doorway and left the fortress. About a hundred men followed them out, and there was no cheering; such death had been dealt that day that an atmosphere of sombre silence descended upon them.

Alayna turned to Drustan and Aniik, who were the only survivors of those who were guarding the door from the now-extinct Scarra.

"How did we survive?" she asked, but neither of the others had the answer.

In fact, it had been the Casters that had saved them; the very spells that they had cast around the citadel before the attack of the first ArchCasters had protected them from the part of William's power that he had got from Vanyol, so anything inside the fortress was shielded and the magic passed over them like water over rock.

As she looked around, Alayna saw a single body instead of the piles of dust on the ground. She breathed in sharply, threw her weapon to the ground, and ran towards it.

William opened his eyes, and everything around him was white. He sat up, and then stood up on the nothingness. It was curious; for the first time since he could remember he didn't feel tired or hungry on in pain. He just felt nothing.

He didn't feel like any air was passing his lips, but somehow he was breathing.

As he looked around, he walked around until he heard a voice behind him.

"William?"

He turned, and he couldn't believe his eyes.

"Mum?"

His mother smiled warmly and opened her arms, and they embraced. He released her and they walked together in silence until another figure appeared, but William couldn't tell who it was.

"I'll leave you two alone," said his mother.

"But Mum…" he began.

"I'll always be with you. Just call me, and I'll be there. I'll always be here; I love you so much."

With the last of her words, she walked two steps and disappeared into the whiteness. He turned back towards the figure, and it seemed to come into focus.

It was Ranson.

William couldn't believe his eyes.

His father smiled and beckoned for his son to walk beside him, and they did so.

"Do you know when you asked me why you were chosen when you weren't one of the Children of the Elements?"

William nodded.

"Well I think I know now," said his father, taking his right wrist and lifting it up so William could see.

"The Ancients believed in another, fifth element. That element is Spirit."

Sure enough, on his right wrist, burning with golden light, was a circular symbol. It had never been there before, but there it was; as bright as day.

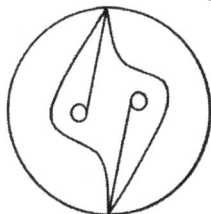

"You see, son. It was never your abilities that made you special, it was your heart, your soul; your Spirit. You chose to give your own life to end the war and save countless others. That's why the earth chose you to unite the Children; because you had a strong Spirit; stronger than mine and stronger than anyone else's. You were chosen because you always make the right choice even when it's impossible to do so. I'm so proud of you.."

William felt a warmth in his heart that he hadn't felt for nearly a year, when he was with his mother back in Tursus, but then he felt a deep sadness for all those he was leaving behind.

"I can't go back, can I?"

"No," replied his father. "It's completely impossible." Then he smiled slightly. "But when has that ever stopped us before?"

Alayna cradled William's body in her arms. He had no open wounds to speak of; his face was burned and scabby, and he was covered in bruises from the fall, but nothing to suggest a fatal strike. It was as if his spirit had just left his body.

Her tears fell hot and silent, but she knew that he was gone. She couldn't muster the strength to bury him, or ask anyone else to, so with a bit of help from Aniik, she stood up and began to follow the last of the United Resistance as they walked sombrely back to Styron's base.

And so magic passed from the world, along with anything born of magic. The Scarra were destroyed and all sorcerers vanquished, and the Stone and it's power along with it. The powers that the earth bestowed upon those chosen few have been returned to it once and for all; from dust they once came, and to dust they were reclaimed. And so our story ends at the end of the story of the Casters, our story ends with a boy called William.

And then his fingers twitched.

THE END

Afterword

I'll keep this very brief, because if you're reading this then you've finished the book so you'll have done enough reading.

Well, thank you so much for taking the time to read my book, I truly hope you enjoyed it.

My name is Matthew Vaughan and I finished this book at 16 years old. It's taken just under two years to complete and I began at Easter in 2013. I originally began simply to see if I could do a 200 page story, but I just couldn't stop until the story finished well so I continued on and ended up reaching 390 pages. I put together the covers myself, and between myself and a very supportive friend designed the map.

Various characters were based on those around me, with their permission of course, and they are categorically my favourite creations. You all know who you are. However, any other characters were not based on any real person, living or dead.

I am also planning to write some additional short stories to go with the book that just didn't fit the final cut, so feel free to email me with ideas, what you thought of the book or any other questions on whitefireauthor@gmail.com and I'll always reply as soon as I can.

The last thing I want to say is simply thank you for everyone who has supported me. I genuinely couldn't have done it without you.

Thanks again, Matthew Vaughan.

Map

Clas Muîr Map

Key

: = William's
journey

x = Point of
interest

☆ = Teleportation

🌲 = Forest

⛫ = ArchCaster
fortress

⛫ = The Torridon

〉〉 = River

∧ = Mountain

)(= Valley/
Mountain Pass

Selaxe's Palace

West
Realm

Styron's
Death

Rael's
Village

Kracian
Pass

Kelthane's Palace

Glossary

Chapter 1

Caster (**car**-ster)
noun. A magical law-enforcer of the Three Realms.

ArchCaster (**ark**-car-ster)
noun. The title that the Three Traitors gave themselves after they conquered the Three Realms.

Torridon (**tor**-id-don)
noun. The fortress that is the base of the Order of the Casters in the centre of the Three Realms.

Kelthane (**kell**-tain)
noun. The ArchCaster in control of the South Realm after the Fall of the Casters.

Solaxe (**sol**-ax)
noun. The ArchCaster in control of the West Realm after the Fall of the Casters.

Vanyol (**van**-yol)
noun. The ArchCaster in control of the East Realm after the Fall of the Casters.

Clas Muîr (**class** m-yeer)
noun. The island made up of the Three Realms; the world in which the book takes place.

Chapter 2

Tursus (**ter**-suss)
noun. The village that William grew up in.

Chapter 3

Delsus (**del**-suss)
noun. The river system that goes through the East Realm (also known as the Tiamo), and the name of the forest that takes up most of the area of the Realm.

Ranson (**ran**-sun)
noun. The name of the man that William is travelling with.

Chapter 5

Scarra (**scar**-a)
noun. A terrifying, animalistic creature that lives in the forests of the East Realm.

Melnhir (**mel**-neer)
noun. William's sword, originally his uncle's; a short, wide-bladed, hand-and-a-half weapon.

Triscant (**triss**-cant)
noun. Ranson's sword; a long, thin-bladed, two-handed weapon.

Chapter 7

Kanen (**can**-en)
noun. The mountain within which the East Realm Resistance set up their base of operations.

Besiarites (**bez**-ee-ar-rites)
noun. The elite soldiers of the East Realm Resistance.

Raimos (**ray**-moss)
noun. The leader of the East Realm Resistance.

Garston (**gar**-ston)
noun. The lieutenant of Raimos, 2nd-in-command of the East Realm Resistance.

Chapter 12

Aniik'arim (a-**neek**'a-**reem**)
noun. The dark-skinned man that William meets in Vanyol's prison. ("Aniik" (or "Kei") is the forname, "arim" is the family name.)

An'Tiamo (an'**tee**-a-moe)
noun. The tribe that lived on the Tiamo (or Delsus) river. "An" means "on" in the language of the tribe.

Chapter 13

Alayna (a-**lay**-na)
noun. The girl that William meets in Vanyol's prison.

Chapter 15

Draoidh (**dray**-ag)
noun. Translates as sorcery or magic (i.e. Stone of magic) in the language of the Ancients.

Cyfarwydd (**Ky**-far-wyth)
noun. Translates as "story" in the language of the Ancients.

Chapter 16

Bevyn (**bev**-in)
noun. The young man who helps William hide while on the ship; translates as "good, young fighter" in the language of the Ancients.

Chapter 19

Rǽl (**ray**-el)
noun. The Child of Earth; translates to "earth" in the language of the Ancients.

Styron (**sty**-ron)
noun. Ranson's friend from decades before in the Resistance, and Eithne's father.

Chapter 20

Eithne (ee-**ith**-nee)
noun. Child of Fire and Styron's daughter; translates "white fire" in the language the Ancients.

Chapter 21

Dawyr (**dar**-weer)
noun. The Child of Water; translates to "water" in the language of the Ancients.

Galawaine (**gal**-a-wain)
noun. Ranson's instructor from the Order of the Casters before it was destroyed.

Greia (**gray**-a)
noun. A girl from Dawyr's village; translates as "tragic love" in the language of the Ancients.

Chapter 22

Èadhar (ee-**ay**-dar)
noun. The Child of Air; translates to "air" in the language of the Ancients.

Chapter 23

An Deireadh (**an dare**-ra)
Translates as "the end" in the language of the Ancients

39564177R00220

Made in the USA
Charleston, SC
13 March 2015